A unt Sunny had this way of looking at Zinnie that was like the tide pulling back the ocean to reveal spinning shells and churning sand. Her gaze brought Zinnie's truth tumbling to the surface, snails and all. She thought that she was just mad about what had happened, but with Aunt Sunny's understanding eyes meeting her own, Zinnie began to feel tears well up.

the Brightest Stars of Summer

LEILA HOWLAND

Illustrated by Ji-Hyuk Kim

HARPER

An Imprint of HarperCollinsPublishers

Library of Congress Control Number: 2015950816
ISBN 978-0-06-231873-2

Typography by Kate J. Engbring
17 18 19 20 21   OPM   10 9 8 7 6 5 4 3 2 1
❖
First paperback edition, 2017

To Henry, the brightest star in my sky

1 · A Young Star

It was guaranteed to be one of the highlights of the summer, maybe even of the year, maybe even of their lives, and Zinnie didn't want to miss a single moment. She plucked her mininotebook out of her back pocket, uncapped her favorite purple pen, and took a good look around.

She was at a special early showing for the cast and crew of the movie *Night Sprites* because her very own and soon-to-be-famous older sister, Marigold, had a part in it. Marigold played a small role, but she had got to say two whole sentences on camera, and it was a pretty big deal.

Being in a movie was Marigold's dream come true, and it only took one glance at her enormous smile, made extra shimmery today by the lip gloss their mother had allowed her to wear for this special occasion, for Zinnie to be certain that her sister was truly a star.

Zinnie couldn't help but feel that she'd had a big hand in making it happen. After all, it had been her idea to have a talent show last summer in the town of Pruet, Massachusetts, where the director, Philip Rathbone, had a vacation home, and where the three Silver sisters had spent a few fun-filled weeks at their aunt Sunny's cottage. And it was Zinnie who'd written the play in which Marigold had performed so outstandingly that Mr. Rathbone had noticed her. And it was Zinnie again who encouraged Marigold to send Mr. Rathbone her headshot a few weeks later, along with a letter telling him how nice it had been to meet him.

Zinnie had even helped Marigold write the letter, making sure it had both personality and good grammar. Zinnie was pretty certain that it had been that letter that had sealed the deal and made Mr. Rathbone think of Marigold when, after the rest of the movie had been filmed, he'd decided that the story needed an opening scene that wasn't even in the book: a scene where a normal, human girl was sitting by a tree reading, not knowing that she was falling into a dream woven by the Night Sprites.

Zinnie imagined Marigold's letter and headshot landing in Mr. Rathbone's mailbox on the very day he had the idea. She could just picture him sitting at a big desk, puzzling over which young actress would play this small but crucial role. Then his eyes growing wide with delight as he opened the envelope containing Marigold's headshot and realized he'd actually met the perfect girl that summer. "Mildred, get this girl in here for an audition right away!" Zinnie imagined him saying to an assistant, just like the old movies she and her dad saw at the cinema that showed classics every Tuesday night.

Regardless of how it had happened, Marigold had gotten the part on the spot. And now, a few months later, here the Silver family was, making their way down the aisle of the movie theater to see Marigold on the big screen in what was sure to be the biggest hit of the summer.

This wasn't any old Cineplex at the mall; it was a fully restored historical movie theater from the 1940s in downtown Los Angeles, grand and ornate. Zinnie thought it was perfect for the exclusive advance screening of a major Hollywood movie. She paused in the aisle before following her dad down the row to their seats. She narrowed her eyes, hoping to land on the perfect details to capture this epic moment. Mrs. Lee, her sixth-grade English teacher, always said that when it comes to writing, "It's all about the details."

Red curtains hang gloriously in front of the screen, Zinnie wrote in the dim light. *Velvet seats snap open like hungry mouths.* She read her work over and imagined Mrs. Lee smiling out of the corner of her mouth and tapping her pencil to her lips the way she did when she thought something was really good.

Mrs. Lee was a real author. She'd had an actual book published. Zinnie had seen it at the library and at the bookstore. It had even won an award and had one of those shiny gold stickers on it. Zinnie wasn't sure if she wanted to write books or plays or—like her father—movies, but she knew that she wanted to be a writer and that getting into Mrs. Lee's Writers' Workshop in the fall was a top priority. Mrs. Lee selected ten students from the seventh and eighth grades, and those students spent the afternoons attending plays and films and going to museums in Los Angeles, visiting bookstores and libraries, and, of course, writing. They even took a group field trip to England over spring vacation, and Zinnie was dying to go on it. One of the best parts was that the members of the Writers' Workshop were excused from mandatory afterschool sports.

This was an even bigger deal to Zinnie than the trip to England. She'd endured soccer last fall, and that had been almost as bad as basketball in the winter, though not as terrible as track in the spring. Track was lonely and boring, and it didn't help that she was always in the very back, "bringing up the rear," as Miss Kimberly said when Zinnie finished far behind everyone else. Zinnie had come to truly hate that expression.

Getting into the Writers' Workshop was not going to be easy. Students could submit a poem, a play, a story, an essay, or even a graphic novel. The work was supposed to be submitted by the end of the school year, but Mrs. Lee said that she understood how sometimes the summer could offer a new perspective, so she'd read applications through July tenth, at which point she was going on her annual summer retreat to Laguna Beach, where she planned to finish writing her latest novel. During the final school assembly, Mrs. Lee said that the only rules were that the writing had to feel true and original. "And it really needs to be the very best example of your work," she'd added, standing at the podium in one of her signature colorful scarves.

Zinnie wasn't going to need the extra time. She'd turned in a story on the last day of school. It was about a band of young warriors from a forgotten land, seeking to overthrow a demon king by unlocking spells that had been dormant for centuries. Zinnie felt good about it: it had action, plot, and, she thought, good use of setting, something they had focused on in English class this year. Mrs. Lee said that a writer is, in a way, always writing, and that little notes she'd taken over the years had sometimes been exactly the inspiration she'd been looking for later.

"Let's sit down," Marigold said. "It's going to start any minute!"

"Okay," Zinnie said, and scooted down the row, taking a seat next to their dad. Marigold, their mom, and finally the youngest sister, Lily, who was decked out in a fairy costume, followed her down the row.

Since Mrs. Lee always said that three was the magic number, Zinnie wanted to capture one last detail before the movie started. She looked around the theater. There were crystal chandeliers, golden balconies, and a ceiling with angels painted on it. Even with the splendor around her, Zinnie turned to Marigold for the final detail for her notebook. With her beauty and confidence and unpredictable moods, Marigold was an endlessly fascinating subject, especially today.

Marigold tossed her long, shiny hair and snapped a selfie with her phone. She leaned toward Zinnie, and before Zinnie even had a chance to pose, she took a picture of the two of them, giving Zinnie a little rush. There was almost nothing that Zinnie liked better than to be included in her sister's glamorous world, and Marigold had been in the best mood all day.

She'd even offered to let Zinnie borrow anything she wanted from her closet. *Anything.* This was unheard of. Zinnie had been bold enough to ask to borrow the jean jacket, the one that had become Marigold's unofficial weekend uniform. Perfectly shrunken and faded, it was her trademark piece. Zinnie had been expecting rejection, but Marigold said, "Sure," and handed it to Zinnie as if she had a million of them. For a second

Zinnie wondered if she hadn't aimed high enough. Was there something else she could have asked for?

The theater lights dimmed. Marigold beamed as she stared up at the screen. *Future star shines bright in the darkness,* Zinnie scribbled in her notebook, even though she could no longer see the paper.

2 · A Bad Feeling

The movie had only been playing for a minute or two when Marigold started to get a bad feeling. She couldn't explain it, but as the music swelled and she watched the scenery unfurl on the giant screen— the turquoise sea, the rocky beach, the steep cliffs—she became a little queasy.

She had asked her mother once why sometimes she knew which way something was going to go, good or bad, right before it happened. Like the time she'd known that she was going to get that part on the TV show *Seasons* before she'd even stepped into the room to audition. Or when she'd felt in the pit of her stomach that seventh grade was going to be a really tough year even before the first bell rang. "That's your intuition," Mom had said. "Your gut instinct. And you should always listen to it."

Right now, her gut instinct was telling her that something was wrong. The first scene was supposed to take place at the edge of the forest, where a girl was sitting under a tree, reading a book. A girl played by Marigold. But the landscape in those fast and sweeping panoramic views suggested that the girl was being skipped over and the audience was being taken directly to the lagoon where the queen of the Night Sprites lived. The bad feeling landed in her belly like a penny at the bottom of a fountain.

Marigold had an important line in this movie. It was the first in the film: "Where does the magic of a summer evening come from? It's hidden deep in the twilight, though perhaps is closer than you ever imagined." She had practiced it until it was like a favorite song playing on a loop as she walked to school or drifted off while doing homework.

Now, a few months after shooting her scenes, she was more than ready to hear that line outside her head. She was expecting it to fill the theater, just as she had envisioned so many times. But instead of her voice opening the movie, Xiomara's song flowed from the speakers.

Marigold's scene had been cut.

Wait. What?

This couldn't be happening to her! Or could it? Everyone said that bad things happened in threes. She didn't believe it, but here it was: the third bad thing.

The TV show Marigold had been on for six whole episodes had been canceled this fall. Then two weeks ago her agent, Jill, had announced that she was quitting the business and moving to Costa Rica to discover the meaning of life. Jill had assured her that a part in the summer's hottest blockbuster would mean that she'd be able to find another agent in no time, and Marigold had believed her. But now she wasn't even in the movie!

Marigold wanted to reach up, rewind the action, and zoom in on the tree under which she was meant to be sitting. But of course she couldn't. All she could do was grip her velvet armrests and try not to cry.

Marigold could still see that tree where they had filmed just two and half months earlier in Griffith Park, the huge park in the middle of Los Angeles. The tree had tangled, knotty roots that rose above the ground to create a shady, comfortable reading nook for a girl her size. On that perfect day in April, as one of Mr. Rathbone's assistants adjusted Marigold's costume, Marigold had wondered how many trees they'd looked at before they found this one. *It's the best tree,* she thought as she relaxed against the cool bark, *for the best day.*

She'd arrived early on the set. A guy with crazy pants had done her hair and a lady with light and careful fingertips had applied her makeup. Marigold was more nervous than she'd thought she would be.

Her mouth was dry and her hands were clammy, but she wasn't so nervous that she forgot her lines. And when Mr. Rathbone called "Action!" Marigold was such a natural that she'd done the scene in just one take.

Marigold had returned from spring break ready to tell everyone about her big day. For weeks it was all she could talk about. It wasn't just because she wanted to relive her dream on a daily basis—it was also because she thought it would give her that something extra she needed to be accepted by the girls in her class.

Her intuition had been right about seventh grade. It was different from sixth in a way that was hard to put her finger on. It wasn't just because they were actually allowed to choose some of their classes (French or Spanish? pottery or dance?), or even that they were allowed to use their phones during the school day. It was something much bigger and more difficult to name.

In sixth grade, all thirty-five girls in her class at Miss Hadley's School had pretty much been friends. Some girls were closer than others, like Marigold and her best friend Pilar, but overall there weren't any groups. She didn't think twice about where she sat at lunch or who she walked to gym class with. And the birthday party rules from elementary school were still in place: girls invited either the whole class or just one or two close friends.

In seventh grade things changed.

The year had started off okay, but as the fall crept toward winter, cliques started to form. There was one group calling themselves "the Cuties" who were all on the swim team and who'd gone on a ski trip together over winter vacation.

In the week they'd spent at Mammoth Mountain, they seemed to have shared a lifetime's worth of secrets and what they called "location jokes." Marigold learned these were jokes she'd only understand if she'd been at the *location* where the joke happened, and they'd all happened during the ski trip. By the time spring vacation rolled around, the Cuties were wearing their hair the same way, sitting together at the smaller lunch table (the one with only enough room for eight people) closest to the windows, and constantly saying the word "amazing."

Marigold, who'd always been confident, was suddenly timid about speaking up in front of the Cuties—and she'd gone to kindergarten with most of them. She was also weirdly shy about using the word "amazing." It was like those girls owned the word, which didn't make any sense. How could anyone own a word?

She thought there was no better way to get her classmates' approval than to make sure that they knew she was going to be in the *Night Sprites* movie. Her entire class had read the books, and it seemed like the whole world was waiting for the film, which would be released on July first—the day her life would change forever.

Marigold started talking about being in the movie every chance she could get: in homeroom, in the locker room, walking to class. "I just can't wait until July first!" she'd said more than once. This did get everyone's attention, but only for a few days. After listening to several stories about "the shoot," the Cuties lost interest, and they still didn't invite her to sit at their table.

It wasn't until Pilar talked to her in the lunch line that Marigold finally started to understand.

"People think you're bragging," Pilar said as she grabbed a yogurt and put it on her tray.

"Do *you* think I'm bragging?" Marigold asked. Pilar bit her lip as she selected a turkey sandwich. "Pilar?"

"Maybe?" Pilar said, looking up at Marigold from under her long, dark eyelashes.

"I think everyone is jealous," Marigold said, picking out a ham and cheese on whole wheat. Pilar froze, her brow pinched. "I mean, not you, but everyone else. The Cuties for sure. They're such jerks."

"They aren't so bad," Pilar said, and then she checked to see if anyone had overheard. Marigold felt her throat constrict. Was Pilar becoming one of them?

It was true that Marigold had been spending less time with Pilar since she'd been cast in *Night Sprites*. She'd had a bunch of auditions that she'd missed school for, and she was now taking an improv class and a voice-over class in addition to her acting class. It was also true that Pilar had asked her to hang out a lot and she'd almost always had to say no. Had Marigold been a bad friend without realizing it? Didn't Pilar understand how important acting was to her?

The truth, Marigold knew, was that she hadn't signed up for all the extra classes just because acting was her passion. It also gave her an excuse not to fit in.

"I'm so busy this weekend because I have auditions," she'd said once when she wasn't invited to a birthday party. (Pilar had been invited to that one.) Another time she'd said, "I have to go to acting class after school today," when she knew a bunch of girls from her class went to the new frozen yogurt place that let you sample every flavor, but didn't ask her to come along.

Marigold realized that even if Pilar did get more invitations, she probably still really missed having her best friend around. Marigold had an idea.

"Hey, do you want to try the Cupcake Café this weekend? We can do a taste test and see if the cupcakes there are as good as the ones at the Farmers Market."

"I went last weekend," Pilar said.

"Without me?" Marigold asked.

"It's been open for a whole month, Marigold."

"But we were going to go together, remember?"

"I already asked you to go twice and you said you were busy."

"I was," Marigold said, her voice high and pleading.

"You're always busy," Pilar said as she grabbed an orange juice and headed toward the seventh-grade tables.

"But I really was," Marigold said, following her friend.

Pilar said "Hi" to the Cuties as she passed their table and they said "Hi" back, but to Marigold's relief, Pilar didn't sit with them. Instead the two of them sat at their regular table with the usual girls. But for that whole lunch period, Marigold felt like Pilar wanted to be somewhere else.

Now Marigold was the one who wanted to be somewhere else. Anywhere but here in this fancy, old-fashioned movie theater, watching her dream go down the drain. She grabbed her mom's hand.

"They skipped it," she whispered.

"Maybe they moved it," Mom said. A tear rolled down Marigold's cheek. "Do you want to leave, honey?"

"No! We need to stay in case it's in there somewhere," Marigold said.

"We'll stay," Mom said, and wrapped an arm around her daughter.

The rest of the movie was torture. Marigold couldn't enjoy a single scene. Zinnie, on the other hand, loved it. She was laughing like crazy when Xiomara entertained the ravens and crying when it appeared that all hope was lost. Marigold kept shooting her dirty looks, but they were wasted—Zinnie didn't even notice. Not until the very end, when she turned to Marigold and, as if it was just dawning on her that something was amiss, said, "Hey, wait a second. Where was your scene? Did I miss it?" And Marigold had to cover her face with both hands to keep from screaming.

"Do you want to stick around and talk to anyone?" Mom asked, stroking Marigold's hair.

"I just want to go home," Marigold said, still hiding her tear-stained face. "I want to call Pilar." How could her dream be taken from her like this? How was she ever going to face her classmates? Now no one would know about her most perfect moment on earth, sitting under that tree, saying her lines like a real movie actress. Now the only people who would ever know that she was in the best, most successful movie of the year were the handful who had been there on that April day. It was, she thought, the cruelest location joke of all.

3 · Detour at the Freeway Café

"You can have the rest of my bacon," Zinnie said, offering her plate to Marigold. Zinnie knew that her bacon, as perfect as it was (extra crispy and deliciously drenched in maple syrup), couldn't make up for Marigold's terrible day yesterday, but she hoped it would at least make this day a little better.

"I wouldn't turn that down," Dad said, taking the last bite of his fried eggs. "You know how Zinnie is about her bacon."

"Honey," Mom said to Marigold, "you need to eat something."

In an attempt to boost Marigold's spirits, Mom and Dad had taken the girls to the Freeway Café for breakfast. Zinnie didn't even have to look at the menu. She knew she wanted the French toast special. Lily had a waffle with extra whipped cream and a cherry on top.

Dad got the fried eggs with grits on the side. Mom ordered flapjacks instead of her usual veggie omelet. But Marigold just asked for dry whole wheat toast and water—no ice. Zinnie thought it was the most boring breakfast ever, especially considering they were at the home of the doughnut breakfast sandwich (which sounded good and looked good, but gave Zinnie a stomachache).

"If Marigold doesn't eat it, then can we give it to Bowser?" Lily asked, referring to the little dog that was up for adoption that they'd seen on their way into the diner. The pet store next door was having its annual adopt-a-dog fair, and Lily had instantly fallen in love with a beagle.

"If Marigold doesn't eat it, I will," Dad said, patting Lily's head. "Bowser is better off with dog food."

"It's the perfect amount of burned," Zinnie said, and pushed her plate toward Marigold, but Marigold just listlessly stirred her ice-less water with her straw and stared out the window. Zinnie almost didn't recognize her sister today. Marigold's eyes were puffy from so much crying, her hair was pulled back in a tangled ponytail, and she was wearing baggy leggings and an old sweatshirt. Normally Marigold wouldn't even sleep in these clothes. And nothing seemed to be cheering her up. Telling her jokes hadn't made Marigold feel better. Praising her acting skills hadn't helped. Offering to be her butler for twenty-four hours hadn't worked either. Maybe syrup-soaked bacon would do the trick.

"The world's best older sister deserves the world's best bacon," Zinnie offered one last time, glancing at Marigold to make sure the compliment had registered. Last night at dinner Zinnie had innocently mentioned that she thought the *Night Sprites* movie was good. She knew almost as soon as she had said it that it'd been a mistake. And sure enough, Marigold had declared her a traitor.

She still wasn't forgiven, because even now Marigold wasn't making a move toward the bacon. Zinnie decided to eat it herself.

"I thought that was for me," Marigold said.

"But you didn't . . . ," Zinnie said, with her mouth full. "I asked you and—"

"You shouldn't give someone something if you're only going to take it away," Marigold said, bursting into tears.

"Sorry," Zinnie said.

"Why was I cut?" Marigold asked, slumping into the booth and dabbing her eyes with a napkin. "I guess I'm just not a good actress!"

"You're a great actress," Dad said.

"Sweetheart," Mom said, placing a hand over Marigold's, "I know how disappointed you are. But I'm sure this has nothing to do with your talent."

"Mom's an editor, so she knows," Zinnie said.

"It's true," Mom said. "Scenes are usually cut from movies because the director or the producers don't think they add to the story."

"As artists, we have to pick ourselves up, dust ourselves off, and find a way to keep going," Dad said. "And we have so much to look forward to this summer."

The summer was going to be a busy one, and Zinnie couldn't wait. Marigold was going to an acting camp in Topanga Canyon, where she would be doing an actual Shakespeare play. Zinnie was going to a creative writing camp, called Summer Scribes, at Miss Hadley's. The camp was taught by Mrs. Lee herself. For two whole weeks the Scribes would be exploring L.A. for inspiration, reading great books, and writing, of course. Lily was taking swimming lessons and going to camp at the zoo.

But of course what they were all looking forward to the most was their family visit to Pruet at the end of the summer. They were going for three days, the weekend before school started. Zinnie didn't see how three days could possibly compare to last summer, when they'd had nearly three weeks of freedom and fun at Aunt Sunny's. There'd been clambakes, sailing adventures, and a dance at the casino—which was what the people in Pruet called the town hall. Zinnie had written a play. Marigold had found a boyfriend. Lily had swum in the ocean. And they'd all put on a talent show. It had been, without a doubt, the happiest summer of Zinnie's life.

They all wanted to return for a nice long visit this summer, but things were different this year. Aunt Sunny had received a grant for the environmental organization she'd started, the Piping Plover Society, and she was overseeing the establishment of a bird sanctuary. It was a full-time job, so she wasn't available to watch the girls like she had last summer. And Aunt Sunny's cottage was a little too small for the whole Silver family to stay for longer than a couple days. Besides, Mom and Dad both had jobs in Los Angeles.

"Camp starts next week," Mom said. "Think about how fun it will be to perform onstage with the Topanga Players, Marigold! You'll get to do Shakespeare."

"Most actors prefer the stage to the screen," Dad said.

"I can't go to acting camp NOW," Marigold said. "I'm DONE with acting. Forever."

"What?" Zinnie asked.

"Obviously Ronald was wrong about me," Marigold said. Zinnie bit her lip. Ronald was Marigold's acting teacher, who didn't think Zinnie was talented enough to be in his class. Zinnie was not a fan. "And if Jill thought I was really so great, maybe she wouldn't have moved to Costa Rica. Even Mr. Rathbone thought the movie was better without me! Why would I want to keep acting?"

"I don't think now is the time to make that kind of decision, honey," Dad said.

Zinnie was about to plead with Marigold not to give up—her sister's talent was nothing short of extraordinary—when Mom's phone rang. Zinnie felt her heart light up as Aunt Sunny's face with her round glasses and cheerful smile appeared on the screen. Zinnie really couldn't wait to see her. How was she going to wait until the end of the summer?

"Aunt Sunny!" Lily shouted and clapped.

"I'll call her as soon as we get home," Mom said, tucking the phone in her purse. The Silvers had a strict rule about not answering phones at the table.

"Come on, Mom," Zinnie said. "She never calls!"

It was true. Aunt Sunny preferred sending letters and postcards and, at least once a month, a package. Sometimes it contained a shell she'd found on the beach. Other times she sent books that she thought the girls would enjoy, or a treasure she had unearthed in her attic. On Christmas she had sent a bunch of ornaments that had been hers as a child. And of course in every package was a batch of her famous surprise brownies, which were rich, gooey, and chocolaty with a peppermint kick.

"We all want to talk to her," Marigold said, her eyes brightening for the first time since yesterday.

"I think we can make an exception," Dad said. "After all, it's Aunt Sunny."

"Well, okay," Mom said, happy to give in as she picked up the phone. "Hello!"

The rest of the family watched in silence as Mom listened. Seconds later, a huge smile broke out on Mom's face and a joyful laugh escaped her lips.

4 · The Wild West

"I can't believe Aunt Sunny's getting married to Tony!" Marigold said, leading the way along the shady path through the sycamore and oak trees.

After the surprise phone call from Aunt Sunny, the Silver family had headed to Griffith Park for some fresh air and a chance to digest their breakfast and the big news that Aunt Sunny was getting married in less than a month. They were on the wide dirt trail that snaked up the steep hill through the chaparral to the observatory. Outside the observatory the views stretched out over the sprawling city in every direction, from the San Gabriel Mountains in the east to the ocean in the west. Inside the observatory were all kinds of cool exhibits and a planetarium.

But to Marigold the whole point of coming to Griffith Park was to be outdoors. Her favorite season here was the spring, after the rain, when the air was cool and the butterflies and bees fluttered among wildflowers. Right now, in the middle of June, it was almost too hot for a hike, but for the first time since yesterday, Marigold wasn't totally and completely bummed out to the point of not even bothering to accessorize.

"I've never been to a wedding," Zinnie said. She'd found a long stick, which she'd declared her walking stick, and she tapped the ground with it as she walked behind Marigold.

"Why are they getting married so soon?" Marigold asked.

"Because love is the eternal flame that draws the heart like a moth!" Zinnie said, quoting the *Night Sprites* movie. Marigold glanced over her shoulder to give Zinnie a look of warning. She was not in the mood for *Night Sprites* quotes.

"Sorry," Zinnie said, wincing. "I couldn't help it. It's just such a good line!"

"Tony's son, Paul, is in the army," Mom said, defusing the tension. "And he's heading back to Syria for a whole year or more. So when Tony proposed last night, he and Aunt Sunny decided to get married as soon as possible. Tony couldn't imagine a wedding without Paul. And of course Aunt Sunny can't imagine a wedding without you three girls as part of the ceremony, which is why we are going to go to Pruet earlier than we planned."

"I can't wait to be a flower girl," Lily said. She was holding Dad's hand and swinging his arm. "I'll give everyone roses as I walk down the aisle. Will I get to carry a basket?"

"I'm sure Aunt Sunny won't object if that's what you want," Dad said as a pair of joggers running downhill split apart to pass them.

"And it makes total sense that Zinnie and I will be bridesmaids, since we fixed them up," Marigold said, wiping some sweat from her brow.

Zinnie had been the one to talk Aunt Sunny into the idea of seeking love again since her husband, Ham, had died many years ago. And all three of them had opened Aunt Sunny's eyes to the fact that Tony had a crush on her. But Marigold thought that she probably deserved the most credit for the romance. Normally, Aunt Sunny didn't wear makeup or anything fancier than shorts and T-shirts, but on the night of the town dance, Marigold had found a closet full of vintage outfits and selected the perfect ensemble for Aunt Sunny, complete with dangly earrings and silver shoes. They were flats, but still. Aunt Sunny had looked beautiful that night and Marigold was certain that was when they had fallen in love.

"We could open a matchmaking business!" Zinnie said as they entered a welcome stretch of shade.

"You can call it the Kissing Store," Lily said, kicking up dust as she ran in front of Marigold and batting her eyelashes like a love-struck cartoon character. "Everything inside will be pink and purple hearts. Like, even the couches and chairs. And we'll have puppies there, too. To help people fall in love!"

"Good idea, Lily," Marigold said. "Mom, do you think Aunt Sunny will let me design my own bridesmaid dre—" But she couldn't finish her sentence, because ahead, coming down the very path that the Silvers were hiking up, was a group of girls Marigold recognized even from a distance.

The Cuties.

They were easy to identify by their matching bobbed haircuts, coordinated outfits, and synchronized laughs. They had probably just been to see the new planetarium show. As they came closer, Marigold realized there was a new member of their clique. She had a jet-black bob and was a wearing a T-shirt Marigold would've recognized anywhere because she had a matching one. *Pilar.*

Marigold had texted her last night and asked her to hang out. Pilar had told her that she had to stay home to pack and get ready for her trip to Mexico, where she was going to get to see her grandmother. But that had been a lie! She'd gone hiking with the Cuties! The worst part was, she'd cut her hair without even checking with Marigold!

She's one of them now, Marigold thought. Her pulse quickened and her mouth went as dry as the drought-stricken dirt beneath her feet. The momentary forgetfulness of being cut from the movie came to a screeching halt. She felt the pain of not being in *Night Sprites*, but also the betrayal of Pilar, and on top of that the prickly embarrassment of having boasted about her movie role. Now her whole class would think that she was not only a bragger, but also a liar and a fake. And eighth grade, she'd heard, was even more grueling than seventh. How was she going to handle it without Pilar by her side? In the heat of the midday sun, Marigold thought she might collapse.

"Marigold, are you okay?" Dad asked. "You look pale."

"I think I see a deer!" Marigold said in a hoarse whisper, the idea coming to her in a moment of panicked clarity. She pointed into a wooded area. "Shhh, be quiet and come look! Hurry, quick! Oh yes, way over there. There's a whole family of them!"

"Cool," Zinnie said as they all followed Marigold off the path in search of the fictional wildlife. "But I don't see anything . . ."

"Shhh! We have to be silent because we don't want to scare them," Marigold said.

A cold sweat dampened her face as she heard the Cuties approaching. She knew she was going to have to see them at some point. The movie was coming out on July first, which was so soon, and the shame and disappointment that were now private would soon become public. *I'm safe for the moment,* she thought as they walked by. She was hiding behind a sycamore tree, but she couldn't hide forever. She gripped the tree and held her breath. The sound of Pilar's laughter echoing though the canyon was like a beesting right on her heart.

5 · Middle-of-the-Night Mother-Daughter Meeting

"Sorry, but you can't go to Pruet early," Mom said as she filled the teakettle and placed it on the stove. "You have camp."

"Please, Mom," Marigold said. "I really think that I could be a big help to Aunt Sunny. Just hear me out."

Marigold glanced at the clock on the microwave. It was 1:07 a.m., way past her bedtime—and her mom's too. But Marigold hadn't been able to sleep. She wanted to get out of Los Angeles—as far away as possible as soon as possible.

Sometime after midnight, after pacing around her room at least a hundred times, she thought of the perfect escape: Aunt Sunny's. Not only was it far away from all her problems, but Aunt Sunny probably needed help getting ready for her wedding. Marigold had woken Mom up to talk through the idea. At first Mom just told her to go back to bed, but Marigold was as distraught and determined as she'd ever been. She begged Mom to listen to her, until finally Mom agreed and they headed to the kitchen for a middle-of-the-night mother-daughter meeting.

"I think you'll really regret not going to camp," Mom said now, turning on the stove to heat the tea-kettle. She took two mugs from the cabinet and put them on the counter. "Shakespeare in a cool outdoor theater with a bunch of other great kids? Sounds awe-some to me."

"But I don't want to act anymore," Marigold said.

"That's how you feel right now, and it's under-standable. You've had some setbacks." Mom placed chamomile tea bags in the mugs. "But what would Ronald say? What would Jill tell you to do?"

"Ronald always says that show business is a hard road, and if there's anything else you can do that makes you happy, you should do it. Even you and Dad have said that. And Jill would probably tell me to move to Costa Rica!"

"Okay." Mom acknowledged this point with a smile. "But you've been looking forward to this for months."

"And then there's the deposit to think about. It was expensive, and I doubt we'll be able to get it back at this point."

"I'll pay you back with babysitting," Marigold said.

"That's a lot of babysitting," Mom said, leaning against the counter. "Is this really just about acting?"

"Not exactly," Marigold said. "There's this clique at school. The Cuties."

"Ah," Mom said. The water in the kettle rumbled. "Tell me more."

"They dress alike and have inside jokes that they call 'location jokes' and they're all on the swim team together and they talk about boys a lot."

"Boys?" Mom asked as the teakettle whistled. "Do they have boyfriends?"

"I think so," Marigold said.

"What do you think they mean by boyfriends?" Mom asked. She poured the hot water over the tea bags.

"I'm not really sure," Marigold said, thinking about it.

"What does having a boyfriend mean to you?" Mom asked. She carried the steaming mugs to the table and sat next to Marigold.

"I guess it means hanging out with a boy who you really like who also likes you back. And you dance together at the dances and go to the movies together and stuff." Marigold grabbed the bear-shaped container of honey and squeezed some into her tea.

"Is that what it means to these girls?" Mom asked, blowing on her mug of tea.

"I wouldn't know. It's not like they invite me

anywhere. They sit at a lunch table with only eight seats, so no one else can sit with them."

"These girls sound mean, honey," Mom said,. "Why do you care what they think?"

"They're the cool kids." Marigold sipped her tea.

"I'm going to let you in on the secret to being cool," Mom said. "Just be yourself." Mom beamed as if this would solve all of Marigold's problems.

"Mom," Marigold said, "you sound like a cheesy TV show."

"Fine, don't believe me," Mom said. "But I'm right."

"No one wants to be unpopular."

"All you really need is one good friend. And you have Pilar."

"Not anymore," Marigold said, feeling her lower lip start to tremble.

"What?" Mom's sympathetic look brought tears to Marigold's eyes. Marigold told Mom about how Pilar had been with the Cuties yesterday—there hadn't actually been any deer.

"Oh, sweetheart, you and Pilar can work this out," Mom said, touching Marigold's cheek. Her hand was warm from holding her mug. "You've been friends for so long. Why don't I take you two to the Farmers Market tomorrow for some frozen yogurt?"

"She's going to Mexico to see her *abuela* really soon. I think the day after tomorrow."

"You need to talk to her before she leaves. But this

is another reason you should go to camp. You'll make tons of new friends there."

"Not if I'm totally miserable." Marigold sighed. "Remember when you said that I could quit acting if it stopped being fun? Well, it's not fun anymore."

"I just want to make sure that dropping out of camp is about acting and not about the girls in your class." Mom looked deep into Marigold's eyes.

"It's both," Marigold said, wiping her teary face with the backs of her hands. "I thought that if I was in the movie, the Cuties would think I was cool and they'd want to be friends with me, even if I didn't want to be friends back. And because I'm not on *Seasons* anymore and I'm not in the movie, I can't stop worrying that I'm not good enough. What if I'm not cool enough or good enough?"

"Of course you're cool enough and good enough. You know what?" Mom said as she smoothed Marigold's hair behind her ear. "I think you're right. I think a couple weeks in Pruet is exactly what you need."

"Thank you, Mom," Marigold said, throwing her arms around her mother's neck and hugging her. "Thank you so much."

6 · Chopped

"Wow!" was all Zinnie could say as she stepped inside the bathroom and shut the door behind her. For a second she wondered if she was sleepwalking, because what she was looking at just didn't feel real.

Even though Marigold had been acting stranger than ever, even though she had been wearing clothes she normally wouldn't be caught dead in, even though she'd claimed she had seen an entire family of deer yesterday that not a single other person had, nothing could have prepared Zinnie for the sight of her sister sitting in the lotus position on the sink counter in her pj's, taking Mom's extra-sharp desk scissors to the last lock of hair that hung below her shoulders.

"Gah!" Zinnie exhaled as the shiny tress fell to the bathroom floor.

"What do you think?" Marigold asked as she shook out her new, uneven bob. She was cheerful for someone who had just chopped off what she had once referred to as her "golden mane of splendor."

"Well," Zinnie said, catching her breath. "It's . . . different." It was different for Marigold, anyway. It was the same length as the hair of that clique of girls in Marigold's class.

"Exactly. It's a whole new me," Marigold said.

Her whole life, Zinnie had envied her sister's gorgeous hair. Unlike her own, which grew out instead of down and required lots of goo for frizz management, Marigold's straight hair had luscious weight and appealing shine. And now it wasn't even long enough for a ponytail.

"I'll go get the broom and dustpan," Zinnie said, taking in the piles of hair on the bathroom floor. The waste was criminal.

"I'm not going to throw it away," Marigold said. "I'm going to donate it."

"Good idea," Zinnie said as she bent down to collect the hair. "But what about your career? You've always said your hair was one of your greatest assets."

"What career?" Marigold said. "I'm not an actress anymore."

"But you're going to acting camp next week," Zinnie said. She placed a handful of hair on the counter as neatly as possible for some lucky wigmaker.

"No, I'm not. I asked Mom last night and she talked to Aunt Sunny, and Aunt Sunny said that if I want to go to Pruet early to help her get ready for the wedding, I can."

"Just you?" Zinnie said. "That's not fair."

"Relax. We can all go. It's up to us."

"Really?" Zinnie asked, delighted. She'd been dreaming of her return to Pruet ever since last summer. She couldn't wait to walk along the harbor to the town beach, where her friend Ashley worked at the snack bar. Or to float on her back down the estuary as the sun warmed her face. Or to go to a clambake and eat lobster, corn on the cob, and fresh clams dripping with butter. Or to gaze up at the stars from the pear orchard while Aunt Sunny told stories of her sailing adventures. And of course she couldn't wait to see Aunt Sunny and give her a hug.

So the news that she would get to visit Pruet twice this summer, once for the wedding and again before school started, gave her a jolt of happiness. Or maybe, even better, they would have one extra-long visit to Pruet. She was about to ask Marigold what the exact plan was when Mom knocked on the door.

"Zinnie? Honey, are you in there?"

"Yes," Zinnie said, opening the door. "Is it true—"

"Wait," Marigold interrupted. "I haven't told—"

But it was too late. Mom was standing in the doorway, holding what looked like a magazine.

"Oh . . . ," Mom said. "What happened here? Zinnie gave you a . . . trim?"

"I had nothing to do with this," Zinnie said.

"I did it myself. I wanted a new look," Marigold said. "For a new me."

"I see," Mom said, and took a deep breath. "We could've made you an appointment."

"I wanted a new look *right away*," Marigold said. "Before I could change my mind. What do you think?"

"I wish you had asked me," Mom said. She put down the magazine and stood behind Marigold. Then she combed her hands through her daughter's hair. "But I gotta say, I think it's cute. It's a little . . . choppy, though. We can see if someone at the salon can fix it up for you. Actually, I hear bobs are coming back into style."

As Mom placed her hands at an angle under Marigold's hair, evening it out and tilting it forward with her palms, Zinnie realized that even with this self-styled haircut, Marigold looked glamorous.

"Is it true that we can go to Pruet next week, Mom?" Zinnie asked.

"That's what I was coming to talk to you about, Zin," Mom said with a smile.

"Yay!" Zinnie said, too excited to let Mom finish. "I can't believe that we're going twice this summer!"

"We aren't going twice. Way too expensive," Mom said.

"So we'll stay the whole summer?" Zinnie asked.

"I wish," Mom said. "Dad and I have to work, and Aunt Sunny is going on her honeymoon right after the wedding. But if you'd like to go early and stay until the wedding, that's fine. It was Marigold's idea, and when I called Aunt Sunny, she said she'd love the extra help getting ready for her big day."

"Of course I want to go!" Zinnie said.

"Helping the bride prepare is totally part of a bridesmaid's job," Marigold said, changing her part to the other side of her head and checking out the effect in the mirror. "I looked it up online."

"I know how much you've been looking forward to writing camp," Mom said.

"It's called the Summer Scribes," Zinnie said. This sounded much better to her than "writing camp."

"You can stay here with us if you'd like and then just go to Pruet for the wedding," Mom said. "It's up to you."

"I can't do both?" Zinnie asked.

"Not unless you can be in two places at once," Mom said. "This summer you get to choose. By the way, this came today."

Mom handed her the magazine, which had been facedown on the countertop. It was *Muses*, the publication that Mrs. Lee's Writers' Workshop produced at the end of the year. Zinnie had been anxiously awaiting its arrival ever since school ended.

"Cool," Zinnie said, taking in the cover artwork, a photograph of the blood moon everyone had stayed up late to see.

Meanwhile, Mom was enjoying playing with Marigold's new haircut. She made two lopsided pigtails that stuck straight up in the air. Marigold made a face to match.

"Zinnie, will you tell me a story, only not one with any witches this—" Lily started as she came into the bathroom. But she didn't finish her sentence. She took one look at Marigold and burst into giggles.

7 · To Go or Not to Go

Zinnie flopped back onto her bed and stared at the ceiling, her copy of *Muses* clutched tightly under her arm. After an hour spent reading it cover to cover, one thing was clear: the story that she had turned in to be considered for the Writers' Workshop didn't belong. Zinnie's stories and plays all involved fairies, magic, and even—she blushed at the thought—talking animals. There was time travel, at the very least. "Spell of Warriors," the work she had so proudly handed in to Mrs. Lee during the last week of school, was no exception.

But *Muses* was full of writing about real people and actual places. There was the narrative of the girl who had just arrived a few years ago from El Salvador, written in both Spanish and English; a series of character sketches of the people who lived in another student's Little Tokyo neighborhood; a story about a family who got lost on a camping trip; a funny essay about when all the kids in the Writers' Workshop first landed in England for their annual retreat and they had jet lag; an interview with one girl's great-grandmother, who had been in an internment camp in the 1940s; and a collection of poems called "The Wandering Question," which Zinnie didn't understand at all.

Zinnie was now certain that she was going to have to change her writing style if she wanted to get into the Writers' Workshop. Her only hope was to email Mrs. Lee and ask her to ignore her submission from last week. Then she'd have to attend Summer Scribes and write something new—something *real*. There was no way she could write something *real* on her own. Zinnie wasn't sure she'd ever even had any *real* ideas. Summer Scribes was the only way she stood a chance of getting into the Writers' Workshop. And Zinnie *had* to get in. She'd never wanted something so badly in all her life.

Throughout *Muses* were photographs of England, and even though her writing didn't seem to belong, Zinnie could so easily picture herself in those shots, standing with the other girls among the mysterious rock pillars at Stonehenge, walking through the grassy ruins of Tintern Abbey, and visiting Shakespeare's thatch-roofed home in Stratford-upon-Avon. Zinnie could envision herself scribbling away in her notebook as her imagination burst open in the English country-side. Instead of feeling left out like she did on the sports teams, she would fit right in.

But if she went to Summer Scribes, then she wouldn't be able to go to Pruet for more than a few days. The thought made Zinnie's heart ache. She was wearing the oversized Cape Cod T-shirt she'd gotten at the Pruet general store last year before the drive to the Boston airport and the long flight back to Los Angeles. She brought the soft sleeve to her nose and inhaled. Even though the T-shirt had been washed a hundred times, she believed its threads still held the scent of the Massachusetts coast: the sun-drenched dunes, Aunt Sunny's living room, the salty air, and even the faintest hint of a waffle cone. She closed her eyes and sniffed again.

She could almost see herself in her flip-flops and rash guard—the surfer-style bathing suit she pre-ferred—with a towel slung over her shoulder, walking home from the town beach. Or opening the gate to the pasture where the hairy cows wandered, with a dirt road that led to the beach with the rolling dunes, the big waves, and the estuary. Even though last year had been her first trip to Cape Cod, the idea of a summer with only a weekend-long visit to Pruet didn't seem like summer at all. She needed at least a week there in order to make it count.

But was it worth sacrificing her only hope of getting

into the Writers' Workshop?

Mom had told her "you get to choose" between Pruet and Summer Scribes like it was a good thing, but the decision already had a weight that was getting heavier by the minute. No matter which option Zinnie went with, she'd have to give up something awesome. Ever since she could remember, she'd wanted to make her own choices: what clothes to put on in the morning, what to eat for dinner, what activities to join after school. But as she'd gotten older and been asked to make more of her own decisions, she'd noticed how much easier it was to just have someone tell her what to do. She closed *Muses* and stuck her thumb in her mouth—an old, secret habit.

"Knock, knock," Dad said, tapping on her door. "Can I come give you a good-night kiss?"

"Sure," Zinnie said, wiping her thumb on her pajama bottoms as Dad opened the door.

"Uh-oh," Dad said after taking one look at his fretful daughter.

"What?" Zinnie asked.

"I see a worry line," Dad said. Zinnie pressed a finger to the place between her eyebrows where a line appeared when she was anxious.

"I don't know what to do," Zinnie said as Dad sat next to her on the bed. "I really want to go to Summer Scribes."

"That's fine," Dad said. "You can stay here with us

and then go to Pruet with Mom and me. You won't miss the wedding. There's no chance of that."

"But I'll miss going to the beach every day and jumping in the waves and climbing the dunes. I'll miss Aunt Sunny's stories. I'll only have three days to get Edith's ice cream. There probably won't be time to collect any shells. And Ashley told me she'd show me a hidden rope swing, but now that's out!"

"Then go to Pruet, honey," Dad said, and rubbed her back.

"But then I won't be able to concentrate on my writing enough to write the best thing ever so that I can get into the Writers' Workshop in the fall. And then I won't get to go to England and I'll have to play soccer and basketball, and, ugh, run track. And I really hate track." Zinnie's breath became shallow at the memory of "bringing up the rear." She was now nearly in tears. "Look," Zinnie said, opening *Muses* to the page with the picture of the girls on a double-decker bus. "They go to England over spring vacation, Dad. *England!* Do you know how bad I want to go to England? Do you know how many stories I could think of there? And all year long I'd get to meet real authors and go to plays and take field trips to interesting places."

"That sounds great, Zinnie. But what makes you think you need to do this summer camp to get in? Didn't you already write something for this program?"

"It's not good enough. I see that now."

"You're such a good writer. That play you wrote last summer was dynamite. That chicken character brought down the house."

She knew he was trying to make her feel better, but bringing up Gus the dancing chicken only triggered her biggest fear. She felt her voice climb higher in her throat. "The girls in the Writers' Workshop do real writing. I need to learn how to write about people and serious things. Not made-up warriors and dancing chickens and fake fairies."

Dad raised an eyebrow. "I don't know about that."

"It's true," Zinnie said, covering her face and shaking her head in despair.

"Okay. Let's take a deep breath," Dad said, placing a strong, reassuring arm around her back. "Close your eyes. Come on, we'll do it together." Zinnie closed her eyes. "In," Dad said, and they inhaled deeply. "And out." He made a shushing noise as they exhaled in unison. "In," Dad said, inhaling loudly, "and out." He shushed again. They repeated the cycle until Zinnie's heart stopped galloping.

"First of all, there's no such thing as 'real' writing and 'fake' writing," Dad said. "Good writing is good writing. I know that for a fact. And Mrs. Lee knows that, too, I'm sure."

"Then how come nothing in here," Zinnie said as she held up *Muses*, "is like anything I've written? I need to go to Summer Scribes. But I really don't want to miss out on going to Aunt Sunny's." She was starting to get worked up again. "What do I do?"

"Everyone is always missing out on something. Right now, there could be a really cool asteroid flying across the sky and we're missing out on seeing it."

"Really?" Zinnie said, opening her bedroom curtains.

"There *could* be," Dad said, drawing the curtains closed again. "My point is that we aren't actually missing out on anything, because we're here, in our home, hanging out together."

"I'm confused," Zinnie said, too tired for any kind of lesson. "I just want to know what to do."

"When I have a tough decision to make, I write out a question and put it under my pillow, and when I wake up, I usually know what to do."

"Really?" Zinnie asked.

"Really," Dad said.

"I guess I'll try it," Zinnie said. It was the only solution she had.

"It's worth a shot, right?" Dad said, handing Zinnie her notebook and a pen.

She wrote, *Do I go to Pruet early or stay in LA?* in her notebook and tore the page out. "Like this?"

"Exactly," Dad said. "Now fold it up and put it under your pillow."

She did as he said and then, exhausted from thinking, climbed under her covers. "I hope this helps."

"Me too," Dad said, handing her the book on her bedside table, a four-hundred-pager called *The Misty Trails of Dragons*, which she was almost done with.

"I still don't get why it works," Zinnie said, turning on the little reading lamp that was clipped to her bed frame.

"I like to think it's the work of dream fairies or the moon spirits. But, shhh! I wouldn't want Mrs. Lee's Writers' Workshop to hear me say that."

"Ha-ha," Zinnie said. "Very funny."

"Love you," Dad said.

"Love you, too," Zinnie said as Dad kissed her between the eyebrows and shut off the light.

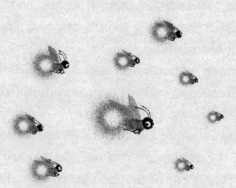

8 · The Illuminated Path

That night, Zinnie dreamed that she was walking down a twisting path in a dark forest. She was scared because the plants and animals were all strange. Then she realized that she had one of Aunt Sunny's field guides with her and she was able to identify the life around her. As she walked on, recording her discoveries in her notebook, dappled light illuminated the path. She knew that she didn't need the field guide anymore because although it was unfamiliar, she understood this world.

Then the path opened up. At the end of it was the dune in Pruet that she loved so well. She ran to it and climbed it. With each step her feet sank so deeply into the warm sand that it became almost comical for her to keep going, but she did. She was laughing as she reached the top. And there she saw the beach with the estuary, and miles of Atlantic Ocean, and her sisters playing in the waves. Aunt Sunny was there, too, standing in the surf.

"Come on in," Aunt Sunny called from below.

"But I forgot my bathing suit," Zinnie called back. "I won't be able to go in."

"That's okay," Aunt Sunny said, gesturing for her to join them. "I brought an extra one just in case!"

Zinnie ran down the dune, so happy that she lifted off the sand and actually started to fly.

When Zinnie woke up, she could feel the sun on her cheeks. At first she thought she was in Pruet about to take a swim with her sisters in the chilly ocean, but as she blinked awake and her room came into focus, she realized that she was in her bed in California. Pruet and all its summer treasure was thousands of miles away. She sat up and grinned, knowing that it wouldn't be far away for long.

That evening she wrote an email.

Dear Mrs. Lee,

Because of a last-minute opportunity to visit my great-aunt Sunny in Pruet, Massachusetts (she's getting married!), I am afraid that I will no longer be attending Summer Scribes. My mom said that she talked to the school, but I wanted to write and tell you that while I am very excited to see my aunt, I am also very sad to miss out on camp. It was pretty much the hardest decision of my life! Also, I know I sent a story already, "Spell of Warriors," but could you please delete it? I've thought about it a lot and I don't think it's a good story to submit. I can't tell you how much I want to be a part of the Writers' Workshop next year and I know I need to turn in my very best work. I think I need to write something new. Since I won't be attending Summer Scribes, do you have any advice for me?

Sincerely,

Zinnie Silver

She received a response the next morning.

Dear Zinnie,

We had quite a waiting list to get in, so your spot was snapped right up. Though we will miss you in class, I am glad you are going to spend some time with your aunt. How exciting to go to a wedding, and Cape Cod is beautiful. Many famous writers have found inspiration there, including Tennessee Williams and Eugene O'Neill. I have no doubt that you will do the same. Also, it's fine to submit a new story if that's what you'd like to do. It just has to be in by the deadline of July 10th. My only advice is to write a little something every day, keep your eyes open, and let yourself be surprised. Stories are everywhere. Some are hidden and some are in plain sight. Don't be afraid to go looking! I look forward to reading your work. Remember, I can only accept ten students into the Writers' Workshop, which is really very few.

Best wishes,

Candace Lee

Zinnie felt a twinge of anxiety as she read that last line. *Only ten students!* There were five seventh-grade spots and five eighth-grade spots. New spots only opened up for the eighth graders who chose to leave the workshop or who, in Mrs. Lee's words, "weren't taking full advantage of the opportunity." It hardly ever happened that an eighth grader left, so it was extra-important that Zinnie get in this year. Going to Pruet had seemed like such a good idea when she'd woken up from her dream, but now she wondered if she'd made a mistake.

Her spot in Summer Scribes had been filled, so it was too late to change her mind. She'd made her choice and she was going to have to stick to it. She could only hope that it would lead to inspiration the way the path in her dreams had led her to the dune, and that her words would be her wings.

9 · Coast to Coast

"Thank you for joining us on Atlantic Airlines," the flight attendant said over the loudspeaker. "We have now reached our cruising altitude of thirty thousand feet. We'll be coming by shortly with snacks and beverages. A menu with available items can be found in the seat-back pocket."

"Remember, Mom and Dad said no soda," Marigold said to her sisters as they reached for their menus. "Too much sugar."

"I always get cranberry juice anyway," Zinnie said.

"They didn't say anything about cookies," Lily said, pointing to a picture of one on the menu.

"That's true," Zinnie said.

"We can split it," Marigold said, determined to be the responsible older sister.

It was almost two weeks later and the three Silver

sisters were on their way to Pruet, where they'd spend another two weeks helping Aunt Sunny get ready for her wedding. They were settled into row 34, with Zinnie on the aisle, Lily in the middle, and Marigold by the window. Lily liked the center seat because she enjoyed being right in the middle of the sister action. Zinnie and Marigold had had to flip a coin for the window seat. Zinnie wanted to be by the window because she liked the view when they crossed the Rocky Mountains. Also, despite everyone telling her it would never happen, she was still hoping that they would fly close enough to another plane so that she could wave to the other passengers.

Marigold had other reasons. She wanted to watch Los Angeles shrink into a maze with ant-sized cars and teardrop swimming pools until it disappeared. She wanted to relish the moment they escaped into the clouds and soared into the blank blue sky. So back in terminal 3, she'd been delighted when her dad had flipped a coin, and she'd won.

As she pressed her forehead against the window and stared at the sky, she was relieved, knowing that with every minute there was more space between her and Los Angeles. *Night Sprites* was coming out in theaters tomorrow and she wasn't going to have to be there. The billboards advertising the movie were everywhere from Santa Monica to Pasadena.

It seemed like every single bus had a picture of

the star, Amanda Mills, with her glittering wings, on the side of it. Thankfully, there were no billboards or city buses in Pruet. There wasn't even a movie theater. It was true that the director, Philip Rathbone, had a summer home in Pruet, but he was going to be so busy promoting *Night Sprites* that he wouldn't be there.

Maybe even more than wanting to forget her acting disappointment, Marigold didn't want to see the Cuties—especially once they realized that she wasn't in the movie. Maybe they already knew, Marigold thought with a shiver. Maybe Pilar had told them. Marigold's heart pinched as she remembered her last meeting with Pilar at the Cupcake Café. During their middle-of-the-night mother-daughter meeting, Mom had encouraged Marigold to talk to Pilar so they could clear the air before they went their separate ways for the summer. Marigold called Pilar the next day and asked her to hang out.

"It's important," Marigold said on the phone, sensing that Pilar was trying to think of an excuse. "It's about our friendship."

"Okay, meet me at the Cupcake Café," Pilar said.

Mom drove Marigold to the café, which was right around the corner from Pilar's house, and waited outside in the car.

They both ordered the vanilla cupcake with chocolate frosting, and then they faced each other in silence until Marigold finally said, "I like your haircut."

"Thank you," Pilar said, peeling the wrapper off her cupcake. "I like yours too."

"Thanks," Marigold said. This was already so weird. It seemed like just yesterday they would have planned their haircuts out together, and now they were being as polite as almost-strangers.

"I saw you at Griffith Park with the Cuties!" Marigold finally said after what felt like a whole minute of awkward silence. "How come you lied to me about having to pack for Mexico the other day?"

"I guess I knew you'd be mad," Pilar said. "I'm sorry."

"Are we still best friends?" Marigold asked.

"I don't know," Pilar said. "You basically ignored me this spring. It really hurt my feelings. I mean, did you expect me to not make any other friends? The Cuties at least want to hang out with me."

"I'm really sorry," Marigold said. "I want to hang out with you now. Can we just go back to how it used to be?"

"Don't you only want to hang out with famous people now?" Pilar asked, leaning back in her chair and crossing her arms.

"No. Not at all! I'd so much rather hang out with you!"

"Really?" Pilar smiled.

"Yes!" Marigold said. "I've missed you so much."

"Me too!" Pilar said. She stood up and hugged her. Marigold hugged her back. Pilar smelled just like her house—pleasant and clean and a little perfumy. Marigold fought back tears as she realized how much she had missed their pajama parties and shopping trips.

"So, are you going to be going to the premiere and stuff?" Pilar asked.

"Well," Marigold said, "here's the thing. I'm not in the movie anymore. I was cut out of it."

"Oh my gosh," Pilar said. "I'm so sorry."

"I'm definitely not a movie star," Marigold said. "But the good news is that we can hang out all the time now."

"Oh," Pilar said. "Now I feel like you want to hang out with me just because your plan to be famous fell through!"

"It's not true," Marigold said. "You're my best friend."

"Only because you're not in the movie!" Pilar sighed. "Look, I need some space this summer. To think things over."

"Um, okay. Are you going to be best friends with the Cuties now?" Pilar shrugged. "Can you at least tell me why they don't like me?"

"They think that you think that you're soooo great. It's like you don't think you're a normal, regular girl. Maybe you should try to be more . . . ordinary." As mad as Pilar was, Marigold could tell that she was trying to give her advice. "At least that's what you have to do if you want to have any friends in eighth grade.

"I'll call you when I get back from Mexico in August," Pilar went on. She picked up the cupcake with one hand, tucked her wallet under her arm, then put her keys and her phone in the other hand and walked out the door.

She needs a nice bag, Marigold thought. *Maybe a clutch.* Then she stared at the table in disbelief at the conversation. She had no appetite for her cupcake.

As soon as Marigold climbed into her mom's car, she burst into tears.

Now, on the airplane, Lily tugged on her sleeve.

"How long is this ride, Marigold?" Lily asked, chewing the sugar-free gum that Mom had bought them to keep their ears from popping during takeoff and landing.

"Four hours and forty-four minutes," Marigold said.

"Oh," Lily said. Marigold reached into her carry-on bag and pulled out some activities for her youngest sister: stickers, drawing paper, and a book about puppies. Lily opened the puppy book and began to read. "Four hours and forty-four minutes is a lot of time to read about puppies."

"You can color, too," Marigold said. "Just let me know when you get bored." Then she turned on her iPad, switched it to airplane mode, and opened a diary app that she'd downloaded last night. Now that Los

Angeles was safely behind her, it was time to get started on her plan.

Marigold was going to give herself a makeover, inside and out, and she was going to record it in her digital diary. The haircut was just the beginning. She would return to school with a new look and a new attitude, and maybe even start going by the less distinctive name Mary.

This summer she was going to practice how to be more ordinary. After all, changing over the summer was something that people did. Girls had left the sixth grade looking like kids and returned in September as full-blown teenagers. Even though Marigold was on the late-bloomer side of the whole looking-like-a-teenager thing, why couldn't she go away and return as the kind of girl everyone wanted to be friends with? She tapped her iPad on and started to make a list of things she thought she needed to do in order to transform.

1. Be more ordinary.

2. Dress casual.

3. Don't show off or try to get attention.

4. Find something else to love besides acting.

She leaned back in her seat and examined this list. It was shorter than she would've liked, but she wasn't sure what else to do to make sure she stopped behaving like she thought she was "sooooo great." She decided that this was okay for now. Maybe not being a famous actress wouldn't be so bad. There were lots of people who didn't care about being actresses or looking like movie stars, and they seemed perfectly happy. She glanced over at Zinnie, whose eyes were glued to the pages of her enormous novel about dragons. There was a small stain on her T-shirt, and even though Marigold had taught her how to do her hair, she still just always put it up in a messy ponytail. Marigold opened her list again and added under the first point: **Dress more like Zinnie.**

Can I go that far? Marigold wondered. *Probably not. That's a little too extreme, but I bet I can find something in between.*

And in Pruet there was Peter Pasque, the red-haired boy who'd taken her sailing last year. He didn't care about acting or Hollywood. He hated the spotlight. When he'd sung "Rocky Raccoon" last year at the talent show, his face had turned bright red and he'd looked totally miserable.

She smiled as she thought of the two of them sailing close to the beach and how fun it had been when the wind picked up and it had felt like they were flying. Now that she was thinking of him, she remembered that he'd told her that at first he'd thought she was stuck-up. They'd lost touch once school started, but he would be so happy to see that she was on her way to being perfectly average. And if he was her boyfriend again this summer, she'd definitely have stuff to talk to the Cuties about.

"Hi, girls," the flight attendant said as she came around with the beverage cart.

Marigold quickly shut her iPad and put it in her seatback pocket. Technically, it was hers and she didn't have to share it, though it was going to be hard because her sisters always wanted to get into her stuff. Zinnie had brought her laptop, and Marigold hoped that would keep Zinnie from trying to use the iPad and discovering her diary.

"What would you like to drink?" the flight attendant asked.

"Cranberry juice, please," Zinnie said.

"Apple juice, please," Lily said.

"Sparkling water and a cookie to share, please," Marigold said.

"Yes, ma'ams, coming right up," the flight attendant said, and she gave the girls their drinks and a cookie the size of a dinner plate. "Oh, and someone on the last flight left this behind, and I thought you older girls would be interested."

She handed Marigold the latest issue of *Young & Lovely* magazine.

"Thanks," Zinnie said, reaching for it and quickly turning it upside down on her tray table. But it was too late. Marigold had seen the cover, which had the *Night Sprites* cast on it. Marigold felt a twinge in her chest so sharp that for a moment she was sure that the cabin pressure had dropped and they were plummeting below the clouds to the hard earth they had so recently left behind.

10 · A Room of Her Own

Zinnie could practically feel her curls rise an extra inch as she and her sisters bounded out of Aunt Sunny's old station wagon and into the humid evening, but the last thing she cared about right now was her hair. They were back in Pruet, where the air smelled sweet and green and it felt like summer existed all year long. Of course, Zinnie knew that wasn't true. New England was famous for its seasons. Aunt Sunny had sent them pictures of the red, orange, and yellow leaves in autumn, her cottage covered in snow at Christmastime, and the garden unrecognizably muddy and brown after long spring rains. But there was something about this place right now, with its warm, mossy stone walls, boat-dotted harbor, and dune-covered beaches that made Zinnie feel as if she was stepping into an eternal summer.

She breathed in the Pruet air. It was almost six p.m., and as she listened to her sisters and Aunt Sunny chatting about which bag belonged to which sister, the sun was casting long shadows across the lawn and the insects were practicing for their twilight chorus. The hollyhocks and roses bloomed in shades of pink and red, and the hydrangea bushes created a ruffled hedge of purple pom-poms that made Zinnie feel like cheering.

It had been a long ride from the airport in Boston, but they had so much to tell Aunt Sunny that Zinnie had hardly noticed the time. They hadn't stopped talking since the first sight of Aunt Sunny at the baggage carousel, where she'd greeted them in her sun hat, boat shoes, and Piping Plover Society T-shirt. The sisters regaled her with stories all the way through the noisy tunnel that ran under Boston Harbor, and along the freeway, which Aunt Sunny called the highway, and down the narrow country roads by the sea.

First Lily listed the many reasons why she thought she should have a dog. Then there was a great discussion about Marigold's haircut, which Aunt Sunny called "smart."

"I'm never acting again," Marigold told her. "This is the start of a whole new me."

"I see," Aunt Sunny said.

Then Zinnie explained how cool the Writers' Workshop was and how much she wanted to be a part of it.

"In order to get in, I have to write something amazing," Zinnie said.

"What a task," Aunt Sunny replied.

Finally they all wanted to know what Aunt Sunny wanted as a wedding present.

"Lily, I was counting on you to scatter rose petals for me," Aunt Sunny said.

"I can do that easy," Lily said.

"I was hoping that Marigold would read a Shakespearean sonnet during the ceremony, and that Zinnie might write something for me, but now that I've heard your stories . . ."

"I'll do anything else, anything at all," Marigold said. "But I can't perform."

"Oh dear," Aunt Sunny said.

"I'll be your wedding organizer," Marigold said.

"That would be helpful," Aunt Sunny said.

"Do you think maybe I can read the sonnet instead of writing something?" Zinnie asked. "Because I already have to write the greatest work of my life while I'm here."

"That *is* quite a challenge. Very well, then," Aunt Sunny said. "I'll need a lot of help making that wedding cake."

"You're going to make the cake yourself?" Zinnie asked.

"We're going to make it together. That can be your gift to me," Aunt Sunny said.

"How come you didn't pick us up from the airport last year?" Zinnie asked when they arrived at Aunt Sunny's cottage. It looked like something out of a fairy tale. Aunt Sunny unloaded Zinnie's suitcase from the trunk, and Marigold and Lily dashed inside to use the bathroom. Last summer, a driver had picked them up in Boston and taken them to Pruet.

"I'm a bit of a country mouse," Aunt Sunny said, grabbing Lily's duffel bag and tossing it over her shoulder. "I've always been afraid of driving in that Boston traffic. It can get awfully hairy. But after you girls visited last summer, I made a promise to myself to step out of my comfort zone and try new things."

"Like getting married again," Zinnie said, smiling up at her.

"Exactly," Aunt Sunny said, giving Zinnie's hand a squeeze.

"Was driving in the traffic as scary as you thought it was going to be?" Zinnie asked as they walked inside. Last summer, Aunt Sunny's house had seemed so strange, but this year she instantly knew its wooden walls and familiar smell, like something was always baking. She was filled with a warm, happy feeling.

"While I can't say I see myself driving a taxicab around Boston anytime soon, it wasn't as scary as I thought it was going to be," Aunt Sunny said, pausing in the entryway to pick up the mail. Zinnie noticed that where once there had been a picture of a boat, there now was photograph of Sunny and Tony holding hands in the garden. "Also, there's something about love that gives you courage."

"Interesting," Zinnie said. She liked this line and thought she might jot it down in her notebook later. Mrs. Lee had told her that writers were great thieves, as they often stole bits of conversation for their work.

"Would you pick up the newspaper for me?" Aunt Sunny asked, pointing to the *Buzzards Bay Bugle* that had fallen to the floor.

"Sure," Zinnie said, bending to pick it up. She almost gasped as she saw that on the front page was a picture of Philip Rathbone strolling along the harbor. The headline read:

Hollywood Director Takes Respite from Blockbuster Movie Fanfare in Pruet

"I'd better put this in the recycling," Zinnie said, not wanting Marigold to learn that Philip Rathbone was here.

"I haven't had a chance to read it, actually," Aunt Sunny said. "I was going to give it a glance after dinner."

"But Aunt Sunny," Zinnie said, pointing to the picture of Mr. Rathbone, "Marigold can't see this. You have no idea how sad she's been. There were two days when she didn't even brush her hair."

"Your mom told me all about it. Poor dear," Aunt Sunny said, taking the paper, folding it in half, and tucking it under her arm. "Such disappointment can be devastating. We'll try to refocus her energy while she's here. I'm going to keep you girls busy, feed you well, and make sure you get plenty of sun and time at the beach. Hopefully that will put the wind back in her sails. Speaking of food, I know how much you love clams, so we're having them for dinner," Aunt Sunny continued as they made their way into the living room with the luggage. "Tony is picking them up fresh from Gifford's Fish Store, along with some corn, beans, and tomatoes."

"Yum!" Zinnie said. It would be a perfect Pruet dinner. Zinnie could hear her sisters chatting away upstairs, where she was certain they were getting settled in the same attic bedroom they had slept in last summer. But before she could rush up the stairs to join them, Aunt Sunny beckoned Zinnie to follow her through the living room and into what had once been her office. Last year, Aunt Sunny's big desk was in here, along with lots of pictures of boats that her late husband had built and bookshelves crammed with old science books and field guides. Now it was empty except for a small green desk and a chair. The window looked out on the lawn.

"What happened to all your stuff?" Zinnie asked.

"It's in my office at the Piping Plover Society," Aunt

Sunny said. "Tony is moving in after we get married. And since we're living in my house, we thought Tony needed a space that was just for him. I know that you plan on writing a great work this summer. It was Virginia Woolf who said that a writer needs a room of her own, so while you are here, this is your room."

"Thanks," Zinnie said, though she wasn't sure who Virginia Woolf was. Probably the girls in the Writers' Workshop knew. Zinnie vowed that she would look her up as soon as she had a chance. Maybe she'd post a few of her quotes around her desk. The room was pretty much perfect the way it was, with a nice big window, a desk that fit her, and a comfortable chair. Aunt Sunny had even provided Zinnie with a cup full of freshly sharpened pencils, a stack of loose-leaf paper, and a rock.

"What's this?" Zinnie asked, holding the rock and turning to see Aunt Sunny smiling at her from the doorway. "A paperweight?"

"I suppose you could use it as a paperweight. I thought it would be something nice to hold on to when you're thinking of just the right word. I found it on the beach this spring. It reminded me of you somehow."

Zinnie examined the rock. It was smooth, cool, and freckled, and it had a pleasant weight. Zinnie wasn't sure exactly what Aunt Sunny meant when she said it reminded her of Zinnie, but she knew it was a good thing. A wise thing, even.

"I'm going to make sure that you have time for writing while you're here, but right now I think you should get settled upstairs. Tony will be here any minute with the groceries, and I have to make dessert."

"What kind of dessert?" Zinnie asked.

"It's a surprise," Aunt Sunny said with a wink, which of course, gave it away. Back in Pruet and Aunt Sunny's surprise brownies—Zinnie didn't think the day could get any better.

"Hiya—anyone home?" Tony called from the entryway. "Clam delivery here!"

"Tony!" Zinnie exclaimed, and she ran to greet her soon-to-be new great-uncle. He was walking toward the kitchen carrying a tote bag that was bursting with vegetables and, Zinnie imagined, fresh clams that they would eat tonight, served just how she liked them—with plenty of warm butter.

"Hi, Zinnie!" Tony said as he placed the groceries on the kitchen counter.

"How are you?" Zinnie asked.

"All the better for seeing you," Tony replied, and gave her a hug. He smelled like a day at the beach. Marigold and Lily flew into the kitchen and also gave him a hug. Aunt Sunny followed, beaming as the sisters gathered around her almost-husband.

"Is it just me," Tony said to Aunt Sunny as she kissed his cheek, "or does this town feel a little brighter now?"

"It's definitely not just you," Aunt Sunny said, reaching for her apron. "The weather report says that some California sun has arrived in Pruet—and lucky us, it will be shining bright from now until our wedding day!"

11 · Ordinary Clothes

It was like the country air had some sort of medicine in it, because Marigold had awakened in the morning sunlight of the attic bedroom feeling better than she had in days. Or maybe the extra brownie that she'd had for a midnight snack was what put her in such a good mood. Aunt Sunny had wrapped the surprise brownies in plastic and placed them in the fridge after supper in case "certain sisters who were still on California time" got hungry late at night.

Lily had no problem adjusting to the East Coast time difference, but Marigold and Zinnie hadn't been able to fall asleep. They sat up for hours discussing all the people they wanted to see the next day (Peter, Ashley, Jean, Edith), the places they wanted to go (the town beach, the beach with the dunes and estuary, the yacht club, Edith's Ice Cream Shop, the Pruet general store, the library), and the things they wanted to do (swim, sail, eat ice cream), until they realized that it was almost midnight, which of course reminded them of the midnight snack that was waiting for them.

They crept downstairs so as not to wake anyone. But Aunt Sunny must've known they were going to visit the fridge, because she had left a light on in the kitchen. They poured tall glasses of cold milk and ate the chilled brownies in silence as the kitchen clock ticked and a single night bird chirped somewhere in the blue-black sky on the other side of the windows. When they were finished, they found themselves deliciously exhausted. They debated brushing their teeth, decided against it, and stumbled into their beds and drifted off to sleep.

Now the smell of coffee and the sounds of Aunt Sunny making breakfast rose up from the kitchen. Marigold was surprised that she was the first one awake. She was usually a late riser. Lily was curled up in her bed with Benny the bunny in her arms. Zinnie was stretched out on top of her covers with a smile on her face. Marigold guessed that she was dreaming of ice cream. Since privacy was rare in Pruet, where she shared a room with her sisters, Marigold pulled her iPad out from under her bed and opened her digital diary.

She reviewed the list she'd written on the plane, thought for a moment, and wrote:

Today I'll find a new thing to love instead of acting. Marigold paused. How was she supposed to do this? She thought about other activities she'd tried. She'd been on the swim team at one point. She didn't exactly love it, but maybe if she practiced more, she could learn to. After all, the Cuties were all on the swim team. She wrote that maybe she would go for a long swim at the town beach today.

She also wrote about how she would try to see Peter as soon as possible. A smile spread across her lips as she typed his name. It was going to be fun to see him again, and because he was an ordinary boy, she'd probably become more ordinary just by spending time with him.

She realized that writing in the diary gave her a feeling similar to that of sharing something with a friend. Maybe if she kept writing in her diary, she wouldn't miss Pilar so much. **A diary is like a friend that will never betray you,** she wrote.

Even though she was hungry for one of Aunt Sunny's breakfasts, she kept writing. She decided that in addition to practicing swimming and looking for Peter, she would wear ordinary clothes today. She went into her dresser drawer and picked out a plain green T-shirt and shorts. Because Aunt Sunny had no full-length mirror in the house, Marigold used her iPad to snap a selfie. Her haircut looked really cute with the T-shirt's unusual neckline, which she had barely noticed before. In fact, this T-shirt looked way better on her with short hair than it had when she'd had long hair.

She took it off and chose a simple blue dress to try on instead. Marigold had plucked the dress off the sale rack at Target. It was so marked down that it had cost less than the toilet paper Mom was buying that day! When she'd tried it on at home, she'd realized it fit weirdly at the waist and was a little too long to be really flattering, but somehow they'd never returned it. Now she slipped it over her head and took another selfie, hoping that she had finally found the outfit that would make her as ordinary as possible. But she must've grown an inch since the last time she'd tried the dress on, because now it fit her well. She would even go so far as to say that it looked good on her.

She returned to her diary to consider her problem. How was she going to look ordinary when her outfits were all so cute? She peered over at Zinnie and typed:

Good thing Zinnie is here. She doesn't care about clothes at all!

Marigold started to open Zinnie's drawer but stopped herself. She always made such a big deal about Zinnie not looking through her stuff or taking her clothes. She imagined that Zinnie would be really mad if she went through her things without checking with her first. She watched her sister's chest rise and fall with her breath. Zinnie was so sound asleep, she would never know. Marigold decided to take a quick peek.

She grimaced as she looked inside the drawer. It was chaos. Zinnie hadn't even been on the East Coast twenty-four hours and she'd already made a mess. Had she just dumped the contents of her suitcase in there? Had her clothes even been folded to begin with? Marigold picked a balled-up T-shirt out of the mess and held it up. It was a Miss Hadley's Field Day T-shirt. Taking another quick glance at her sister to make sure she was sleeping, Marigold put it on over the blue dress and took a picture to see how she looked.

Yuck! she thought when she saw the picture. She might as well have been wearing a paper bag! The gray shirt completely robbed her complexion of color. The sleeves made her arms look short. And the rest of the shirt hung bulkily around her middle. She tapped on the diary app.

I just tried on one of Zinnie's T-shirts, and it looked terrible!! I can't go this far. Poor Zinnie. I worry that she won't ever find a — boyfriend because she really is such a spaz.

Almost as though Zinnie could hear her sister's thoughts, she stirred. Marigold quickly tossed the iPad on the bed, pulled the T-shirt off, and put one of her own T-shirts on. She had started to stuff Zinnie's shirt in the drawer when Zinnie sat up, yawned, and asked, "What're you doing?"

"Just getting dressed," Marigold said, turning around

and doing her best to look innocent. Now she was glad the drawer was so disorganized, because the stuffed-in T-shirt wouldn't stand out.

"You look . . . stressed," Zinnie said, rubbing her eyes.

"I'm not," Marigold said, leaning against the dresser.

"Oh, can I use your iPad?" Zinnie asked. "I need to Google Virginia Woolf."

"Aunt Sunny doesn't have Wi-Fi, remember?" Marigold said. Her iPad was glowing on the bed, leaving the page of her digital diary on full, bright display. She clenched her jaw and willed the iPad to go to sleep. Marigold had always been a more guarded person than either of her sisters, but there was something about the public embarrassment of being cut from the movie that made her privacy feel more valuable than ever. "Besides, you have your laptop."

"Oh, yeah," Zinnie said, and then she sat up straight, her eyes brightening as she seemed to wake up all of a sudden. "Do I smell pancakes? Is Aunt Sunny making her silver dollar pancakes?"

Zinnie hopped out of bed and was running down the staircase before Marigold could respond. Marigold breathed a sigh of relief, grabbed her iPad, and shut the cover.

"What are you hiding?" Lily asked. Marigold turned and was surprised to see her littlest sister sitting on the edge of her bed with Benny the bunny in her lap.

"What do you mean?" Marigold asked. "I'm not hid-ing anything. And how long have you been awake?"

"You look like you're hiding something," Lily said. "Like when Dad buys those Snickers bars he doesn't want Mom to see and he puts them way up on that shelf with the popcorn machine we never use."

"He does that?" Marigold asked. Lily nodded. "Hey, do you smell those pancakes?"

"Pancakes!" Lily said. "Yum!"

"You'd better go get some before Zinnie eats them all," Marigold said as she chased Lily out of the room, making chomping sounds.

As soon as Lily was bounding down the stairs, Marigold put the iPad deep in her dresser drawer under a pile of neatly folded T-shirts. Then she care-fully laid out an adorable blue gingham dress for Lily to wear for her first day of nature camp. At least one of the Silver sisters needed to look good. She was about to head to the kitchen when she decided to take another security measure just in case someone had the urge to snoop. She took the iPad back out of the drawer and set up a password.

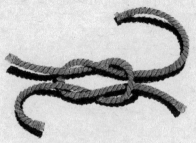

12 · Preparations

By the time Marigold made her way downstairs, her sisters were already on their second helpings of blueberry silver dollar pancakes.

"Why are you so fancy today?" Lily was asking Aunt Sunny, who was pouring more batter on the griddle. Marigold would hardly say that Aunt Sunny was fancy, but she was definitely more dressed up than usual in a khaki skirt, a button-down shirt, and even a pair of earrings.

"I have to go to work," Aunt Sunny said. "The Piping Plover Society has become quite an organization—we have our own offices and with computers and a copy machine and everything."

Marigold could feel Zinnie eyeing her as she took a seat at the table.

"Why are you so . . . unfancy today?" Zinnie asked.

"Are you feeling okay?"

"I'm dressing casual this summer," Marigold said as Aunt Sunny put three hot pancakes on her plate.

"Why?" Zinnie asked.

"Just because," Marigold said.

"Speaking of getting dressed," Aunt Sunny said, and checked her watch, "Lily, you need to finish up and get ready for camp. We have to leave in fifteen minutes."

Lily nodded and dutifully stuffed her last pancake in her mouth.

"I put your clothes on your bed," Marigold said as Lily carried her plate to the sink.

"And don't forget to brush your teeth," Zinnie added.

"I know, I know," Lily said as she left the kitchen. "Jeesh."

"Let's talk about our bridesmaid duties," Marigold said to Aunt Sunny.

"Okay," Aunt Sunny said as she sat down with her coffee and a pad of yellow paper. "First on the list is making the cake."

"What kind of cake?" Zinnie asked.

"Lemon blackberry with cream cheese frosting," Aunt Sunny said. "My mother's recipe."

"Oh, yum!" Zinnie said.

"We can start today," Aunt Sunny said.

"But we won't be eating the cake until the wedding," Marigold said. "Won't it get stale?"

"My mother always said that cake baking should

never be rushed, and we have a lot of baking to do. And then we have to assemble the layers and frost and decorate the tiers. We'll make as much of the cake as possible in advance, freeze it, decorate the layers the day before the wedding, and then put it all together on the big day."

"So we'll do the baking today?" Zinnie asked.

"We have to make six cakes, two for each tier, so I think we'll do half of them tonight and half tomorrow. I don't have enough cake pans to make them all at once. Our first task will be to find the recipe! It's in one of my recipe boxes, and I'm just praying that it didn't get lost over the years."

"We can always just use another recipe," Marigold suggested.

"I have my heart set on this one," Aunt Sunny said. "This was my mother's favorite. Every summer, as soon as the blackberries were ripe, we'd go to Davis Farms and fill two baskets with the juiciest, sweetest blackberries in the world. Of course, we inevitably ate half of them by the time we got home, which is why Mom always had us fill two baskets. Using this recipe will be my way of having my mother and sisters with me. We're going to have eighty guests, but oh, how I'll be missing those three. Especially Beatrice."

As Aunt Sunny bowed her head for a moment, Marigold and Zinnie exchanged a melancholy glance. Beatrice was Aunt Sunny's much older sister, and she was also their grandmother. Grammy, as they called her, had passed away in the fall. The girls hadn't been close to their grandmother, who lived in Florida. Zinnie remembered visiting her when she was very little, but for the past several years she hadn't been well enough to have visitors. But once, many years ago, she had been a great beauty and, their Mom said, a whole lot of fun.

"It's really sad she missed your wedding," Marigold said. "Mom said that she used to love parties."

"She certainly did," Aunt Sunny said. "She was such a social butterfly before she became ill."

"How are you going to fit eighty people in here?" Marigold asked.

"We're going to put up a party tent right there," Aunt Sunny said, pointing to the lawn. "There'll be a dance floor and a buffet and even a platform where Tony's band is going to play. And we'll have ten tables where people will eat their dinner. We'll need place cards so people know where to sit, and of course tablecloths and napkins. I have a great collection of them in the attic, but they need to be sorted. Can you believe all of this hadn't even occurred to me? I'm so glad you girls are here to help!"

"We need balloons, too," Zinnie suggested. "Everyone loves balloons."

"Balloons are festive," Aunt Sunny said, "but they also create debris and pose a hazard for wildlife, and as the director of the Piping Plover Society, I'm afraid I can't have that."

"I didn't know that," Zinnie said.

"How about shells and flowers as decorations for the tables?" Marigold suggested, realizing that arts and crafts was something normal that she could be good at. "You have a whole garden full of flowers, and we can collect shells at the town beach."

"Marigold, that's a lovely idea!" Aunt Sunny said. "But I want to make something very clear. As glad as I am for your help and as much as I need it, you girls are here to relax and have fun. Kids are so overscheduled these days. I'm hoping that you girls will follow your whims, climb the trees, ride the waves. When we were your age, my sisters and I thought of our own adventures every day. We had chores, but for the most part our time was ours. That's what I wish for you."

Marigold smiled. This sounded perfect to her.

"Oh gosh, now look at the time. I've got to get to work. I've packed you both lunches. They are in the fridge. Don't forget to pick up Lily at three o'clock."

"Of course!" Marigold said.

"And would you mind stopping by the yacht club for me? Jean and Mack make the most delicious blackberry jam, which they serve for yacht club brunches. Jean said she'd be happy to give me some jars of it for the wedding cake."

"No problem," Marigold said. Jean and Mack were

Peter's parents. Mack was the manager of the yacht club. Stopping by to pick up the jam would give her the perfect excuse to see Peter.

She had everything to look forward to: a day at the town beach, the possibility of seeing Peter Pasque, and the chance to reinvent herself, one ordinary outfit at a time.

13 · The First Mission

J ust as they had done many times last summer, Zinnie and Marigold walked down the road to the beach. Zinnie kept her eyes peeled and her mind open. She had her notebook and pen in her back pocket as she looked for a story. "Remember, stories are everywhere," Mrs. Lee had written in her email. "Some are hidden and some are in plain sight." Zinnie ran her hand along the stone wall, its texture rough under her fingers. She looked at the names on the mailboxes. She observed the flowers in the gardens they passed, the telephone wires above her, and the sound of Marigold's flip-flops slapping her heels as she walked beside her. Where were the stories?

When they reached Harbor Road, she studied the boats at their moorings. The clouds cast shadows on the water, creating dark patches on the bright-blue surface. She squinted into the sun to check out the wooden sign for the general store. The red letters had been repainted since last summer. She noticed the grass growing through the cracks in the sidewalk, the station wagon that drove by with a wet, happy dog leaning out the window, and a pile of lobster traps in the back of a truck. She saw the details and she made notes in her notebook, but without imagining wind spirits in the clouds or fairies in the stone walls or the voice of that dog shouting out a joke, she just couldn't find the stories.

"Holy moly, is that who I think it is?" Ashley called from behind the snack bar as Zinnie and Marigold placed their towels on their old spot at the town beach.

"Yup!" Zinnie called back as she kicked off her sneakers and headed toward the snack bar. With the warm sand between her toes, a cool breeze on her face, and the sight of her old friend waving at her, Zinnie couldn't stop smiling. It was good to be back. She and Marigold had come to the town beach almost every day during their visit last summer. Here the water was perfect for swimming, the sand was ideal for lounging, and there were cold, delicious treats when Zinnie was thirsty or had a snack attack.

"Hi!" Zinnie said, running the last few steps to greet her friend. "You didn't forget about me, did you?"

"Uh, no," Ashley said, reaching into the freezer and

handing her a red ice pop. Last summer, Ashley had always saved a red one for her. They were the most popular flavor and often sold out before lunch. "You're unforgettable. How long are you in town for?"

"Two weeks," Zinnie said, taking the delicious treat. "My aunt Sunny is getting married and I'm a brides-maid. My sisters and I came early to help her get ready. Today we're collecting shells for decorations. What have you been up to since you won first place in the talent show?"

"I joined the chorus at school and I was even asked to sing at the mall last Christmas."

"That's so cool!" Zinnie said, proud that she'd had a role in her friend's success. After all, Zinnie was the one who'd organized the talent show.

"Where are your sisters?" Ashley asked.

"Lily is at camp and Marigold is right—" Zinnie looked toward where their towels were, but Marigold wasn't there. Zinnie scanned the beach until she saw a flash of her sister's hot-pink bathing suit in the water out by the floating docks. "Oh, there she is," Zinnie said, pointing.

"She's doing laps?" Ashley asked.

"I guess so," Zinnie said. She'd hoped Marigold would be her old self once they'd arrived in Pruet, but she was still acting totally strange.

"At the beach? Weird. That's what the old ladies usually do," Ashley said.

"She hasn't really been herself lately," Zinnie said with a sigh as she watched Marigold switch to the breaststroke. "Anyway, I have to go collect shells."

"There aren't a lot of good shells around here. You have to climb over the jetty," Ashley said, pointing to the long line of rocks that extended into the water. "And look on that part of the beach where there aren't as many people."

"Got it," Zinnie said. "See ya!"

Even though Marigold called them "the ugliest things on the planet," Zinnie was so glad she was wearing her water shoes, which were like tight-fitting mesh sneakers, as she climbed over the jetty. The pile of rocks was uneven and a little jagged, and she nearly stubbed her toe as hopped to the other side. There were hardly any other people over here, just a couple of ladies reading magazines in beach chairs. She picked up some shells as she waded in the water.

Farther away was a boy who appeared to also be looking for shells. He was walking slowly through the shallow water with his head down. He had longish hair that fell in front of his face, but she could tell by the way he was moving that he was looking very carefully. He paused, wiping his eyes. Zinnie thought she saw his shoulders shake. *Is he crying?* she wondered as she walked into the surf up to her ankles. She couldn't tell. But by the way he turned away and buried his face in his hands, she guessed that he didn't want anyone to see him. Respectfully, she looked away. The tide pulled on her feet as it drew back to reveal a tumbling layer of sand, swirling with little stones, shells, and even some spinning hermit crabs.

Zinnie plucked a few shells out and examined them in her hand. Most of the shells looked the same: small, fan-shaped, and pale pinkish, which was why the shiny rectangles of metal stood out so clearly even as the water foamed. She put the shells in her bucket and then bent to pick the shining objects up and see what they were before they were carried back out into Buzzards Bay by the waves. She realized the rectangles of metal were connected on a chain. It was some kind of necklace. It fit neatly in the palm of her hand and had a name, "Cima, Paul," a number, and the words "O Positive" and "Christian." She rinsed it again and held it up. *Here's a story,* she thought. Then she heard the splashing sounds of someone running toward her.

"You found them!" She looked up to see the boy from down the beach.

Zinnie thought the boy was probably her age, maybe just a little bit older. With his shaggy brown hair, the way he had loped through the waves to reach her, and the friendliness of his impossibly big brown eyes, he reminded her of a Labrador puppy. She was pretty sure that he was the kind of boy the girls in her class would call cute. As he stood there beaming at her for finding this necklace, she couldn't help but match his grin in both size and wattage.

Because she went to an all-girls' school and only had sisters, she didn't have a lot of boys who were friends. Actually, she didn't have any. When she was really young, she'd wanted nothing to do with boys. They seemed so rough and different. They chewed with their mouths open, couldn't seem to sit still and have a conversation, never wanted to play her make-believe games long enough for her, and always seemed to want to be hitting things.

Now that she was twelve, she knew that boys weren't all maniacs and gross eaters. She was well aware of the fact that a bunch of girls in her class had completely reversed their position on boys and now wanted to kiss them. She had even seen—with her very own eyes—Marigold kiss Peter Pasque last summer. But it wasn't something that she thought she was ready for. When Zinnie saw kissing on TV, she thought it looked messy and strange. She had absolutely no interest in touching mouths with anyone. But now, with this grinning boy in front of her, his nose scattered with freckles, and his eyes sparkling with mischief, she was definitely interested in having a boy as a friend. After all, her dad had been a boy once, and he was her favorite person in the world.

"You're looking for this?" Zinnie asked, offering him the necklace.

"Yes!" he said, taking it and clutching it tightly. "Thank you, thank you! I mean, seriously! You just saved the most important thing in the world to me." Zinnie couldn't believe it, but his smile grew even bigger. "You're my hero."

"I am?" Zinnie started to giggle.

"Yes!" Then he started to giggle, too. The sun was now directly overhead, and light was bouncing off of the water in every direction as the two of them stood there laughing.

"Why are we laughing?" Zinnie asked.

"I don't know!" the boy said. "I'm just so happy."

"Because of a necklace?" Zinnie asked.

"Actually, these are my dad's dog tags," the boy said.

"Dog tags?" *Maybe he really is part Labrador,* she joked to herself.

"People in the military wear them in case . . . something happens to them. These are an old set. My dad gave them to me and I never ever take them off, even though he's home right now. But then this morning, when I was out here, my friend told me that shiny things in the water attract sharks."

"Sharks?"

"Don't worry," he said. "I don't think there are any around here."

"You don't *think*?" Zinnie said, heading for dry land. She was only in up to her ankles, but still.

"Seriously," the boy said, catching up with her. "They're pretty rare." This didn't make Zinnie feel much better, and she walked a few more steps away from the water. "I just got freaked out. So I took the dog tags off and left them on the sand. And when I came back, they were gone. I'd been looking for them for hours and . . ." The boy took a breath and looked away. "I didn't think I was going to find them."

"I thought you were crying when I first saw you," Zinnie said. The boy turned bright red. "Sorry, I didn't mean to embarrass you."

"It's okay. It's just that these dog tags are really important. It's weird, but they make me feel like he's safe even when he's off fighting. So losing them is like . . ." He looked away again.

"Don't make me cry now, too," Zinnie said, feeling choked up. She took a deep breath and gathered herself. "Look, the important thing is that we found them, okay?"

"Okay," he said, wiping his eyes. "Sorry. I'm not usually a crybaby."

"Don't worry. I cry all the time. Well, not all the time. But when I'm sad I do. Everyone does."

"Not guys," the boy said.

"You should see my dad," Zinnie said. "He cries when he looks at our baby pictures or whenever my sisters and I give him Father's Day cards. And you're not going to believe this, but he also cried at the movie *Annie*."

"The one about the orphan?" he asked. Zinnie nodded. The boy's grin returned. "No way."

"I swear," Zinnie said. "He's very sensitive." She tilted her head and held her hand above her eyes to shield them from the sun. "I'm Zinnie, by the way."

"Max," the boy said. At the very moment Zinnie extended her hand to shake, he held up his hand for a high five.

"Whoops," Zinnie said, reaching up to give him five just as he went low for the handshake.

"Gah!" Max said as they switched again. They laughed.

"High five or handshake?" Zinnie asked. "Let's try to coordinate."

"Handshake first," Max said. They shook. "Then bring it up"—they raised their hands together and then pulled them apart once they were over their heads— "and high five!" They high-fived.

"A secret handshake," Zinnie said.

"Totally," Max said. His eyes narrowed as he looked over her shoulder. "Shoot. That's my mom. I was supposed to meet her like an hour ago at the house. If she knew I lost the dog tags, she'd be so upset."

"Your secret is safe with me," Zinnie said.

"One more time?" Max said, holding out his hand

for a shake. They did their secret handshake again before Max ran down the beach, hopped over the jetty, and turned around to wave.

As Zinnie watched him go, she wondered if this light and happy feeling meant that she liked Max in a boyfriend-girlfriend way. How was she supposed to know? She'd heard the girls in her class talking about butterflies in their stomachs. She walked back toward the beach towels, putting a hand to her tummy to feel if anything was flying around in there. She didn't think so. It just felt like her belly, though she did notice that her stomach was grumbling. She was looking forward to the peanut butter and jelly sandwiches, fresh blueberries, and surprise brownies that Aunt Sunny had packed for their lunch.

"Where were you?" Marigold asked. She was lying on her towel faceup, slightly out of breath, her cheeks flushed.

"Looking for shells," Zinnie said. "Ashley told me the good ones were over there." She hadn't collected as many as she'd hoped to, but she had a dozen or so, which she emptied from her bucket and laid out on the towel. "Why were you swimming laps?"

"I'm going to try out for the swim team in the fall," Marigold said.

"But you hated swim team," Zinnie said, sitting on her towel and arranging the shells in different patterns.

"I'm giving it another try," Marigold said, squeezing the water out of her hair.

"But you used to say all that stuff about the chlorine in your hair and—"

"Zinnie! It's just . . . It's what I'm doing. Okay?"

"Fine," Zinnie said, digging her toes into the warm sand. "Whatever." She was so happy about finding the dog tags and meeting Max that Marigold's annoyance evaporated off her skin as quickly as the droplets of water in the midday summer sun.

"Did something happen to you?" Marigold asked, propping herself up on her elbow.

"What do you mean?" Zinnie asked, piling sand on her feet to fully bury them.

"You've got this big smile on your face," Marigold said. "Like you just ate Aunt Sunny's brownies or something. Did you eat both the brownies while I was swimming?"

"No," Zinnie said. "The thing is—"

She was about to tell Marigold about Max, but something inside her made her stop. Right now, what had happened belonged completely to her. She had found a treasure and met a boy with a smile like a superpower, and he had called her his hero. It was a perfect moment that was somehow still taking shape. She felt that if she spoke about it too soon, it would seem less wonderful.

Sometimes Marigold had a way of acting as if

things that felt like a big deal to Zinnie were really no big deal, and implying that Zinnie would see this if only she were a little older and a little cooler. Zinnie didn't want Marigold to do that about Max, so she decided to hold her happiness inside and let it ripen like a peach.

"Well?" Marigold asked. "What's the thing?"

"Nothing," Zinnie said. "Except I'm ready for lunch."

14 · A Brush with Rathbone

"You dressed me too fancy today," Lily said with a frown when Marigold and Zinnie arrived to pick her up from camp. Her arms were crossed and she was sitting slightly apart from the other six-year-olds at the picnic tables outside the casino. "The casino" was what the people in Pruet called the converted barn that functioned as the town's gathering space. It was where they held dances, bingo, and even the talent show last year. Lily's camp, the Young Naturalists, met there every day. They used the big room inside as a classroom and ventured out to the inlets, tidal pools, marshes, and farms around Pruet for field trips.

Zinnie couldn't help but giggle when Lily stood up to demonstrate that the gingham dress Marigold had picked out for her had a splat of mud on the back and a dirty hem. But Lily wasn't giggling. She was pouting, and the same worry line that Zinnie got when she felt anxious creased Lily's brow.

"I'm supposed to wear shorts and a T-shirt," Lily said, taking Marigold's hand and waving good-bye to her counselors. "We went to a pond today to look for frogs, and tomorrow we're going to a marsh to look at birds."

"Sorry," Marigold said. "It's just that it looked so cute on you."

"Did the camp counselor say anything when she saw you were wearing a dress to camp?" Zinnie asked.

"She asked me if I thought it was a good idea to wear a dress to go for a nature walk, and I said, 'Yes. Marigold says dresses are good for all occasions.'"

"It's true," Marigold said. "I wear sundresses when I go for walks."

"She doesn't mean at the mall, Marigold," Zinnie said, shaking her head.

"And then she said that the dress might not look the same at the end of the day. I guess she was right. There's mud everywhere and it's not funny."

Zinnie and Marigold exchanged a concerned glance.

"Did something happen at camp?" Marigold asked.

Zinnie thought it was remarkable how much Marigold sounded like Mom sometimes.

"I can't believe I was wearing a dress today!"

"I'm so sorry," Marigold said. "Tomorrow we'll put you in shorts and a T-shirt, okay? I didn't know either."

"The other kids all talk the same, too," Lily said. "I sound different."

"What do you mean?" Zinnie asked.

"They sound like Aunt Sunny. They say *'summ-ah'* instead of 'summer' and *'muth-ah'* instead of 'mother.' Oh, and they all have the same lunch boxes with Princess Arabella or Lumberjack Joe on them. I was the only one with a brown-paper lunch bag."

"We'll make sure you have a lunch box for tomorrow, okay?" Zinnie said.

"We will?" Marigold asked. "A Princess Arabella or Lumberjack Joe lunch box might be hard to find in Pruet."

"We'll try our very best," Zinnie said. "I bet Aunt Sunny can get one."

"Okay," Lily said as she kicked a rock along the road.

"You know what will make you feel better?" Zinnie asked, pointing to the ice cream cone–shaped sign above the door of Edith's Ice Cream Shop.

"Ice cream!" Lily exclaimed as they walked inside and the little bell above the door rang, signaling their arrival.

"But we can only get one scoop each," Marigold said, "so we don't ruin our appetites."

Aunt Sunny had told them this before they left for the day, but Zinnie had been hoping Marigold would forget. Edith's ice cream was the best in the world and

Zinnie had been waiting all year for another taste. How was one scoop going to be enough?

"Well, if it isn't the three sisters from California!" Edith said as Marigold, Zinnie, and Lily walked through the door. Edith's faithful dachshund Mocha Chip barked a friendly hello. "What a sight for sore eyes. Come on in and try some of my new flavors."

"New flavors?" Zinnie asked as Lily dropped to her knees and embraced Mocha Chip, who immediately licked her face like she was the best ice cream flavor of all.

"Edith, do you know when the sailing team finishes practice?" Marigold asked.

"In about fifteen minutes, I reckon," Edith said, glancing at the clock. "That's when I get my afternoon rush. So you girls came just in time to beat the line."

"Can I use your bathroom, please?" Marigold asked. "I really have to go."

"Sure thing," Edith said, and handed her the key from behind the counter.

"What kind of new flavors?" Zinnie asked as she sidled up to the counter and sat on one of the spinning stools.

"Try this," Edith said, handing Zinnie a plastic spoon with a sample.

Zinnie tasted it. It was a familiar flavor, but she couldn't quite place it. "It's kinda weird but I like it. What is it?"

"Sweet summer corn," Edith said with a grin. "These unusual flavors are all the rage this summer. Over on the Vineyard they're even serving zucchini blossom ice cream. Corn is about as far as I'll go. Would you like a scoop?"

"Yes, please," Zinnie said.

"And for you, honey?" Edith asked Lily as she handed Zinnie her ice cream.

"Peppermint stick, please," Lily said. Zinnie knew she liked it mostly because it was pink. Mocha Chip was now curled up on Lily's lap. "Good boy," Lily said, scratching behind his ears as Edith brought her a small dish of peppermint stick.

"Hey, remember last summer I suggested you make pickle ice cream?" Zinnie asked.

"I sure do," Edith said, returning to the counter. "I thought you were nuts."

"Turns out it wasn't so nuts after all," Zinnie said, holding up her corn ice cream cone. "I mean, corn?"

"You're going places, kid," Edith said as she wiped down the counter. "I told you that last year. Don't forget little old Edith when you end up with your name in the papers."

"I won't," Zinnie said with a smile. There nothing little about Edith. She was as tall as Zinnie's father and was quite round, too. Just then she saw Philip Rathbone standing outside the shop and talking on his cell phone. At that very moment, Zinnie heard the toilet flush. *Poor Marigold,* she thought. *The last thing she needs is to be reminded of* Night Sprites*!* Even though Pruet was a very small town, what were the chances of running into Philip Rathbone? He lived in a huge house on a private road. Zinnie felt sure he also had a private beach. She was determined that her sister not have to see the man who had, as Marigold had put it, "crushed my heart and destroyed my dreams." The bathroom doorknob turned and, ice cream in hand, Zinnie jumped in front of Marigold, blocking her view of the window.

"Open your mouth and close your eyes and I will give you a big surprise!" Zinnie said, flinging her hand over Marigold's eyes. Remarkably, Marigold did as Zinnie instructed. Zinnie placed the cone of ice cream at Marigold's lips.

"Yum," Marigold said after taking a lick.

"It's one of Edith's new flavors," Zinnie said, craning her neck to see if Mr. Rathbone was going to come into the shop. She couldn't tell. He wasn't opening the door, but he wasn't walking on either. He was just sort of hanging around in front of the shop, pacing back and forth and chatting. Zinnie kept her hand over Marigold's eyes. "You have to keep your eyes closed until you guess the flavor."

"Will you play this game with me next?" Lily asked.

"Sure," Zinnie said. "What do you think, Marigold?"

"I don't know—this could take a while," Marigold

said, taking another lick.

"That's okay," Zinnie said.

"Is it almond?"

"Nope," Zinnie said. "Guess again."

"Um . . . kiwi?"

"Kiwi? Are you crazy? Not even close." Zinnie turned her head again to see what Mr. Rathbone was doing. It looked like he was wrapping up the conversation. He was! With great relief, she watched him end his call, put the phone in his back pocket, and move on. "I'll give you a hint. It comes on a cob."

"Duh! Corn!" Marigold said.

"You got it," Zinnie said, and removed her hand from Marigold's face.

"That was too easy!" Lily said.

"It's true," Edith said. "You gave it away."

"That's okay," Zinnie said. "Next time I'll make it harder."

"Corn ice cream?" Marigold asked with a smile on her face as she studied Edith's new, more daring menu. Zinnie took her seat at the counter again and watched with satisfaction as her sister ordered beach plum sherbet, blissfully unaware that the man who had so cruelly dashed her hopes had moments ago been just steps away.

15 · Peter Pasque, Five Inches Taller and Twice as Handsome

"Welcome back!" Jean said when the girls walked into the yacht club office, which was on the second floor of the club and had a great view of the docks and the harbor. Jean was on the computer and Mack was doing paperwork.

"Great to see you," Mack said, and stood up to shake their hands.

"We're so happy to be here," Zinnie said.

"Here's the jam for the wedding cake," Jean said, handing Marigold a shopping bag. "We're looking forward to the big day."

"We are, too," Marigold said, but her attention was now focused on the view of the harbor, where the sailing team was making its way back to the docks.

"Where's Peter?" Lily asked. "I can't wait to see him!"

"Practice is finishing up. He should be here any minute," Jean said. "Why don't you girls go say hi. I forgot to tell him you were coming early, so it will be a surprise."

"I wonder if Peter will still be as handsome as a prince," Lily said, taking Marigold's hand as they crossed the yacht club lawn.

"I guess we'll see," Marigold said.

Her heart raced at the thought of seeing Peter again. Last year he had given her his beat-up Red Sox hat. At first she'd thought it was gross. It was faded and tattered and even a little bit grimy, but on her last day in Pruet, when he placed the hat on her head and told her to keep it, she loved it. By then she couldn't separate her feelings about the hat from her feelings about Peter, and she liked him a lot. *A lot* a lot.

"Do you think he'll take you sailing again?" Zinnie asked.

"I hope so," Marigold said.

"I think he's going to be my boyfriend," Lily said.

As the sailing team lowered their sails and the kids hopped out of the boats onto the dock, Marigold wished she'd worn Peter's hat today. All the boys and most of the girls were wearing baseball hats. Red Sox, of course! She would have fit right in. Also, he would know that she had changed from being what he thought of as a fancy L.A. actress who always dressed up and had to look her best to someone who was more like him: ordinary in the best way.

Marigold watched the kids tie up their boats at the small dock that was just for the sailing team, and she tried to pick out Peter. Where was he? Because of the hats, she couldn't identify him by his red hair. The group was laughing and joking with a togetherness that reminded Marigold of the Cuties. Ugh! She didn't want to think of the Cuties right now, and she did her best to force them from her mind.

"Where's Peter?" Zinnie asked.

"Yeah, I don't see him," Lily said.

"I don't know," Marigold said. It wasn't until the group reached the lawn that Marigold could tell he was the one in the bright-blue T-shirt and cargo shorts.

"Peter!" Lily called.

Peter turned to see them. He seemed confused for a second, and then he smiled and waved.

"He looks like a real teenager now," Zinnie said.

"He does," Marigold said. He had grown so much. He had to be at least four inches taller. He used to be sort of skinny, but he wasn't anymore. His shoulders were broader, his legs looked stronger, and his arms had bigger muscles.

"Marigold, Zinnie, and Lily," Peter said, separating from the group and walking toward them. His voice was deeper than it used to be, and while it was hard to tell after a year apart, she was pretty sure that he had fewer freckles. *He's twice as handsome,* Marigold thought.

"Hi," Marigold said. There was a light breeze and the afternoon sun cast a warm, golden glow. For a moment she wished she still had long hair.

"Hey," Zinnie said, and she and Peter high-fived.

"You look like a prince," Lily said.

"Thanks, Lily. You look like a princess," Peter said.

"And I can dance like one, too," Lily said.

"Let's see," Peter said.

As Lily twirled across the lawn, Zinnie laughed and Marigold smiled. One of the things Marigold liked best about Peter was how kind he was to Lily, who had a huge crush on him.

"So, how are you?" Marigold asked.

"Good," Peter said. "It took me a second to recognize you."

"I cut my hair," Marigold said, and then she blushed. *Duh! That's so obvious. S*he wondered if there was something else besides her short hair that made her look different from last summer. Did she look older, too?

"We didn't recognize you at first either," Zinnie said. "You grew!"

"Five inches," Peter said.

"We're going to Edith's," One of the girls from the group called to Peter. She had a long, loose ponytail, a too-big Pruet High School T-shirt, and a sweatshirt wrapped around her waist. "Are you coming, Pete?"

Pete? Marigold thought. The name sounded weird to her ear. To her he was Peter. Or *Peet-ah*, as he pronounced it.

"I'll catch up with you in a minute," Peter said to the girl.

"Okay," the girl said, and joined the rest of the team.

"I wasn't expecting to see you today," Peter said, sticking his hands in his pockets. "My mom said you'd be back, but I didn't think it was until later."

"We came early," Marigold said. Lily was now leaping around the flagpole, still showing off for Peter.

"Because Aunt Sunny is getting married, and we're helping with the wedding," Zinnie said.

"So here we are! Ta-da," Marigold added, and struck a pose. She felt instantly silly with one hand on her hip and the other in the air. And even though she'd been sure that Peter would like her better if she was a casual girl, she now wished she'd dressed up. She remembered why she liked fashion so much. It gave her outside confidence when her inside confidence was lacking.

"So . . . aren't you in a movie?" Peter asked Marigold. When he said "aren't," it sounded like *"ahh-nt."*

"Not anymore," Marigold said. Then she changed

the subject. "Do you think you could take me sailing again?"

"Um, sure," he said.

"Great," Marigold said. "How about tomorrow?"

"I'm working in the dining room tomorrow and the next day," Peter said. "But maybe the day after that."

"Okay," Marigold said, though three days felt like an eternity.

"Do you girls want to come to Edith's?" Peter asked.

"We just came from there," Zinnie said.

"And we can't ruin our appetites for dinner," Lily said.

"Okay," Peter said. Marigold thought he looked a little relieved.

"Glad you girls are back. But I better go. I gotta meet the team. I'll see you later," Peter said.

"Bye, Prince Peter!" Lily said.

"See ya!" Zinnie said.

"Can't wait to go sailing!" Marigold called. But Peter was already halfway across the lawn, and he didn't look back.

16 · Lunch Box Blues

"I really hope Aunt Sunny and Zinnie find a Princess Arabella or Lumberjack Joe lunch box," Lily said to Marigold as they searched through Aunt Sunny's recipe card collection for the one that was labeled "Priscilla's Summertime Cake."

"I hope they have one, too," Marigold said, though she was doubtful that Smith's Market had the lunch box Lily wanted so badly. Smith's was the only grocery store near Pruet, and even though it was also kind of like a general store, selling everything from gardening supplies to beach towels, it was pretty small.

The other places Aunt Sunny had called were all sold out. When Sunny had called Smith's, they said they might have one, but the workers were too busy to go and check at that moment. So Aunt Sunny and Zinnie went to see for themselves. They had to stop by anyway to pick up cake flour, sugar, butter, and eggs for their big baking plans. Aunt Sunny pretty much knew the recipe by heart, but she still wanted to follow her mother's instructions "to the letter." It was her wedding cake, after all, and she wanted it to be just right.

"I can't be the only one without the lunch box again," Lily said. "It will be too terrible. I'm already the only one who doesn't go to Cross Street Elementary!"

"Let's keep our fingers crossed," Marigold said. "And in the meantime, keep looking for a recipe title beginning with a *P*. 'Priscilla' begins with a *P*." Marigold was starting to worry that Aunt Sunny had lost the recipe for the cake. She and Lily had looked through all these cards twice and they hadn't found it yet.

"Who is Priscilla again?" Lily asked.

"She was Aunt Sunny and Grammy's mom, our great-grandmother. She was Aunt Eleanor's mom, too, but none of us ever knew Eleanor. She died before I was born." As Marigold heard Aunt Sunny's car rumbling down the driveway, she said a silent prayer that Smith's had had a Princess Arabella or Lumberjack Joe lunch box.

"They didn't have it," Zinnie said a few moments later when she and Aunt Sunny walked in with their arms full of groceries.

"Oh no!" Lily said.

"I'm sorry, dear," Aunt Sunny said. "They're sold

out. Did you girls find the recipe?"

"Not yet," Marigold said. Aunt Sunny bit her lip in concern. "But we'll keep looking."

"They did have a lunch box with Jennifer Rabbit on it," Zinnie said.

"Jennifer Rabbit is for babies!" Lily said, covering her face with her hands.

"Zinnie and I will go to the library tomorrow to see if we can order one online," Marigold said in a soothing voice as she rubbed Lily's back. She sensed a tantrum coming on.

"But what about tomorrow?" Lily said through her tears. "What am I going to do about lunch tomorrow?"

"Lily, my girl, how about if you take a basket instead of a lunch box?" Aunt Sunny suggested as she put the groceries away. "I have a great collection, and you can pick out the one you like the best."

"Everyone will laugh at me if I bring a basket!" Lily said. She flung herself on the table in a fit of sobs, and the recipe cards fell from the table and scattered on the floor. Zinnie bent down to pick up them up as Marigold pulled Lily onto her lap.

"How about if I draw Princess Arabella on your lunch bag?" Marigold suggested as she held Lily tight. She knew just how Lily felt. It was no fun not fitting in.

"That's a fantastic idea," Aunt Sunny said. "I even

have some glitter you can add to make Arabella's dress sparkle."

"That would look so pretty," Marigold said. She felt Lily's tears subsiding.

"Do you think you can draw a good-enough picture?" Lily asked, wiping her eyes.

"Definitely," Marigold said. "Want to give it a try?"

"Okay," Lily said, nodding. "But we're going to have to use a lot of glitter. Probably all the glitter that Aunt Sunny has."

"Found it!" Zinnie said, holding up the recipe card they'd been searching for. "Look, it was stuck to the back of the one for Mrs. James's Johnnycakes."

"Oh, thank goodness," Aunt Sunny said, taking the card from Zinnie. Her eyes filled as she read it over.

"Is that the right recipe?" Marigold asked. "Are you okay?"

"Yes," Aunt Sunny said, dabbing her eyes. "It's just the sight of my mother's handwriting. Makes me miss her. I can't tell you how relieved I am. Lily, you get the measuring cups and spoons. Marigold, you get the mixing bowls. Zinnia, you wipe down the table. I'll grab the aprons and put on some music. It's time to get baking!"

17 · The Boyfriend Question

The next day at the town beach, Marigold waited until Zinnie had climbed over the jetty. Then she pulled her iPad out of her beach bag and opened her digital diary. She had a lot to write about and she hadn't had a moment to herself since they'd returned to Aunt Sunny's yesterday afternoon. First she and Lily had looked for the cake recipe, then Marigold had to comfort Lily about the lunch box situation, and then they'd had to do so much baking. In total, they needed to bake six cakes to make three tiers: two twelve-inch, two nine-inch, and two six-inch. They'd only made half of that last night and it had still seemed like they'd made enough cake for several birthday parties.

Lily didn't have the patience to wait for the cakes to be finished for Marigold to make her Princess Arabella lunch bag. So after they'd helped with the batter,

Marigold had drawn Princess Arabella on the plain brown bag while Zinnie and Aunt Sunny finished the cakes. Lily got pretty excited about the glitter, and when she held up the bag to show Aunt Sunny, silver and gold glitter ended up in the cake pans along with the batter. Marigold was worried that Aunt Sunny might get mad, but she just laughed. It wasn't enough glitter to hurt anyone, Aunt Sunny said, and anyway, what could be more appropriate than a little sparkle in a wedding cake?

Once the cakes were in the oven and the dishes were done, and Lily was in bed, Marigold was planning to write in her diary. Zinnie was working away in Aunt Sunny's old office, so it really was the perfect time. But Marigold heard clicking sounds coming from the living room and she was too curious to ignore them. She discovered Aunt Sunny making her wedding dress.

"Come and join me," Aunt Sunny said. She was working at a sewing machine. "I'd love your company."

Marigold sat on the nearby sofa and watched as Aunt Sunny sewed lace onto fabric. They sat together for a while without saying anything. Marigold never felt like she had to talk when she was alone with Aunt Sunny. Marigold observed Aunt Sunny carefully moving the fabric through the machine, transforming a plain piece of cotton into a sweet wedding sash.

"Maybe I can make a dress this summer, too,"

Marigold said after what must've been at least a half hour of quiet, except of course for the sound of the sewing machine.

"I'd love to help you make something while you're here, but a dress is pretty complicated. Why don't we start with something simple?" Aunt Sunny suggested.

"Like what?" Marigold asked.

"A pillowcase is simple," Aunt Sunny said. Marigold wrinkled her nose. She didn't have much interest in pillowcases. "There are lots of things you can make," Aunt Sunny went on. "Your first step will be to find a pattern. Tomorrow you can do a little research at the library. Go online, search for simple sewing projects, and see what you come up with."

"Good idea," Marigold said, pulling a light throw blanket over herself and snuggling down on the sofa as Aunt Sunny went back to work. She must've fallen asleep there, because she woke her in the same place with the sun warming.

This morning, Marigold had made sure to slip her iPad into her beach bag before she and Zinnie left for the day. First, they went to the library. They ordered a Princess Arabella lunch box for Lily using their parents' online account. Then Marigold researched simple sewing patterns and printed a few out: a headband, a bag, and an apron. After that, both girls looked for wedding decorations. Marigold looked online and

Zinnie searched the magazines. Marigold found a picture of flowers arranged in jars like the ones that Aunt Sunny used when she made jelly. There was a whole box of those jars on a shelf in the pantry.

Once they arrived at the beach, they had a very busy morning collecting shells. After they'd filled up their buckets halfway, they rinsed the shells in the water, laid them to dry on Zinnie's towel, and strategized about the decorations. Imagining the towel to be a tablecloth, they tried out various designs. They built small towers, discussed putting shells in jars, and even talked about gluing the shells to candles. At last they decided that arranging the shells in a heart shape around a vase of flowers would look best. They weren't sure what kinds of flowers. They would have to look in Aunt Sunny's garden when they returned.

Because they had different types of shells, each table would be unique, which they thought Aunt Sunny would appreciate. Marigold had even found a piece of sea glass during her shell search. She thought that if they could find nine more pieces before the wedding, they could work a piece into each of the designs, making the sea-themed tabletops even more beautiful. Of course, sea glass reminded Marigold of Peter. He had a whole collection of it, including a rare red piece that Marigold had given to him as a gift last summer. And thinking about Peter had made her want to write in her diary.

Luckily, Zinnie was now on her way over the jetty to look for more shells. Once Zinnie was out of sight, she opened her iPad and typed in her password.

Dear Diary,

Being an ordinary, normal girl is harder than it looks! I don't know how people do it. This morning I picked out my red one-piece, which I know is not nearly as pretty as my striped tankini, but in order to not draw attention to myself, I have to make these kinds of choices.

Marigold continued to write in her diary, relaxing into the idea that her diary was her new best friend. She wrote about seeing Peter and how much he had grown. She wrote about his cute accent and his red hair. She also wrote about how something felt different between them. It wasn't like he'd been mean at all. It was just that he seemed kind of far away even though he was right in front of her. It was probably because they hadn't seen each other in so long, she told herself. She guessed that things would get back to normal when they went sailing together.

They'd had so much fun sailing together last year. She felt a tingle of excitement just thinking about it, but she wasn't sure if he was her boyfriend or not. What exactly was a boyfriend? She knew that she and Peter *liked*-liked each other last summer, because they'd kissed and because, well, she could just tell. But had his feelings changed? Did boyfriends and girl-friends ask each other "Will you go out with me?" How did it work?

Pilar would know. Marigold suddenly missed Pilar so much she thought she was going to cry. Would they ever be friends again? Marigold wasn't sure how she was going to get through eighth grade without her. She wasn't even sure how she was going to get through the summer. Who was she supposed to ask about boy-friends? Aunt Sunny? It seemed too embarrassing to talk about with her. Should she look it up online?

Marigold barely had time to finish her thought when she saw Zinnie coming back toward her.

"I forgot my water shoes!" Zinnie called.

Marigold quickly closed the iPad, tucked it in her bag, and pretended to look very busy with the shells. For a moment Marigold wondered if she could talk to *her* about boyfriends. Zinnie could be smart about unexpected things because she read so much.

"Hey, Marigold," Zinnie said as she reached for a pile of seaweed, which she put on her head like a floppy, ridiculous wig. "Check it out! Am I gorgeous or what?"

Never mind, Marigold thought, though she couldn't help but laugh at the sight. *Never mind.*

"Guess what!" Marigold said as soon as she spotted Lily, who was waiting for her sisters all by herself at a lone picnic table. She looked even sadder than yesterday. Marigold hoped she would cheer up once she learned that a Princess Arabella lunch box was on the way and would arrive at Aunt Sunny's tomorrow.

"We ordered you the lunch box," Zinnie said, but Lily still looked miserable.

"Aren't you happy?" Marigold asked.

"No. I got poison ivy!" Lily said, and she stood up to show her sisters the rash on the backs of her legs. "And it really itches."

"What's poison ivy?" Zinnie asked.

"It's like poison oak," Marigold said.

"But it looks different," Lily said. "The other kids all know what poison ivy looks like because they live here."

"What did your counselors say?" Marigold asked as they started to walk down the road to Edith's.

"They said it must've happened yesterday, because it takes twenty-four hours to show up," Lily said. Her mood seemed to lift instantly as the sailing team emerged from the yacht club. They must've ended practice a little early today. "Look, it's Peter! Peter, I'm over here!"

Peter waved and walked over to them.

"They're probably on their way to Edith's, too," Zinnie said. Marigold's heart skipped a beat. She hoped so.

"Hi," Marigold said. "We're going to Edith's. Are you?"

"Some of the team are going for ice cream, but the

rest of us are going to the beach."

"Sounds fun," Marigold said. She waited for an invitation, but none came.

"Peter, I have poison ivy—can you believe it?" Lily said. "Let me show you."

Lily showed Peter the red rash on the backs of her legs.

"What a *bum-ah*," Peter said. "At least it's not contagious. Make sure to put plenty of calamine lotion on it."

"I really don't like camp," Lily said.

"I'm so sorry to hear that, Lily," Peter said. "Maybe next *sum-ah* you'll come to sailing camp instead."

"That would be wonderful," Lily said. "Especially if you were my counselor."

"I'm really looking forward to going sailing the day after tomorrow," Marigold said. "Should I meet you at the dock? At this time?"

"Sounds good," Peter said.

"It looks like everyone on your sailing team is going to Edith's except her," Zinnie said, pointing to the girl with the loose ponytail who'd called him Pete.

"Um, I kind of have to go," Peter said. Marigold noticed that Peter's ears were turning pink. "See you later."

That night, after they'd made the second batch of cakes and the house smelled like a cupcake factory,

Marigold gave Lily a cool bath with special oatmeal powder that Aunt Sunny said would make her feel better. Marigold's mind was on Peter and how he seemed to be acting so differently this summer. Did it have something to do with him being more grown-up? She'd thought that he would definitely like her now that she was more ordinary, but her plan didn't seem to be working. She was wondering if she should wear a dress for their sailing adventure when Lily spoke up.

"I want to go home," Lily said.

"What? Why?" Marigold asked, though she already knew. Lily was having trouble making friends.

"Kids don't like me here."

"That's crazy," Marigold said. "You are the sweetest girl in the world."

"I am?" Lily asked.

"Yes! Remember when you made me those cookies when I was feeling sick? Or how you always bring treats to the dogs in the neighborhood? Or what about when you helped your teacher clean the white-boards?"

"That's true," Lily said. "I am a sweet girl."

"Why don't you show that to the kids at camp? Do something really nice for someone there tomorrow and see what happens."

"Okay," Lily said.

As Marigold shampooed Lily's hair, she had an idea. She needed to take her own advice and do something nice for Pilar. She needed to remind Pilar that she was a good friend—a best friend, even.

18 · The Lighthouse of Fear

"If you had to write a story about something, what would it be?" Zinnie asked Ashley the next day at the town beach.

They were hanging out at the snack bar. Business was slow lately. More people seemed to be bringing their own snacks. Ashley thought she needed to create better displays to bring in more customers, and she was currently arranging a bowl of fruit. Zinnie was lending a hand by making a sign.

"I'd write a thriller," Ashley said as she artfully positioned fruit in the bowl. "The kind that keeps you up at night. A real nail-biter."

"Really?" Zinnie said as she drew an ice pop and colored it a vibrant shade of red. "I never would've thought about that. I don't like superscary stuff."

"Are you kidding? Thrillers are the best!" Ashley

added some pears to the bowl. "I know what I'd call my story: 'The Lighthouse of Fear.'"

"Are lighthouses that scary?" Zinnie asked. She'd always thought of them as quaint and old-fashioned. She had a cute T-shirt with a picture of a lighthouse on it.

"Of course they are," Ashley said, her eyes growing wide. "Oh, my God. You've never been to Pruet Point Lighthouse, have you?"

"No," Zinnie said, thinking about the lighthouse that they passed on the way to Smith's Market. "The one with the red stripe on it?"

"That's the one," Ashley said. "And I'm not surprised your aunt didn't take you there, because it's totally haunted."

"Who do people say is haunting it?" Zinnie asked as she added an ice cream cone to her poster.

"The old lighthouse keeper who—" Ashley abruptly stopped talking and gave Zinnie a *zip-your-lips* signal as a little boy approached the snack stand. "Hi, Carson," Ashley said to him in sweet voice. "How are you today?" He ordered a bag of chips and Ashley served him with a smile. Once he was safely out of earshot, she continued. "I don't want to scare the little kids. But anyways, as I was saying, rumor has it that the old lighthouse keeper's wife was so lonely that she tried to jump from the window into the sea on a winter's night. The lighthouse keeper pulled her back in and nailed the window shut so she couldn't jump. And to this day you can still hear him hammering and her screaming, "Get me out! Get me out!"

"Ahh," Zinnie said as a shiver went through her.

"I'm telling you, this is bestseller material!" Ashley's eyes glinted with mischief. "I'll take you there and we can check it out, if you dare."

"At night?" Zinnie asked, dreading Ashley would say yes.

"No way!" Ashley said, finishing off her fruit display with a perfect yellow banana. "I want to live to see the tenth grade! We're going during the day. Just tell me when you're ready."

"Don't hold your breath," Zinnie said.

19 · The Boy in the Backyard

After the beach, Zinnie and Marigold went to the library. Now that she'd decided she was going to make a bag for Pilar using Aunt Sunny's sewing machine, Marigold wanted to find something that fit her taste. Meanwhile, Zinnie researched the Pruet Point Lighthouse. She couldn't find anything about its being haunted, and she didn't believe in ghosts anyway. She did want Ashley to take her there, however, because it would make an interesting setting for a story. Then Zinnie checked out Mrs. Lee's book. She thought that if she read it again, it might help her come up with an idea. As Zinnie tucked Mrs. Lee's novel into her bag, she wondered if maybe she would be a novelist some-day, too. Maybe even a bestselling one with gold stickers on her books.

Lily seemed to be in better spirits when they

picked her up from camp.

"Today was both good and bad," she said, toting her handmade Princess Arabella bag for the second day while she waited for the lunch box to arrive in the mail. It was crumpled, but she still seemed happy with it. "It started out really good but turned bad at the end."

Lily told them all about it as they walked back to Aunt Sunny's. She explained that she'd worn long pants to hide her poison ivy, and everyone seemed to have forgotten that yesterday she was known as Poison Ivy Girl. She had even made one friend, a girl named Anna, by sharing her cookies with her. And she had actually learned a lot about shells today during their field trip.

"So, what was bad?" Marigold asked as they passed the field with the horses.

"Everyone was talking about baseball. I said that my daddy liked the New York Yankees."

"Uh-oh," Zinnie said. She knew where this was headed.

"All the other kids *hate* the Yankees," Lily said.

"You can wear Peter's baseball hat tomorrow and they'll forget all about it," Marigold said.

"I feel like I don't know anything," Lily said.

"You know lots of things," Zinnie said.

"But nothing they care about," Lily said as they walked into Aunt Sunny's driveway.

"We care," Marigold said, and draped an arm around her.

"Welcome back, girls," Aunt Sunny said as Marigold, Zinnie, and Lily filed into the kitchen. "Look what arrived today." She held up the Princess Arabella lunch box.

"Thank you!" Lily said.

"Thank your sisters," Aunt Sunny said. "They were the ones clever enough to order it for you." Lily hugged Marigold and Zinnie. Aunt Sunny gave them each a kiss on the head and said, "Today we'll make the frosting."

"I love frosting," Zinnie said, salivating at the ingredients laid out on the table: cream cheese, butter, powdered sugar, and vanilla.

"Great, then you can be the one to add in the sugar. We need sixteen cups, added a little bit at a time. Oh, and Tony will be coming by any minute to start building the stage."

"Yay," Zinnie said as Aunt Sunny put package after package of cream cheese and stick after stick of butter into the bowl of the electric mixer.

"And you'll be happy to know that we finally have the perfect idea for your table decorations," Marigold said. Then she carefully removed the shells from the bucket and laid them on the wide windowsill under the big window, where they had put yesterday's collection. Aunt Sunny's kitchen was starting to look like the beach.

"Oh, thank heavens," Aunt Sunny said, turning on the mixer. "Tell me all about it."

"Those are bivalves," Lily said, pointing to various

shells. She looked up at her sisters with pride.

"See how much you know, Lily?"

"You must've learned that at camp today," Aunt Sunny said. She turned to Zinnie and handed her a two-cup measuring cup and the boxes of powdered sugar. "We need eight of these for sixteen cups."

"I did learn it at camp," Lily said. "We took a field trip to the hairy cow beach and identified shells."

"Did you go swimming?" Zinnie asked as she poured the first two cups of sugar into the mixing bowl. It had been at the hairy cow beach that Lily had stepped into the estuary and was almost carried out to sea last summer. The memory still made Zinnie's pulse quicken and her mouth feel dry. It was why she and Marigold had both enrolled in CPR and water safety classes during the school year. They were the ones who were supposed to watch her. Even though Lily was now a good swimmer, it still made Zinnie nervous to think of her going in the ocean without one of them there.

Four cups, Zinnie counted in her head as she poured. *Six cups.*

"The Young Naturalists don't go swimming," Lily explained. "We're scientists. We go exploring and make scientific observations. See?" She held out a shell-identification chart that she had colored in and labeled.

"I think you have an aptitude for science," Aunt Sunny said.

"A creature used to live in here," Lily said, picking

up a shell. "That's how shells are made."

Eight cups, ten cups, Zinnie counted.

"That's right," Aunt Sunny said. "Life in the sea isn't easy, and the small, vulnerable animals must protect themselves, so they create hard shells to live inside."

"And then they die and leave behind their shells for us to decorate Aunt Sunny's wedding tables with," Lily said brightly as she put the shell back on the windowsill.

Twelve cups, fourteen cups, Zinnie continued as she poured the sugar.

"I don't want to think about the dying part," Marigold said as she went into the pantry for a jelly jar. "We'll use these jelly jars as vases," she said as she came out, "and arrange the shells in a heart around them, like this. And we thought those blue flowers that you have in the backyard would look really good."

"Hydrangeas!" Aunt Sunny said. "I love hydrangeas."

"I'll go pick one," Marigold said, "so we can see what the whole thing will look like. Lily, you make a heart with the shells." Marigold was about to charge out the back door, but she stopped, noticing something. "Who's that boy with Tony?"

"What boy?" Zinnie asked, looking up from the frosting as she poured another two cups.

"Oh, that's Tony's grandson," Aunt Sunny said. "He's

here to help Tony build the platform for the band."

Zinnie stood up to get a look. Tony and a boy were unloading some wood from Tony's pickup truck, which was parked in Aunt Sunny's driveway. Zinnie couldn't see the boy's face because his back was to them, but something about him was familiar.

"Does his grandson live here?" Zinnie asked.

"His father, Paul, is the one in the army, so he's lived in a lot of different places. He did spend the last school year here, however, and he'll be staying again this year with his mom, Cindy, while his dad goes to the Middle East."

"Does Tony have any grandchildren my age?" Lily asked.

"No, just a teenage boy and twin baby girls," Aunt Sunny said.

"I always wanted a twin," Lily said. "Then we could play tricks on everyone."

"I *thought* that was him!" Zinnie said, dumping two whole extra cups of sugar into the bowl as the boy turned around and shook his long bangs out of his face.

"Oops!" Zinnie said. "I think I poured eighteen cups!"

"A little extra sugar never hurt," Aunt Sunny said.

"So I didn't ruin it?" Zinnie asked.

"Not in the slightest," Aunt Sunny said, testing a sample.

"Good!" Zinnie said, then shouted, "Max!" as she ran out into the backyard, the screen door slamming behind her.

Max and Tony were leaning planks of wood against the truck.

"Zinnie," Max said, and smiled one of his solar-system-sized grins. They did their secret handshake and it only took them two tries to get it right.

"Hey, Tony," Zinnie said, her cheeks hurting from smiling so hard.

"Hey there, Zinnie. You two know each other?" Tony asked.

"We met at the beach," Zinnie said. "I was looking for shells and Max was—" Max looked worried for a second. But Zinnie would've never told Tony about the dog tags. "Max was just hanging out. And we started talking. And then we started laughing for, like, no reason. It was funny, right, Max?"

"Yeah, it was—" Max started, but he didn't finish his sentence. It was no longer his smile that was taking up his whole face, but his eyes, which seemed to have doubled in size as he stared over Zinnie's shoulder. Something, or someone, had mesmerized him. Not only were his big brown eyes lit up, he appeared to be holding his breath. Zinnie turned to see what had caught his attention. But she really didn't need to, because she already knew.

It was Marigold.

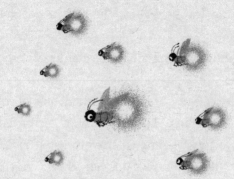

20 · A Case of the Can'ts

"Am I interrupting your writing?" Aunt Sunny asked, knocking on the door of Zinnie's writing room. She was carrying a glass of lemonade and a leather-bound book.

"Nope," Zinnie said, turning away from her laptop. "Come on in." She was actually relieved to see Aunt Sunny. She had been staring at her laptop screen for what felt like days but in reality had only been an hour. She knew because she'd watched each minute pass, hoping that a "real" idea would fly into her mind, but she hadn't had any luck. Zinnie had thought of a story about a baby dragon egg hatching in the middle of mall in Los Angeles, another about a time portal inside someone's locker at school, and another about a girl who found she had the power to control her sister's dreams, but nothing "real." Nothing good enough for her Writers' Workshop application.

She'd decided that she was going to write a short story for her submission to the Writers' Workshop for a couple of reasons. First, there were lots of short stories in *Muses*, so obviously Mrs. Lee must like them. Second, short stories were short! Zinnie didn't have a lot of time to produce the greatest thing she'd ever written, and so far she had nothing. Nada. Zilch. Zippo.

And anyway, how was she supposed to come up with the greatest thing she'd ever written by July tenth when all she could picture was Max's face once he'd seen Marigold? Zinnie had thought that Max would've wanted to hang out with her more than Marigold. He laughed at her jokes. They had a secret handshake. He'd called her his hero! But as soon as he'd seen the beautiful Marigold, it was like he'd forgotten all about Zinnie. Even without her "mane of glory," chic outfits, and a part in a movie, Marigold still managed to be the star.

Zinnie replayed the moment in her mind, wondering if there was anything she could have done differently.

"This is my sister Marigold," Zinnie had said as Marigold approached them.

"Well, hellooo there," Max had said. Then he'd turned bright red and shaken his head. "*Hello there?* Gosh, that sounded weird. Ugh. I meant just, you know. Hey. Hi."

Then Marigold had waved hello.

"This is Max, *my* friend," Zinnie had said, hoping to send Marigold the message. But she was losing Max quickly. She watched his Labrador-like goofiness drain away and be replaced by something else, something more catlike. Something cooler. Zinnie didn't want Max to be a cool cat. She liked his playful, puppyish self. "We met on the beach while I was looking for shells, and it was really funny."

"Where are you girls from?" Max had asked, completely ignoring Zinnie's mention of their beach-time fun. And while he'd said "you girls," Zinnie had the feeling that he was really only asking Marigold.

"California," Zinnie answered. The name of her home state had come out faster and sharper than she'd expected. Even though Marigold didn't seem to notice Max staring, and even though she was obliviously swatting at a mosquito that was circling her head, he'd still been captivated by her. Zinnie wanted her sister to *go away*. Max was her first boy-who-was-a-friend and possibly maybe even boyfriend. She wasn't sure yet. She hadn't decided. But she didn't want Marigold to take him away from her. It wasn't fair.

"Um, Marigold, don't you have some hydrangeas to pick?" Zinnie asked. "Like, now?"

"Oh, yeah," Marigold said, and headed toward the hydrangea bushes with Aunt Sunny's kitchen scissors. Max followed her with his gaze like she was angel who'd descended from heaven.

One of the worst parts about this whole thing was that she couldn't even get mad at Marigold. Marigold hadn't *tried* to get Max's attention. It's not like she knew how much Zinnie liked him and then had put on her prettiest dress and impressed him with stories of her acting career. She'd been wearing shorts and a T-shirt and had barely said a word. In fact, the only thing she'd said was "Oh, yeah," but Max had looked at her as if the words "Oh, yeah" had been penned by Shakespeare.

Thankfully, Tony had told Max seconds later that it was time for him to go home for dinner, because it would've been nothing less than torture for Zinnie to watch him stare all googley-eyed at Marigold for any longer than she'd had to. She couldn't stand sitting across from Marigold during dinner, even when Marigold asked her if she wanted to search for the lacy tablecloths in the attic. Aunt Sunny had said they were "up there somewhere" and they'd be perfect for the buffet table if the girls could "unearth" them. Going through Aunt Sunny's attic was something Zinnie had genuinely been looking forward to. The place was like a giant treasure chest, full of cool old clothes, antique toys, and items that Aunt Sunny had called "relics of a simpler time," like a typewriter, a record player, and something called a Dictaphone.

"No," Zinnie had responded, and cleared her plate. "I need to write. Some of us have work to do."

And here she'd sat for the last hour "stewing in her own juices," as her dad would say. Maybe Aunt Sunny would be able to help. Maybe the lemonade had magical properties. Maybe it would bring ideas the way that her brownies brought surprises.

"How's it going?" Aunt Sunny asked, placing the lemonade and the book on the little green desk.

"Terrible," Zinnie said, pulling on one of her curls. "I don't have any ideas for a short story. Not a single one."

"You have a case of the can'ts," Aunt Sunny said.

"What's that?"

"It's when your mind is so tight and wound up, it feels like you just can't do anything. So then you start *thinking* that you can't do anything and the next thing you know, you're paralyzed. Stuck in a rut with a case of the cant's."

"But it's not that I'm not trying. I'm trying so hard."

"Maybe too hard," Aunt Sunny said. "Your spirit has seemed heavy ever since you saw Max today. Did something happen with him?"

Aunt Sunny had this way of looking at Zinnie that was like the tide pulling back the ocean to reveal spinning shells and churning sand. Her gaze brought Zinnie's truth tumbling to the surface, snails and all. She thought that she was just mad about what had happened, but with Aunt Sunny's understanding eyes meeting her own, Zinnie began to feel tears well up.

"I saw Max first. We met at the beach," Zinnie said.

"I see," Aunt Sunny said.

"I found his—" She was about to tell Aunt Sunny about the dog tags (it was really hard to keep anything from Aunt Sunny), but somehow she managed to stop herself. "I found something that he'd lost, and he called me his hero."

"It must've been something very important," Aunt Sunny said, producing a tissue from inside her sleeve.

"It was," Zinnie said, taking the tissue and dabbing her eyes. "And I've never had a boy friend, and by that I mean a boy-who-is-a-friend, not, like, a *boyfriend-*boyfriend."

"It's perfectly okay to want one of those," Aunt Sunny said.

"I wasn't sure," Zinnie said. "I just knew that I liked him and he liked me. I could feel it, you know what I mean?"

"I do," Aunt Sunny said.

"But then he saw Marigold," Zinnie said. "And he just went gaga for her."

"Hmm," said Aunt Sunny, nodding. Zinnie was relieved that Aunt Sunny didn't say something like "I'm sure that's not true" or "There's no way that happened."

"Max is a very charming boy," Aunt Sunny said. "He has a wonderful smile. And he's a nice person, too. This winter he salted my driveway after every storm."

"That's so nice," Zinnie said, before realizing that she had no idea what Aunt Sunny was talking about. "Wait, why did he put salt on your driveway?"

"To melt the snow," Aunt Sunny said. Zinnie was picturing Max trudging through the snow shaking salt over the driveway with the saltshaker from the kitchen table when Aunt Sunny continued, "In any case, if Max decides to court Marigold, I'm afraid there's not a lot you can do to stop him. But, Zinnia, if ever there was a girl who didn't need to worry about making friends in life, it's you. People want to be around you. There's something irresistible about you. You have star quality."

"Marigold is the movie star, remember?" Zinnie said.

"I'm talking about the stars of the Milky Way," Aunt Sunny said. "The bright photons of heat shining in dazzling constellations. I'm talking about that supernova heart of yours. If Max doesn't see your luminescence, someone else will in a minute." Zinnie couldn't help but linger on Aunt Sunny's word choices, especially "luminescence." Though she didn't know the exact definition, the word itself seemed to glow. Aunt Sunny smiled and said, "You're feeling a little better. I can see it."

"A little. But I'm not going to like it if I have to see Marigold and Max all lovey-dovey."

"Don't get ahead of yourself," Aunt Sunny said. "Heroes are not soon forgotten. Besides, Marigold may not be interested. I thought she liked Peter."

"That's true," Zinnie said, feeling a small weight lifting from her chest. For the past couple of hours she'd forgotten all about Peter. But if Marigold and Peter were boyfriend and girlfriend, then Max would lose interest in Marigold and he and Zinnie could be friends again. Or, who knows? Maybe they would be more. She still wasn't sure about that, but things seemed less terrible than they had a minute ago. She sipped her lemonade, which was tart and sweet.

"And as for your story," Aunt Sunny said after giving Zinnie's forehead a powdery-smelling kiss, "why don't you email your teacher, tell her that you're struggling, and ask her for some advice."

"Teachers are usually good with advice," Zinnie admitted. She noticed the book Aunt Sunny had placed on the table. "What's this?"

"It's a book of poetry with the Shakespearian sonnet that I'm hoping you'll read at the wedding. I've marked the poem with the ribbon."

"Okay, great," Zinnie said. "I'll look at it tomorrow."

Then she finished her lemonade and wrote Mrs. Lee an email. New and technologically advanced neighbors must have moved in, because Zinnie had discovered that if she stood on the very edge of the lawn, back behind the garage, she could pick up a faint Wi-Fi signal. Before bed, Zinnie sent her email.

> Dear Mrs. Lee,
>
> I hope that Summer Scribes is going well. I am having a fun time on Cape Cod. I'm taking many notes about my observations and recording sensory details as you suggested. However, I'm having a really hard time coming up with an idea. Do you have any advice?
>
> Sincerely,
>
> Zinnie Silver

To Zinnie's surprise, Mrs. Lee wrote back right away.

> Dear Zinnie,
>
> How nice to hear from you! I'm so glad that you are enjoying the Cape. Summer Scribes is going very well, but L.A. has been miserably hot, so enjoy your time at the New England seaside for all of us! As for your question, I can tell you that in Summer Scribes we've been talking about transformations, and that almost all good stories have one in them. A simpler way of saying this is that a character changes, usually because he or she is faced with a problem. Can you think of a character who starts out one way and ends up another? For instance, a character may start out scared, but then, in the face of a challenge, she finds herself becoming brave. Of course, this is just one example. The possibilities are infinite. And remember,

sometimes the best stories are right under your nose! I look forward to reading your submission. And don't forget that the deadline, July 10th, will be here before you know it.

Good luck!

Mrs. Lee

P.S. Occasionally, I give writing prompts in class to get students started. Would you like me to send them to you? You can use them when you feel stuck.

Zinnie wasted no time in writing back.

Dear Mrs. Lee,

I would love to get the writing prompts!

Sincerely,

Zinnie

Mrs. Lee was clearly sitting at her computer, because she responded quickly.

Hi, Zinnie,

Great! Here they are. Don't feel you have to tackle them all at once. Start with whichever one grabs you.

1. Write about an argument you've had—but from the other person's point of view.

2. Be a detective! Listen to a conversation. See if you can write down some of it word for word. Characters all have distinctive voices. What do you notice about the way a person talks that you that might not have otherwise picked up on?

3. Go to a place you've never been before and write about it from all five senses.

Have fun!

Mrs. Lee

Zinnie instantly knew which prompt she was going to use first.

21 · Second Chances

Marigold could hardly contain her excitement as she got ready for her afternoon sail with Peter. Zinnie was sitting on her boat bed reading that book by Mrs. Lee, Lily was downstairs helping Aunt Sunny make the lemon syrup that would go between the cake layers, and Marigold was facing the difficult task of deciding what to wear.

Marigold had been thinking of this as a date, but she wasn't sure if that was what it was or not, especially given the way Peter was acting. Again, she wished that she could ask Pilar, who always seemed to know about these things even though she'd never had a boyfriend. It was probably because Pilar always had high school girls as babysitters, which was like having a bunch of older sisters who had to be nice to her. What would Pilar say if she were here now? Would she think Marigold was doing a good job of being ordinary? Marigold missed her so much.

Marigold's "gut instinct," as her mother would say, was to get all dressed up. Finding the perfect dress, or just the right pair of capri pants and matching sandals, or a cute top that would bring out the color of her eyes, was something that relaxed her, so it was actually hard for her to just throw something on, Zinnie style. But if she wanted to be ordinary, she supposed, this was what it was going to take.

She'd been thinking about seeing Peter all day while she and Zinnie went about their wedding preparations. That morning, they'd gone through the attic in search of Aunt Sunny's tablecloths. After Aunt Sunny had taken Lily to camp, Marigold and Zinnie pulled on the dangling cord that lowered the staircase leading to the attic. Marigold thought this staircase, which was hidden in the ceiling until you pulled the cord, was like something out of a mystery novel or a movie. Up in the attic they found a whole dresser full of tablecloths. There were lacy ones, floral ones, plain white ones, and ones that had designs embroidered on them. As Aunt Sunny had instructed, they laid them out, measured them to see which table each would fit, inspected them for moth holes and stains, and then put them in either the "yes" or the "no" pile.

There were also lots of mismatched linen napkins. Marigold applied one of her rules of fashion as she sorted through them, which was that things didn't always have to match exactly. In fact, it was better that they didn't. If she was wearing a bold striped skirt, she wouldn't wear a top that was exactly the same, or even was the same color as one the stripes. She would choose a different color or a smaller pattern. She thought she could mix and match the tablecloths and napkins in a similar way. She imagined Peter coming to the wedding and admiring her work.

After she and Zinnie had their "yes" piles of table-cloths and napkins all sorted by size, shape, and color, they continued their treasure hunt. They discovered a bunch of blank notebooks, which were small, with a blue paper cover and a place to write a name and a class. The notebooks looked strange to Zinnie and Marigold because there wasn't a lot of paper in them.

"They must've used them in the old days for school," Marigold said.

"Oh, I have the best idea!" Zinnie declared. "We can write guests' names on them, and then on the inside they can write their favorite memories of Sunny and Tony and maybe what they wish for them in the future."

"And they can write them while sitting in that super-cute desk," Marigold said, pointing to an old school desk with a chair attached.

They also found a cart with a slide projector, which could somehow be repurposed; a drawer full of old seed packets that would make very cool place cards; botanical charts from the 1970s; and a whole chest of camping equipment—flannel sleeping bags, a camp stove, a tent, and some lanterns. The camping equipment didn't seem to have any wedding decor potential, but never having gone camping themselves, the girls thought it was intriguing and delightful. They discovered a collection of framed flowers. Marigold also found a box labeled "Beatrice," their grandmother's name. She opened it up to discover a glass bluebird, about the size of Christmas tree ornament, sitting in a nest of tissue paper. Marigold was afraid to handle it because it was so delicate. After she showed it to Zinnie, she placed it back in the box. When their stomachs began to rumble, they went down to the kitchen for lunch.

Aunt Sunny surprised them by coming home from work to join them. She had made them chicken salad sandwiches for the day's lunch, and now she sliced up some apples. When Marigold and Zinnie described how many tablecloths they had uncovered, Aunt Sunny explained that they'd been handed down for generations. Some of them had even belonged to her great-grandmother, who used to ride to Boston from Pruet in a horse-drawn buggy.

"A horse-drawn buggy?" Zinnie said. "I'd love to ride in one of those."

"The horse-drawn buggies are long gone," Aunt

Sunny said. "But the tablecloths remain, though I don't think I've ever used them. I've been too afraid they'd get ruined."

"It's almost as if they've *been* ruined if all they're doing is sitting up in the attic," Marigold said, thinking of Aunt Sunny's closet full of vintage clothes, most of which she didn't wear anymore. "It's like you don't have them at all."

"You're right," Aunt Sunny said. "I say we give them a second life."

"They will think they've time traveled!" Zinnie had said. "Like, they went to sleep when there weren't even cars and they'll wake up to airplanes and the internet."

"Let's give lots of things in that attic a second life," Marigold said, returning the conversation to the practical realm. "There's so much we can reuse. Like the old school desk and those little blue notebooks."

"Test booklets," Aunt Sunny explained. "Back when I started teaching, students handwrote their answers to essay questions in those booklets."

"The framed flowers are pretty," Marigold said.

"I pressed those flowers myself when I was just a girl. I loved collecting them, looking up their Latin names, and categorizing them. And of course I loved the way they looked in their frames."

"We can hang them around the wedding tent," Marigold said.

"I wish there was a way to reuse that camping equipment," Zinnie said.

"My sisters and I had such fun camping," Aunt Sunny said. "There was one summer in particular when we slept outside almost every night. We must have been about your age. That summer, the song "Stand by Me" was so popular. We sang it together a million times." Aunt Sunny began to hum the tune, and though they were tone deaf, Marigold and Zinnie both chimed in with the chorus, because everyone knew the words to that song. "It really brings my sisters back." Marigold noticed tears welling in Aunt Sunny's eyes.

"I also found a glass bluebird," Marigold said. "I think it belonged to Grammy."

"Oh, the bluebird!" Aunt Sunny said. "Yes, she loved that bluebird. I bought it for her from a glassblower at a crafts fair, and she said it always reminded her of our summers together."

For a moment, Marigold pictured her grandmother's hands as she last remembered them—soft and wrinkled—holding the glass bird, and she felt a lump gather in her throat. Some grandmothers pinched cheeks, but Grammy used to press the back of her hand lightly against Marigold's face when she saw her. She always smelled like lavender.

"It needs to be at the wedding," Zinnie said.

"On top of the cake," Marigold added.

"I love that idea," Aunt Sunny said, bringing a

tissue to her eyes. "Beatrice will be with me on my wedding day."

After lunch, Aunt Sunny decided to take the rest of the day off. She picked Lily up from camp early to spend some special alone time with her. They went for a swim at the hairy cow beach, and now they were busy with the lemon syrup.

Marigold smiled to herself as she heard Lily laugh downstairs. Even if Lily was having a hard time fitting in at camp, she was enjoying being with Aunt Sunny. As Zinnie turned the pages of her book, Marigold put on a plain white T-shirt and jean shorts.

"Is that what you're wearing?" Zinnie asked, laying her book in her lap.

"Yes," Marigold said. "Why?"

"Don't you think you should dress up a little more?"

Zinnie had been acting strange ever since that boy Max had come over. First, she'd been in a horrible mood during dinner. She hadn't even wanted to go looking through Aunt Sunny's attic, which was something she normally would have loved because of all the old stuff up there. After dinner, she'd stormed off to her writing room and slammed the door. And then, later that night, she'd wanted to stay up chatting about Peter. In fact, she wanted to think of romantic things he and Marigold could do together after they went sailing. Just as Marigold was drifting off to sleep, thinking about her reunion with Peter, Zinnie said one last strange thing.

"Um, Marigold, do you think that you could, like, not talk to Max that much?" Zinnie asked.

"What do you mean?" Marigold asked, half asleep.

"It's just, he's more of *my* friend," Zinnie said. "So could you, just, I don't know, don't try to be his friend?"

"I guess so," Marigold said.

"And if it turns out he likes you, could you promise not to like him back?"

"Uh, okay," Marigold said. It was pretty clear that Zinnie had a crush on Max. It was tempting to tease her, but Marigold decided not to. She remembered her first crush—the movie star Clint Lee. It seemed silly to her now, but she would have died of embarrassment if anyone had given her a hard time about it.

Zinnie's crush was making her act weirder than ever. Her odd behavior was continuing today. Marigold could hardly believe that Zinnie was giving *her* fashion advice—not the other way around.

Hopping up from the bed, Zinnie opened the closet door, and said, "There's got to be something in here that'll look better." Zinnie stepped inside the closet and riffled around through the clothes. "Here!" Zinnie pulled out a sea-foam-green sundress that the old Marigold would have paired with silver sandals and a long, loopy necklace. Marigold let herself touch the fine jersey fabric that draped so well and felt so nice and light on a summer day. But then she backed away and stuck her hands in her jean shorts pockets. She had to stick to her rules.

"Really?" Zinnie asked. "Why not?"

"I'm just dressing more casual this summer, okay?"

"Casual doesn't have to mean old T-shirts," Zinnie said, pointing to Marigold's current ensemble. "You still want Peter to say 'ooh la-la' when he sees you today, right?" Marigold had to admit that Zinnie had a point there. She did want Peter to say "ooh la-la." And seeing the sea-foam-green dress had awakened her fashion sense just enough to open her mind to at least the possibility of a nice shirt.

"Here, this is casual, too," Zinnie said, and held out a sleeveless, coral-colored top with a ribbon trim and a sweet little button closure in the back. It wasn't nearly as nice as the sea-foam-green dress, Marigold decided. It was sort of a happy medium between the dress and what she was wearing right now.

"I guess I could try it on," Marigold said, taking the top to the bathroom to change. Her digital diary wasn't the only thing she was feeling more private about these days.

"Much better!" Zinnie said when Marigold returned. She handed her a pair of navy espadrilles. "And these will look better than those old sneakers."

"Why do you care so much about what I'm wearing?" Marigold asked as she slipped on the espadrilles, which went perfectly with the top. She was proud of

Zinnie for having picked them out.

"I just want you to look, you know, like you," Zinnie said. "You've been dressing like someone else lately. It's practically Halloween around here!"

Marigold added the final detail, the one that was sure to remind Peter of his feelings: the Red Sox hat he'd given her last year.

"I told you—" Marigold started.

"I know, I know. You're going casual this summer," Zinnie said, handing her some lip gloss. Marigold hesitated. "Oh, come on! You know you want to!"

Marigold tried to turn it down, but it was too tempting. She allowed herself this shimmering, cherry-scented indulgence. She looked in the mirror and exhaled. It was a relief to shine, even just a little.

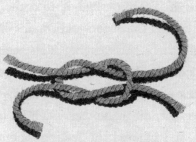

22. The Squall

Marigold arrived at the yacht club in her nicer-than-usual but not-nearly-as-fashionable-as-before ensemble a few minutes early to meet Peter. She was waiting for him in the gazebo on the yacht club lawn. It was the spot that Zinnie had assured her was the most romantic.

"Peter!" Marigold called, waving from the gazebo as he walked down the yacht club driveway. "Today I have your hat," she said, holding it up.

"Oh, yeah," Peter said, smiling. "Are you sure you want to go sailing? I know you don't like to mess up your nails."

"I don't care about that stuff anymore," Marigold said as she followed him down the dock. She was happy he was teasing her. It was friendly and felt familiar. "Can't you tell? I'm much more laid-back now."

"You still look pretty fancy to me," he said. His rowboat, called a "dinghy," was on the dock with the oars inside of it. Peter pushed it into the water and then held it close so that Marigold could climb aboard. "I'm surprised you're not wearing high heels."

"Ha! No one would wear heels with shorts!" Marigold joked back as she stepped into the boat. It rocked under her weight. It made her slightly queasy, but she sat down and ignored the feeling. She didn't want anything to ruin this day. "So, where are we going?"

"Just out to Biscuit Island," Peter said as he jumped in after her. The boat rocked some more as he leaned over to push them away from the dock.

"Biscuit Island? That sounds cute," Marigold said. She put a hand to her stomach and took a deep breath of fresh air to fight the nausea. She remembered suddenly that she'd been a little seasick last summer when they went sailing, but that it had gone away once they'd gotten going. Peter slid the oars into place and began to row toward his sailboat.

"It's just a bunch of rocks, really, but it's still cool."

"Great," Marigold said, taking another deep breath. She didn't want Peter to think she was prissy. And she'd really loved sailing when they went last year. In fact, she'd been thinking that maybe in addition to swimming, she could practice sailing here in Pruet, and maybe start a team at Miss Hadley's.

"It's a perfect day for a sail," Peter said. "Nice breeze."

"That's your boat, right?" Marigold asked, pointing to a little blue sailboat.

"Yes," Peter said, looking over his shoulder. "The one tied to the white mooring." She remembered from last year that not all boats in the harbor could fit at the dock, so most of them were tied to these volleyball-looking things in the water called "moorings."

Peter rowed them up to the sailboat, a Cape Cod cat-boat, he'd told her last summer, and Marigold climbed aboard as Peter tied the dinghy to the mooring. The boat rocked under her and she felt her stomach do another flip. *It's okay,* she told herself as she sat down in the boat. *You'll feel better once we're sailing.*

"I think I remember what to do now," Marigold said as Peter hopped in. "We take this piece of wood out, right?"

"That's right," Peter said, lifting the board from the center of the boat.

Marigold was about to stand up and help him, since she wanted to learn, but her stomach told her to stay seated. As Peter raised the sail and untied the boat from the mooring, Marigold noticed a dark cloud in the distance. She didn't think much of it, because the rest of the sky was sunny.

"All right, Peter said. "Do you want to sail or should I?"

"How about you start," Marigold said, not trusting her stomach.

"Okay," Peter said. There was another small boat, with two girls inside, cruising around the harbor. The girls' sail was full and their ponytails streamed behind them. They waved to Peter and he waved back.

Marigold wished she knew how to sail as well as those girls did. She wished she didn't feel like a beginner.

"Can I take the tiller?" she asked Peter once they started to pick up speed. She was proud of herself that she remembered the correct term for the long, thin piece of wood that steered the boat. The only way to learn, she thought, was to do this herself, even if she did feel a little sick.

"Sure," Peter said. "Just try to keep it at the same angle." Marigold took the tiller and held it steady. "Might as well take the sheet, too." He handed Marigold the rope that controlled the sail. Maybe she wasn't such a beginner after all. "Okay. Now keep your eyes on that pile of rocks. That's where we're headed."

"This is fun," Marigold said. "Thanks for taking me out."

"I'm glad you asked me to. See, there's something I've been meaning to tell you, but I just haven't known exactly how to say it. You know how last year . . ."

But he didn't finish his sentence. A chill came over them as they looked up and saw that the dark cloud that had been in the distance was now directly overhead. The wind suddenly shifted direction, sending the sail clear across the boat.

In her surprise, Marigold dropped the sheet. She reached for it but got tangled in the line and slipped. The sail puffed as the wind switched again and blew from the other direction.

"We got a squall!" Peter said just as a wave hit the boat, sending water over the side, soaking them.

"Ah!" Marigold cried, holding on to the swinging tiller for dear life.

"Give me the tiller," Peter said as he grabbed the sheet. Marigold handed him the tiller and gripped the side of the boat as water sloshed up over her feet and soaked her shorts. Peter pulled in the sail as the boat turned and another wave knocked more water over the side.

"What's a squall?" Marigold asked, her stomach turning all the way over. "Are we going to be okay? I want to go back!"

"I'm trying to get us back,'" Peter said. "But right now, I need you to use that bucket and dump water out of the boat."

"Okay," Marigold said, picking up the bucket and filling it with seawater. She dumped the water over the side and then tried to repeat the action. Just as she was about to lift the bucket, another wave came and that was it. She dropped the bucket, turned her back to Peter, and threw up over the side.

"You okay?" Peter asked as she slumped back in the boat.

Marigold nodded, even though she wasn't okay at all. She felt clammy and gross. She wiped her mouth and turned away, unable to face him. It was pure luck that the wind had been blowing in the right direction. At least her regurgitated lunch had gone out to sea instead of back on her face—or worse, Peter's.

23 · Old Hat

"Do you need some more *wah-tah*?" Peter asked once they were safely on the dock.

"That'd be great," Marigold said, gulping down the last drops from the bottle Peter had on the sailboat. Luckily, she'd been able to rinse out her mouth.

The strangest thing was that it was now a beautiful day again. The squall—which, Peter explained during the awkward rowboat ride back to the dock, was a small, sudden storm that could come out of nowhere—had passed as quickly as it had arrived. Peter had even offered to continue the trip out to Biscuit Island if she was up for it, but she definitely was not. In fact, she didn't care if she ever set foot on a sailboat again. The worst part, of course, was not that their sailing trip had been ruined. It was that Peter had seen her throw up. She felt certain that he would never want to kiss her again.

"So, is that . . . common?" Marigold asked, still feeling ill as they walked toward the yacht club.

"Nah. It took me by surprise. Normally, it'd be no big deal. If I'd anticipated it, you would've barely noticed. Um, are you okay?"

"I think I just need to splash some water on my face," Marigold said.

"There's some mouthwash in the bathrooms at the yacht club, too," Peter said. Marigold nodded and covered her mouth. "I'm not saying you need it, I just thought you might want it because . . . *nevah* mind. Come on in, I'll get you a ginger ale, too."

They were on their way up the steps to the yacht club when a girl's voice called, "Hey, Pete!" They turned around to see the girl with the windblown ponytail.

"How fun was *that*?" the girl asked, grinning. She was totally serious! She had enjoyed the squall! "We had the best time out there."

"It wasn't that fun for me," Peter said. "I was with an inexperienced sailor."

Marigold swallowed hard as Peter's face turned pink. Marigold looked at the ground.

"I had a wicked good time!" the girl said. "My sister is an awesome sailor, but I wish you'd been with me."

Peter's face now turned lobster red. Then, as if noticing Marigold for the first time, the girl turned to her and said, "Hi. I've seen you around but we've never met. I'm Lindsey, Pete's girlfriend."

Girlfriend? "Hi. I'm Marigold."

"Do you guys want to go to Edith's?" Lindsey asked.

"Sure," Peter said.

"Thank you, but I think I'd better go back to Aunt Sunny's," Marigold said, feeling as though she might throw up again. "I have to do a lot of wedding preparations. And Aunt Sunny's making scallops for dinner, so I can't have ice cream anyway. She wouldn't want me to ruin my appetite." She was glad she'd taken improvisation classes this spring.

"Okay," Peter said, his brow furrowed as Lindsey took his hand. "I'll see you later?"

"Yeah," Marigold said, calling upon her acting skills to produce a sweet and carefree smile. "I'll see you later. Thank you for taking me sailing. I really learned a lot." The Red Sox hat on her head suddenly felt like it weighed a hundred pounds. "Um, do you want your hat back?"

"No, that's okay," Peter said. "You can keep it."

Of course he doesn't want his old hat back, Marigold thought as she headed across the yacht club lawn to the road. *He has a new one.*

As soon as Marigold returned to Aunt Sunny's, she flew up the stairs to the attic bedroom. She retrieved her iPad from inside her dresser drawer, tapped it awake, and opened her digital diary. Zinnie knocked on the door, but Marigold told her that she didn't want to talk. Instead she wanted to write about the whole thing. And she did, sparing no detail. She wrote about the squall and throwing up and the moment that she had met Lindsey. She wrote about how she'd thought for some reason that Peter was like Aunt Sunny's house or Edith's Ice Cream Shop—that he'd have stayed the same, just as they had—and then she wrote about how wrong she'd been. She wrote about Lindsey, who was both similar to the Cuties in seeming ordinary, and at the same time different from them, because she really didn't care about fashion. Her jeans were grass-stained! Her T-shirt was two sizes too big! **I must dedicate myself to being more ordinary than ever,** Marigold typed, wiping tears from her eyes. Then she closed her iPad and put her head on her pillow. She gazed out the window, where there was a view of Aunt Sunny's garden blossoming with color. A breeze blew through the open window and a bird chirped in a nearby tree. But Marigold didn't feel like she belonged in this happy country scene. With her fashion sense and love of lip gloss, she didn't fit in here at all. She didn't fit at school. She didn't fit in Hollywood. As she heard Lily calling her to come down to dinner, she wondered if there was anywhere on this earth where she actually did belong.

24 · Gathering Flowers and Collecting Information

"She's back!" Zinnie said, rushing to greet Marigold when she heard the front door open. She had been helping Sunny and Lily with dinner, but she couldn't wait to talk to Marigold. It wasn't just because she was wondering how the date had gone, though of course she was dying to know. Zinnie had to hear if Marigold had used any of the romantic lines that Zinnie had come up with last night, like "Let's tie our hearts in a complicated boat knot so they'll always be together" or "How'd you like to sail away with me?"

But even more urgently, Zinnie needed to talk to Marigold about what she'd overheard that afternoon while Marigold was gone. Zinnie had been trying to complete her submission for Mrs. Lee by writing down a conversation between Aunt Sunny and Lily.

"Just ignore me," Zinnie had said as she sat at the kitchen table with her notebook. "I'm working on a writing exercise, but I need you to pretend I'm not here."

"Okay," Aunt Sunny said. She was washing the saucepan they'd used to make the lemon syrup. Lily spied a box of things the sisters had brought down from the attic. It didn't take her long to discover the framed pressed flowers that Aunt Sunny had made when she was a little girl.

"These are actual, real flowers?" Lily asked, holding up the pansies preserved under glass.

"They certainly are," Aunt Sunny said. "I picked them myself when I was about your age."

"These very flowers?" Lily asked.

"That's right," Aunt Sunny said.

"But how can they have they lasted so long?" Lily asked.

"They're pressed," Aunt Sunny said. "Plants lose their color because of bacteria and fungi, but those things need moisture to live. If you dry and press the flowers, they'll keep for a long time."

"Can you teach me how to do that?" Lily asked.

"I'd love to," Aunt Sunny said, drying her hands on a towel. "Maybe you can start your own collection of pressed flowers to remember this summer by when you're back in California."

"Yes!" Lily said. As sweet as this conversation was,

Zinnie didn't feel like she was getting any great ideas.

"Hi, Tony," Zinnie said, when he walked in with the scallops, corn, and peas.

"How are my girls?" Tony asked, placing the groceries on the counter and giving Aunt Sunny a kiss. Aunt Sunny smiled and blushed.

"Aunt Sunny is going to teach me how to press flowers," Lily said.

"How cool is that?" Tony said, and he tousled Lily's hair. "Your aunt is one smart lady."

"Are you staying for dinner?" Zinnie asked Tony.

"Can't tonight. I have to go see about a job," Tony said.

"That's too bad," Aunt Sunny said.

"Can we start picking flowers now?" Lily asked.

"I don't see why not," Aunt Sunny said, removing her apron and hanging it on its hook. "Come on. Zinnie and Tony, will you join us?"

Tony's phone rang. He glanced at the screen. "I gotta take this, but I'll see you out there in a jiffy." Tony stepped into the hallway.

"I'll come," Zinnie said. "I'm just going to put my notebook away."

"We'll be in the garden," Lily said, taking Aunt Sunny's hand as they stepped out the back door.

Zinnie went to put her notebook in her writing room when she realized that Tony was in there, talking on the phone with the door closed.

"Sunny has no idea," she overheard Tony say. Already this was intriguing. Zinnie pulled out her notebook and started to jot things down. "The old girl is a fixer-upper, but that doesn't mean my efforts won't pay off." *The old girl?* Was he talking about Aunt Sunny? Zinnie leaned her ear against the door. "I can't wait to really get my hands on this property," Tony was saying. "As soon as we sign the paperwork, it'll be mine. I just have to put on a good act until the wedding is over. Then it's 'Bye-bye, old girl, hello new beauty.'"

What the . . . ? Zinnie's heart started to race. Was Tony not who everyone thought he was? Was he a bad person—like a *really* bad person? Zinnie listened to Tony saying his good-byes and then she darted into the garden.

As soon as Zinnie heard Marigold come in the door, Zinnie tried to catch her. Just as she was rounding the corner, Marigold ran upstairs. Zinnie heard her shut and latch the door to the bedroom. Zinnie followed her up, taking two steps at a time, and knocked on the door. Technically it was her room, too, and she really shouldn't have to knock, but something told her to proceed with caution.

"How'd it go?" Zinnie asked, leaning against the door.

"I don't want to talk about it." Marigold's voice

was quiet and small.

"Are you okay?" Zinnie asked.

"Yeah, just don't come in right now, okay?"

"Okay," Zinnie said, resting her hand on the door. "I need to talk to you about some stuff. It's kind of important."

"Zinnia and Marigold, can you please come shell the peas?" Aunt Sunny called from the bottom of the stairs. The sound of Aunt Sunny's voice, so happy and relaxed, broke Zinnie's heart.

"Coming!" Zinnie called back. She went down the stairs to where Aunt Sunny stood, looking expectant.

"How'd it go with Peter?" Aunt Sunny whispered.

"I think she needs some time to herself," Zinnie said.

"Ahh," Aunt Sunny replied, "I see." And she patted Zinnie's shoulder.

"Um, when you marry Tony, does this house become his?" Zinnie asked as they walked to the kitchen.

"Heavens no," Aunt Sunny said. "It becomes *ours*."

"Do you have to share it?" Zinnie asked.

"I want to," Aunt Sunny said. "That's part of the fun of being married."

"Yeah, okay, but he can't just sell it without asking you, can he?" Zinnie asked.

"Good gracious, of course not."

"That's great," Zinnie said, and she sighed with relief.

"Why do you ask?"

"Oh, no reason," Zinnie said. The last thing she wanted to do was upset Aunt Sunny so close to her wedding, but what she'd overheard wasn't sitting right with her. She'd just have to keep her eyes and ears on Tony.

25 · Handsome Horace

Zinnie was dying to ask her about Peter, but Marigold didn't come out of the bedroom until dinner, and then she barely touched her scallops, which were her favorite seafood, or her vegetables, which she usually ate because she'd read that they were good for the hair, nails, and skin. She hadn't brought up the sailing trip once during dinner, and now that Aunt Sunny and Zinnie were clearing the table, Marigold was totally focused on Lily and her flower-pressing project.

"What kinds of flowers did you pick?" Marigold asked Lily as they spread the fresh flowers on the table.

"These these are impatiens and these are forget-me-nots," Lily said. "Aunt Sunny told me they'll press well because they're flatter than other flowers."

"That's right," Aunt Sunny said, drying her hands on a dish towel. "And you've done a good job sorting them. Now, I've got plenty of heavy cookbooks to press them with, but will you go and get some clean sheets of paper from the living room, Lily?"

"Sure," Lily said, and hopped off her chair.

"Time for us to get to work on these tablecloths," Aunt Sunny said as she placed the stack of tablecloths and napkins that the girls had sifted through yesterday on the table.

"Okay, what happened with Peter?" Zinnie asked—she couldn't wait another second.

"It didn't go well," Marigold said, resting her chin in her hand.

"Is Peter not your boyfriend anymore?" Lily asked as she bounded back into the kitchen with the paper.

Marigold shook her head.

"Someone has good ears!" Aunt Sunny said as she took some lemon halves out of the fridge and brought them to the table.

"What?" Zinnie said.

"So he can be mine?" Lily asked.

"Sorry, Lily. He has a new girlfriend," Marigold said.

"Oh dear," Aunt Sunny said, shaking out a white tablecloth with little blue flowers embroidered on it.

"I don't really want to talk about . . . the details," Marigold said. "I'd rather clean tablecloths."

"All right," Aunt Sunny said. "We're going to look for stains and treat them with lemon juice and salt. We'll let the tablecloths and napkins sit tonight and wash them early tomorrow. See? Like this." Aunt Sunny located a faint stain in the center of the table-cloth and rubbed a lemon half on it, and then she shook some salt on it.

"Will you help me with the flowers, Aunt Sunny?" Lily asked, handing Aunt Sunny the paper.

"Certainly," Aunt Sunny said, opening up a big cookbook to a page in the middle and placing a piece of paper inside. "Now carefully arrange your impatiens right here—make sure they don't touch one another or they'll stick together." Lily placed her flowers on the page and Aunt Sunny placed another piece of paper on top of them and then shut the cookbook and put another, heavier, cookbook on top. "We'll leave them there for a month to dry out."

"But I won't be here in a month," Lily said.

"I'll be sure to send them to you," Aunt Sunny said. "But if you don't give them at least a month, they won't preserve well. And you want to remember this sum-mer for a long time, don't you?"

"Yes," Lily said. "I can be patient."

"Okay, now it's your turn," Aunt Sunny said, open-ing another big cookbook for Lily. "Do the same with the forget-me-nots."

As Lily started the process again, Zinnie didn't

think she was capable of waiting much longer to find out who Peter's girlfriend was. "I'm not asking for details, but I need to know—who could Peter like more than you?" Zinnie asked, taking a tablecloth from the pile and opening it. "Seriously, who?"

"A girl named Lindsey," Marigold said. She'd found a big yellowish stain on an ivory-colored tablecloth and she vigorously ran a lemon half over it. "She's on the sailing team."

"You need to get him back," Zinnie said, handing her the salt. "We need to come up with a plan."

"He seems to really like her," Marigold said. Her jaw clenched as she shook more than enough salt onto the stain.

"I think that's plenty, dear," Aunt Sunny said, taking the tablecloth away and putting it in a laundry basket at the end of the table. "We can put all the treated tablecloths and the ones without stains in here."

"You need to sing to Peter. Like this." Lily paused her flower arranging, tucked her thumbs in her armpits to make wings, and made an O with her lips. Then she sang a weird, throaty song. Aunt Sunny and Zinnie laughed, but Marigold seemed to miss the humor. Lily took a bow and smiled proudly. "That's what the male shorebirds do when they want a girlfriend. We learned all about birds today at camp."

"I don't think that would work," Marigold said. "I'm not a shorebird."

"Or a male," Zinnie said.

"Did you ever like someone who didn't like you back?" Marigold asked Aunt Sunny.

"Certainly," Aunt Sunny said, smoothing out a pale-yellow tablecloth with scalloped edges. "Horace Zanks."

"Horace?" Lily asked, bursting into giggles.

"I think you make these names up," Marigold said. "Last summer you told me about someone named Stanley Toots."

"Oh, the Tootses were a very prominent family in these parts until the youngest Toots, the very Stanley I told you about, married a sporty young woman named Sissy, sold the family estate, and moved to Africa."

"Look!" Lily said, pointing to her flowers, which were spaced evenly on the paper.

"Well done," Aunt Sunny said. "Now place the second piece of paper on top of them and close the book."

"Stanley and Sissy Toots?" Marigold asked, raising a disbelieving eyebrow. Aunt Sunny grinned and nodded.

"But what about Horace?" Zinnie asked. Lily laughed again at the name.

"Laugh all you want," Aunt Sunny said as she handed Lily a stack of napkins and a lemon half, "but Horace broke many a heart in this town. Handsome Horace, we called him."

"How old were you when you fell for Handsome Horace?" Zinnie asked as she examined green linen napkins with an ivory trim. She was curious about when most people found a boyfriend or girlfriend.

"I was thirteen," Aunt Sunny said.

"And how did you know you liked him *in that way*?" Zinnie asked.

"I just knew," Aunt Sunny said. "He made my heart go pitter-patter, pitter-patter." She tapped her hand on her chest.

"Like butterflies in your stomach?" Zinnie asked.

"Exactly. I can see him now, with his wavy brown hair and nicely fitting dungarees."

Zinnie's heart had gone pitter-patter when she'd seen Max in the backyard the other day. But didn't it always go pitter-patter when she was happy?

"He didn't like you back?" Marigold asked.

"I asked him to go to the Sadie Hawkins dance with me and he said no, even though he didn't have a date yet," Aunt Sunny said.

"What's a Sadie Hawkins dance?" Zinnie asked, holding up a delicate and lacy tablecloth that had been very well preserved. She put it in the laundry basket.

"That's a dance where the girls ask the boys to be their dates," Aunt Sunny said. "Of course, that happens all the time now. But back in those days it was the boys who asked the girls."

"Did it hurt your feelings when he said no?" Marigold asked.

"It did. I was very blue about the whole thing. I

moped around for a week at least. But he had eyes for Karla Nickerson. All the boys did. She was what we called a knockout."

"When I get a boyfriend, I'm going to call him my puppy," Lily said as she rubbed a stain out of a napkin.

"That's a good name," Aunt Sunny said.

"So you didn't go to the dance?" Marigold asked.

"Of course I did! I took my friend Bill. He had a quick wit and fast feet. He was a very good dancer, so I knew I'd at least have fun. Bill and I danced the night away. We did the jitterbug, the Lindy, the West Coast swing, the bop, and the twist. And of course we boogie-woogied. Oh, we had fun! Poor Karla Nickerson couldn't put one foot in front of the other without tripping. She and Horace sat in the corner all night."

"Did Horace like you when he saw you dancing with Bill?" Zinnie asked.

"He asked me to go for a stroll the next Saturday," Aunt Sunny said.

"Did you?" Zinnie asked.

"I did. We walked along the harbor on a lovely winter afternoon."

"So it turned out he did like you?" Marigold asked. "Once he saw you having so much fun with another boy?"

"I like to think that Horace became interested in

me because he saw me really being myself, dancing and laughing and whooping it up with Bill. Anyway, I learned on that walk that Horace wasn't very bright. I lost interest. I was glad that he had his looks to fall back on."

"And those butterflies in your stomach just . . . flew away?" Zinnie asked.

"That's the thing about butterflies. They don't stay put for long, do they? They flutter around one flower, then they flutter around another."

"They're eating," Lily said. "Butterflies feed on nectar and pollen."

"You are learning so much," Aunt Sunny said, and holding up the basket of linens, she added, "and we have treated all our linens. Tomorrow we'll wash and hang them."

"What happened to Bill?" Zinnie asked. "Did he ever become your boyfriend?"

"We dated for a few weeks in high school, but it turned out we were better off as friends. We're still in touch," Aunt Sunny said, yawning.

"Would you ever get back together with him, like if things don't work out with Tony for some reason?" Zinnie asked.

"That's a weird thing to say," Marigold said.

"Don't you worry, Zinnie. Weddings bring up all sorts of emotions in people, but you can rest assured that things are going to work out with Tony. He's a wonderful man and he brings me a lot of happiness. Now, I don't know about you girls, but I'm about ready to pack up my tent. Why don't we all get in our pj's and I'll show you a postcard Bill sent me from Peru."

26 · The Lost Art
of Hanging the Wash

"You have to hang the tablecloths with the wind at your back," Aunt Sunny said the next morning. She was demonstrating how to pin one of the freshly washed tablecloths to the clothesline that hung between two posts in the backyard. Zinnie, Marigold, and Lily watched. Zinnie had woken up early, and she and Aunt Sunny had washed most of the tablecloths and napkins in the delicate cycle of the washing machine. They'd washed some of the lacy ones in the sink and rolled them in towels to remove the excess water. Aunt Sunny continued, "Otherwise the tablecloth will wrap around and you'll get all tangled up, not to mention wet."

Zinnie nodded as if she were paying rapt attention, but she couldn't stop thinking about Tony. She hadn't yet been able to discuss what she'd overheard with Marigold and she really needed to. With any luck, she'd only have to wait a few more minutes. Lily was all packed and ready to go to camp, her Princess Arabella lunch box in her hand. Aunt Sunny had made sure to give Lily several extra cookies so that she'd have plenty to share. Lily had packed a pendant with a pressed flower inside so that she could show the kids at camp an example of the project she was working on at home. Now Zinnie was just waiting for Aunt Sunny to finish explaining what she called "the lost art of hanging the wash."

"And it would be best if you two worked together so these tablecloths, which we've just made so nice and clean, don't touch the ground," Aunt Sunny said, handing Zinnie a corner. "Zinnia, dear, you take one end and I'll take the other." With a sure hand, Aunt Sunny pinned one corner of a white cotton tablecloth with a wooden pin, and Zinnie pinned the other. The tablecloth flapped in the early-morning sunshine like a loose sail. "It's a perfect day for hanging the wash. We have a good southeasterly breeze, and the bright sunshine will get rid of any lingering stains." Aunt Sunny checked her watch. "I have to get to work and Lily needs to get to camp. We'll see you both this afternoon. Don't forget that the band will be rehearsing here later. Max is going to arrive a little early to work on the platform, so you should expect him around ten or so."

Zinnie and Marigold waved good-bye to Sunny and Lily. As soon as they were out of sight, Zinnie told Marigold what she'd heard. "I asked Aunt Sunny if Tony could just take the property once they were married, and she said that he couldn't."

"Then none of this makes any sense. Tony is so nice. Are you sure you heard him right?"

"I mean, I think so. He called her an 'old girl' and a 'fixer-upper' and said something about putting on a 'good act' until the wedding."

"I know!" Marigold said. "Sometimes people call a boat or a car a girl's name. Maybe he's fixing up a car or a boat as a present for her?"

"I guess that's possible," Zinnie said.

"It's the only thing that makes sense," Marigold said.

"Maybe you're right," Zinnie said. It *did* make sense. "See, this is why I needed to talk to you so badly last night. But you fell asleep before I had a chance."

An hour later, Zinnie and Marigold had hung about half of the tablecloths and napkins and were ready to take a break. Marigold went inside to get them some lemonade and a snack.

"Boo!" a voice said, startling Zinnie. She turned to see Max, in a bright-green T-shirt and jeans, his great big smile almost wider than his face.

"I didn't even hear you!" Zinnie said, laughing.

"What are doing?" Max asked.

"Oh, nothing much, except hanging the wash," Zinnie said. "It's a lost art," she added, quoting Aunt Sunny. She couldn't help but feel happy when she looked at Max, whose eyes were sparkling. "Cool guitar. Can you play me something?"

"Sure," Max said, "What do you want to hear?"

"How about a song for hanging the wash?" Zinnie said with a shrug.

"Okay," Max said, and began to strum a happy tune. "We can make up the words as we go, because I don't know any songs about laundry."

"Oh, oh, oh my gosh, we're hanging the wash," Zinnie sang.

Max laughed and added: "Please, oh please, can I have some squash? It's what I like to eat when I hang the wash."

Zinnie laughed and sang: "If you don't have squash, will you go ask Josh?"

Then they sang together: "Because squash is what we eat when we hang the wash." They burst into laughter.

That was when Marigold returned with two cups of lemonade and a Ziploc bag of cookies.

"What are you guys doing?" Marigold asked.

Max's cheeks flushed. Marigold, however, barely seemed to notice him.

"We're making up a song," Zinnie said. She pulled a tablecloth from the basket and went to hang it on the line. She was so taken with Max and his guitar that she forgot Aunt Sunny's rule. The breeze picked up and the wet tablecloth wrapped around her, soaking her shirt and shorts.

"Uh, be right back," Zinnie said, handing the tablecloth to Marigold. She ran into the house and up to the attic bedroom. Not only was it uncomfortable to wear wet clothes, but also she was worried that her T-shirt was now see-through.

She opened her drawer to put on a dry T-shirt, but she saw that the drawer was almost empty. Since Marigold had been borrowing so many of her clothes, Zinnie hardly had any clean T-shirts left. She had a reputation in her family for packing light, sometimes too light, and with Marigold raiding her drawer, now she had nothing to wear. The only T-shirts in there were ones she wore to bed.

Normally Marigold would flip out if Zinnie borrowed her clothes without asking, and *normally* Zinnie respected that. But things were different this summer. Not only did Marigold want to borrow Zinnie's clothes, she had simply been taking her stuff whenever she wanted to. Zinnie didn't mind. In fact, she was kind of flattered. And in light of this new way of doing things, Zinnie reasoned that it should be perfectly okay for her take something of Marigold's without asking. She wondered why she hadn't thought of it until now. Her heart quickened at the idea of selecting one of Marigold's beautiful things. Maybe she would wear the teal tank top that she'd been envying since Marigold had brought it home from the mall. Or what about the cute pink button-down? Did she want to borrow a dress, even?

She opened Marigold's drawer, where everything was folded as if it were on a display table at the Gap. She reached in to pick out a blue T-shirt from the middle of pile when she felt something slim and hard between the T-shirts. She pulled it out, realizing that it was Marigold's iPad.

She looked out the window to see Marigold outside, hanging the napkins and chatting with Max. Zinnie tucked the iPad back in the drawer. She opened Marigold's closet and considered what to wear. She was curious about whatever Marigold was trying to conceal on the iPad, but she wasn't about to leave Marigold alone with Max any longer than she had to.

27 · Shy Girl in the Key of C

"Nice dress," Marigold said, her nose wrinkled, as Zinnie walked back outside, wearing her sister's sea-foam-green dress. Max was seated on a tree stump, playing Marigold a tune that sounded more serious than their laundry-hanging song, and Marigold was hanging napkins. Zinnie flinched at the sight of Max's adoring gaze set firmly on her sister, but she kept her composure as she strode toward them. She had a new look and she liked it.

Back in the bedroom, Zinnie had used her phone's camera to see what she looked like in the dress. She was surprised to see that the dress didn't just look *not terrible* on her, it looked good. Really good, actually. The color brought out the hazel of her eyes and set off her dark hair. And the hem hit her knees, just like it did on Marigold. She knew that she'd had a growth spurt this winter—but had she had another one this spring? Because not only was she getting a little bit taller (her legs had definitely lengthened), her overall shape was changing, too. She appeared to have developed something of a waist. Had this all happened overnight? How had she not noticed until now? Zinnie decided that she loved this dress.

Zinnie and Marigold had different-sized feet (Marigold's were long and narrow, while Zinnie's were small but wide), so she couldn't wear any of Marigold's shoes. Her sneakers didn't look good with the dress at all, and the ballet slipper shoes that she was going to wear to the wedding were too dressy. So Zinnie decided that she was going to go out to the yard barefoot.

"Kind of dressy for hanging tablecloths, don't you think?" Marigold asked. Zinnie could tell that even though Marigold had been totally comfortable borrowing *her* clothes all week, she was still shocked at seeing Zinnie in her dress.

"As someone I know once said, a dress is suitable for any occasion," Zinnie responded. "And since we share clothes now, I knew you wouldn't mind."

Marigold opened her mouth to reply but quickly shut it.

"I think it's cool when girls don't dress up too much. Like you, Marigold. You're always wearing the kind of clothes that you can run around in and stuff," Max said. Zinnie's spirits lowered a bit as she watched Max focus on Marigold, who was wearing *her clothes*. "I hate getting dressed up. My parents sent me to private school one year and I had to wear a tie every day and I totally hated it."

"I know what you mean," Zinnie said. "I don't like dressing up either."

"But you just said you liked dresses," Max said, confused.

"But I didn't really mean that," Zinnie said. "I meant—" She started to protest more, but stopped when she could feel that she was just making the situation worse. She usually didn't like wearing dresses. This one had been a total exception. As Max bent his head to tune his guitar, Zinnie looked to Marigold to back her up, but Marigold pointed to her sealed lips. Zinnie had told her not to talk to Max, but she didn't mean now, when Marigold could have helped her out.

"Then why'd you say it?" Max asked with curiosity.

"I don't know," Zinnie said, shaking her head.

"Man, girls are so complicated," Max said, and he looked longingly at Marigold. "Well, not all girls. Marigold, do you have any requests? I can play a lot of songs." Marigold shook her head no. Max started to pluck a tune on his guitar and began to sing.

"There is a very shy girl I know, hey, hey, hey. She doesn't like attention, but I can tell she has a lot to say," Max sang. "She doesn't care about dresses or makeup or what her hair looks like at all. She's from a big city, but she's a country girl in spite of it all."

Oh my goodness, he's singing about Marigold, Zinnie thought. She watched Marigold pause in her laundry hanging and blush.

"Okay, so I rhymed 'all' with 'all,' but, hey, I'm making this up as I go along!" Max said playfully as Marigold hung the last of the napkins.

A shy girl? Zinnie thought. *A girl who doesn't care about makeup and stuff? Please!* Zinnie wanted to put an end to the madness and yell, "This isn't true," but she sensed that Max was set on liking Marigold no matter what.

It wasn't every day that Zinnie came across someone as fun and creative as Max. The fact that it was a boy who was her imaginative equal both didn't matter at all (a fun friend is a fun friend!) and mattered a ton (this was Zinnie's first boy-who-is-a-friend or possibly boyfriend). Why did Marigold have to interfere?

Tony's pickup truck rumbled down the driveway.

"Hi there, girls!" Tony called as he parked. He smiled and waved. If he was up to something suspicious, he was a really good actor. "And hello, Max!"

"Hi, Grandpa!" Max said, strumming his guitar.

"Hi, Tony," Zinnie said as she and Marigold exchanged a quick look. "I was wondering, do you know how to fix up cars?"

"I sure wish I did know how, but cars aren't really my thing."

"What about boats?" Zinnie asked. "Do you like to fix up boats?"

"I'm afraid not," Tony said. "You're not going to believe this given where I live, but I'm not much of a sailor. More of a landlubber."

"Interesting," Zinnie said, pinching Marigold.

"Are you looking for a new mode of transportation?" Tony asked. "I could build you a skateboard if you like."

"Grandpa built one for me this fall," Max said. "I painted it black and red. It's so cool."

"No, thank you," Zinnie said. "I'm just trying to learn more about my new great-uncle."

"Well, I'm an open book. So if you have any questions, just ask. Are you ready to get to work, Max?" Tony asked, pulling his own guitar out of the backseat. "And by work I mean play a little rock and roll."

"Yup, I'm coming, Grandpa!" Max turned back to Zinnie and Marigold, flashed one of his sunbeam smiles, and said "I'll see you later."

"See you later," Zinnie said. Even though she had a story to write and a mystery to get to the bottom of, for the moment all she could think about was Max, and the way his smile made something inside her melt like ice cream in the sun.

28 · Hidden Words

"I just can't seem to put it together," Zinnie said to Ashley a couple of days later. She hadn't seen her friend in a few days because Aunt Sunny had kept the sisters busy with wedding preparations. It had been a blast to pick blackberries for the cake at Davis Farms and see the animals there, too. And taste testing lemonade recipes was fun, but Zinnie was glad to be back at the town beach, hanging out at the snack bar. "Tony is up to something."

Marigold was sure that nothing fishy was happening with Tony, and it didn't bother her that he clearly wasn't fixing up a car or a boat. She said Zinnie had probably misheard him on the phone. Zinnie wasn't convinced.

"Why do you think that?" Ashley asked as she handed Zinnie an ice pop.

Zinnie told her what she'd heard him say. "He wasn't talking about a car or a boat. Something isn't right."

"Look, my parents know Tony," Ashley said. "Everyone knows Tony. Before you make any accusations, you need more information. You don't want to cause any unnecessary drama."

"Anyway, you need to focus on your story so you can get into that writing class of yours," Ashley said.

"You're right," Zinnie said. She could feel her worry line forming on her forehead as she furrowed her brow. "I can't think of anything! But I have to write that story soon or I won't have a chance of getting in, and then I'll have to do sports, which I hate. . . ."

"Hey, don't freak out," Ashley said, taking her by the shoulders. "You still have a little time, right?" Zinnie nodded. "We'll think of something. Hey! How about my original idea for a thriller—the Lighthouse of Fear!"

"My teacher did suggest that I go someplace I've never been before and describe it using all five senses. . . ."

"Okay, I'll take ya," Ashley said. "Meet me here in the morning. And make sure to bring garlic."

"Garlic?"

"My nana says it keeps away the bad spirits," Ashley said.

"All right," Zinnie said. "Whatever you say."

Zinnie returned to her towel and pulled out her notebook. Her pen was out of ink, so she looked in Marigold's bag. There was that iPad. Only it was wrapped in a T-shirt, like Marigold didn't want Zinnie to see it. Mrs. Lee's words came back to Zinnie: "Be a detective!"

Zinnie eyed Marigold swimming her laps and then opened the iPad. She was surprised to find a password. Her mother had specifically asked—or, fine, *encouraged*—Marigold to share the iPad even though it was hers. A password did not seem to be in the spirit of sharing. Zinnie knew that a password should keep her from going any further down this road, but Mrs. Lee's words seemed to be telling her to press on and find the story.

Zinnie typed in Marigold's birthday. It didn't work. She typed in their phone number back in Los Angeles. Didn't work. She tried the number of their home address. Nope. Then she thought of a number that Marigold had been obsessed with all year: 0701. The day the *Night Sprites* movie came out. She tapped the numbers and, presto, the iPad came to life. *I really should be a detective,* Zinnie thought, and then noticed that the screen had opened to what looked like a diary. Zinnie's breath caught in her throat and she checked to see that Marigold was still busy swimming.

I shouldn't be doing this, Zinnie thought. She was about to close the iPad when she saw her name. **If I'm**

going to be ordinary, I need to be more like Zinnie, it read. **I can't go that far. Ugh.** Zinnie's heart thumped in her chest. So that was why Marigold was borrowing her clothes! It wasn't because she was going casual or because she admired Zinnie's style. Zinnie didn't feel so bad about invading her sister's privacy anymore. But then it got worse. She read these lines: **Poor Zinnie. I worry that she won't even find a boyfriend because she really is such a spaz.**

Was this true? Was Marigold right? Something was waking up in Zinnie's stomach. Only it wasn't butterflies, it was anger. Zinnie felt her face flush right up to her hairline. Her breath became shallow, and she could hear the air whirring in her ears and the steady thump of her pulse. Could her own sister really have written such mean things about her? Sisters were supposed to have each other's back, not stab them there.

Her rage began to transform into an idea. Mrs. Lee had said that good stories always have a transformation in them. Here was a transformation. Marigold was trying to transform from her regular, glamorous self into someone who was ordinary.

This wouldn't just make an okay story, Zinnie thought. It would make a great story. It was the opposite of most transformation tales, in which an ordinary girl learns that she's a princess, or a losing team tries very hard and practices all the time and then becomes the best team, like in some of Dad's favorite sports movies. Instead it was the reverse. A girl who is so beautiful and special tries to be ordinary. And just as Mrs. Lee had promised, the story was *right under her nose*. The best part was, she wasn't going to have to use her imagination that much. She could just watch Marigold and write what she saw. Relief cooled her anger at her sister. The deadline was just days away, and at last she knew what to write.

29 · A Writer Writes

Later, as Marigold was turning the seed packets into place cards at the kitchen table and Tony's band was rehearsing in the yard, Zinnie went into her writing room with a glass of Aunt Sunny's iced tea and a scone and shut the door.

Just to be extra sure that she wouldn't be interrupted, Zinnie used the hook-and-eye device to lock the door. Then she opened her laptop and started to type the story of an extraordinary girl who wanted to be ordinary. The words flowed. It was easy to describe her sister's extraordinariness in great detail. After all, Zinnie had been observing her for her whole life.

Sounds of Tony's band playing "Here Comes the Sun" drifted in the window as Zinnie tried to capture Marigold on the page. There was her legendary sense of style, her bright blue eyes, her ladylike hands with long fingers and colorful nails. And, of course, her hair! From her the way her nose wrinkled when she laughed to her high-pitched sneezes to the way she leaned just a tiny bit to the left when standing still, Zinnie described how the little things Marigold did came together like notes of music in a great song, the kind that makes you want to sing in the car.

After Zinnie felt she'd painted a portrait of her sister so that the reader could see her in her mind's eye, she experimented with different names: Skylar, Esme, and Zora. Isabelle, Annabel, and Lulu. Sarah, Katie, and Jane. Each one took Zinnie too far away from her sister. She decided to name her character Marianna. It was close enough to keep her source of inspiration bright and alive as she wrote, but different enough so that she felt free to take some liberties.

Taking a sip of iced tea and a bite of the scone, Zinnie wrote about "Marianna's" journey over the past few weeks. She was careful to change the major details. She imagined that Marianna, instead of being an actress cut from a movie, was a talented but somewhat stuck-up ballerina who also happened to have a great love of fashion. The ballerina was cut from a performance when an understudy proved to be just a little bit better. Zinnie described Marianna's longing to forget about ballet and the stage. She was tempted to skip the part about Marianna chopping off her hair, but it worked so well with ballet—because didn't all ballerinas have long hair that they twisted into buns? Yes, she was sure they did. She had to keep that detail.

Zinnie wrote about Marianna's trip from L.A. to a small town in Rhode Island. Marianna was traveling to a much older cousin's wedding. (What else could it be besides a wedding? Zinnie wasn't going to write about a funeral!) She described Marianna's plans to hide her grace and brilliance in order to complete her transformation. Then she wrote about Marianna's reuniting with her boyfriend from last summer, "Pedro," who she was hoping to dance with at this wedding, and how he rejected her. Instead of making Pedro a sailor, Zinnie made him a surfer. They had surfing here, right? Of course they did. She'd seen surfboards on top of cars in Pruet.

She wrote about another boy, "Lawrence." "Lawrence" was the last name of the boy they called Laurie, Jo's boy-who-was-a-friend in *Little Women*, and Zinnie thought her character's name was a brilliant literary allusion. (She had only learned about allusions this spring, and here she was, already using one!) Laurie loved to play Jo's games, just as Max did Zinnie's. The Lawrence in Zinnie's story was falling for Marianna but for all the wrong reasons. He was in love with the personality she was creating, not the person that she was. Zinnie tried to think of something that Lawrence could do to show that he liked Marianna besides singing to her, but since Zinnie had witnessed such a scene so recently, it seemed to find its way onto the page practically on its own.

Zinnie had to type quickly to keep up with her ideas. Her mind was buzzing as her fingers flew across the keyboard. When she finally took a break and looked up from the screen, she saw that the sun had lowered in the sky and Tony's band was packing up. She checked the clock on her computer and realized that she only had a half hour left before they had to pick up Lily from camp. She couldn't believe it. She had been writing for almost two hours and fifteen minutes straight—that was three class periods—and she'd barely noticed. As her imagination waned from a rapid boil to a simmer, she was both energized and slightly exhausted. It was a great feeling.

After a quick trip to the bathroom, and a brief stop at the fridge for a green apple, Zinnie read over her last paragraph:

Marianna was wearing her ordinariness like a mask. As sweet Lawrence sang to her, she touched her hair with nervous hands, forgetting for a minute that it was too short for twirling. She liked being sung to, and yet none of the words rang true. How long could she keep her extraordinariness

hidden? How long can someone not be herself before she gets tired? Or, she wondered with fright, was she even still extraordinary at all?

It's good! Zinnie thought. *I wrote something real and it's good!*

She sighed and leaned back in her chair. She had done it. She had written a story that she was certain gave her a shot at getting into the Writers' Workshop—and with time to spare before deadline! There was only one problem. It didn't have an ending. Did Marianna rediscover her greatness and find a way to get back into the ballet? Or did she lose her extraordinariness altogether? And what about the story line about the two boys? Which one of them was she going to dance with at the wedding?

Zinnie usually liked to give her stories happy endings, but she had noticed that most of the stories in *Muses* didn't have happy endings. Some of them didn't seem to have endings at all. She also thought of Marigold's comments about her being a spaz, and how she wondered whether or not Zinnie would ever get a boyfriend. Zinnie came to the conclusion that a happy ending was not necessarily in order. She wished that she had more time before the deadline for the Writers' Workshop so that she could see how the story finished in real life at Aunt Sunny's wedding, but she had to email this to Mrs. Lee before then.

"Time to pick up Lily," Marigold said from the doorway. Zinnie jumped a little in her chair and slammed her laptop shut. She had forgotten to lock the door again after going to the bathroom. "Jeez," Marigold said. "You're jumpy. Did you finish your story?"

"Uh . . . almost," Zinnie said, spinning in the office chair to face Marigold. "I just need to think of an ending." After writing about her all afternoon, Zinnie noticed that Marigold appeared different somehow.

"Do I have something on my face?" Marigold asked, wiping her mouth and then smiling so that Zinnie could see her teeth. "Is my tongue blue? I just ate a Popsicle."

"No," Zinnie said, studying Marigold's expressions so that she could maybe add another detail to her story later.

"Okay!" Marigold said, placing a hand on her hip. Zinnie also noted that Marigold's left foot was pointed out a bit. "You're looking at me like I'm from another planet or something."

"Sorry," Zinnie said, shaking her head. "I'm just thinking about my story."

"You're not writing about me, are you?" Marigold asked.

"No! No way. I'm writing about . . . time travel."

"Oh, okay," Marigold said, and walked out of the office. As Zinnie followed her through the kitchen and out the back door into the breezy July afternoon, she felt relief that Marigold had bought the lie. But she could also feel the lie itself, crawling across her heart like a caterpillar.

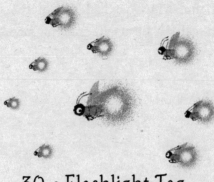

30 · Flashlight Tag

"Fifty-seven, fifty-eight, fifty-nine . . . ," Zinnie called from the stone archway in the pear orchard. "Sixty!"

Marigold lay under the bench with the stone angel sitting on it. She was hiding from Zinnie, who was "it" in this fifth and final round of flashlight tag. Aunt Sunny, who was drinking coffee with the other grown-ups on the picnic blanket, had told them one more game and then it was time for bed. Marigold had a great hiding spot. Under the big tree near the driveway, the bench was still within bounds but far from the stone archway, which was "it jail," the place where, once they'd had been tagged, they had to sit and wait for the last person to be found.

"Ready or not, here I come!" Zinnie called.

Marigold grinned as she watched the beam of

Zinnie's flashlight illuminate the vegetable garden in the opposite direction. She was pretty sure she was going to be crowned the evening's ultimate flashlight tag winner. The reward was the last remaining snickerdoodle cookie.

But that wasn't the only reason Marigold was smiling. Peter was visiting tonight, and he was hiding—she guessed from the way he'd darted off to the right—behind the shed. He, Jean, and Mack had stopped by to bring Sunny a bunch of candles that were left over from their Christmas party. They thought Aunt Sunny could use them for the wedding reception. Aunt Sunny had accepted the gift and insisted that they stay for dinner.

"I've made enough spaghetti for a small army!" Aunt Sunny said. Tony, Max, and Max's parents, Paul and Cindy, were all there for dinner, too.

"I'm in the army, so I can say it's true—Sunny cooked enough food for my whole batallion. And I made tons of meatballs," Paul said, squeezing Max's shoulder. Marigold knew that Max's dad was in the army, and he looked it, too. He had muscles and very short hair. He also had one of the biggest, warmest smiles Marigold had ever seen. It was clear that Max got his smile from him. Max's hair, on the other hand, came from his mom, who was petite, with the same shade of light-brown hair as Max.

"We're Italian," Max said, "so my dad knows how to

make awesome meatballs—and he always makes a lot!"

"I do love meatballs," Jean said. Aunt Sunny had invited the rest of the band—Eduardo, Joe, and Fred—to stay. But they all had to get home to their families. Jean, on the other hand, said, "We'd love to," and offered to run home to whip up a salad.

"Nonsense," Aunt Sunny said. "The girls have already made one. Pull up a seat and make yourselves at home."

They'd had to bring in extra chairs from the living room to fit everyone at the table, and when Aunt Sunny realized that still wasn't enough room, they'd spread a big blanket on the ground and eaten outside, picnic style.

At first Peter was looking down a lot, shuffling his feet and folding the bill of his baseball cap. Marigold had a feeling that his parents had made him come over. But Marigold knew she was acting weird, too. She was so embarrassed about throwing up when she was on the boat. And she really wasn't sure what to say to him.

It was all pretty awkward until Lily blurted out, "Peter, I don't like that you have a new girlfriend. I thought I was next."

Peter knelt down and said, "Lily, I didn't know you would be back in town so soon, or I would've waited for you. You know I'd be so honored if you were my girlfriend."

Lily squealed with delight and flung her arms around Peter's neck.

"How's that camp going, Lily?" Peter asked. "I know you didn't like it at first."

"I love it now," Lily said. "It just took a few days for people to get to know me. Once I shared some of Aunt Sunny's cookies and showed them how to press flowers, everyone wanted to be my friend."

"Of course they did," Peter said.

Marigold's heart melted. Peter was always so nice to Lily, which made Marigold, as her big sister, like him even more although that hardly seemed possible. Plus, when he'd said "honored," it sounded like *"on-ahhd."* Oh, how she'd missed his accent!

To make things even more uncomfortable for Marigold, Max had been following her around like a puppy dog all evening. Marigold was under strict instructions from Zinnie not to talk to him. The problem was that this seemed to make Max even more fascinated by her. First, he'd sung her that song while they were hanging the tablecloths. Then, before dinner, he'd brought her a bouquet of purple flowers because "violets are shy, too" (even though she was pretty sure they weren't violets). And when she'd been charged with gathering salad ingredients from the garden and she had to make a few trips outside, he kept offering to open the door for her, which became weird after the first time. She had two hands and was perfectly capable of opening doors!

She could tell this was driving Zinnie nuts. First, Zinnie had tried to distract him by challenging him to a tree-climbing competition. Then, when Max was trying to make conversation with Marigold, Zinnie interrupted to ask him if he could identify a spider on a rock. Finally, in a really desperate moment, Zinnie started to sing that laundry-hanging song way too loud. "Sing with me, Max!" she said, and did a Broadway-style dance move.

"Uh, a little later?" he'd said. "I'm going to help Marigold peel carrots."

Marigold couldn't seem to shake him loose or discourage him with her silence, so she sighed and handed him a vegetable peeler.

Later, when Aunt Sunny asked Max and Peter if they would find some good rocks to secure the picnic blanket with, Marigold overheard the two boys talking. She was finishing up with the vegetable chopping and they were standing just outside the kitchen window.

"So, you were Marigold's boyfriend last summer?" Max asked Peter. Marigold felt her cheeks turn bright red as she sliced a cherry tomato in half.

"Yeah," Peter said. "I mean . . . sorta. She wasn't here that long."

Sorta? Marigold thought. *They had kissed! Didn't that make her his girlfriend, even if only for a few days?*

"You're, like, the luckiest person I know," Max said.

"She's the prettiest girl I've ever seen. And she's so humble, too."

Marigold smiled at this sweet and surprising bit of information. She popped a tomato into her mouth and wondered if she *could* like him. She was, after all, looking for an ordinary boy, and Max wasn't exactly a movie star, even with that hundred-watt smile of his.

"Humble?" Peter said.

"Yes. And so shy," Max said.

Well, at least she was doing a good job of being a normal girl who didn't try to get attention, she thought, and cut another tomato.

"Are we talking about the same girl?" Peter asked.

"There's only one Marigold here, right?" Max said. "I think the fact that she's so quiet means that she's really deep. I'm hoping that she'll be my girlfriend. I'm going to ask her tonight."

Oh no! Marigold thought, realizing that she didn't want just any normal-boy boyfriend. She wanted Peter!

"But she lives in California," Peter said.

"I wouldn't care if she lived in India," Max said. "We can talk every night on the computer. My mom and dad video-chatted when he was stationed in Turkey."

Marigold sat in between Lily and Aunt Sunny during dinner. Every time Max tried to start a conversation with her, she focused on teaching Lily how to twirl spaghetti onto her fork, or helped her practice her addition and subtraction using peas. But it wasn't just Max who was trying to get her attention. Peter kept asking her questions, or offering to refill her lemonade, or bringing up things they'd done together last summer (or *"summah,"* as he said), like sailing and collecting sea glass. And when Jean and Mack went home because their favorite TV show was on, Peter didn't go with them.

"I'll be home later," Peter said, and then he proposed a game of flashlight tag.

It was just like Handsome Horace! Marigold realized now as she lay under the bench in the dark. Peter liked her again because Max said that he wanted her to be his girlfriend. She watched Zinnie's flashlight illuminate Lily in the vegetable garden.

"Peter is behind the shed!" Lily called out, jumping out from between some tomato plants. Zinnie's flashlight beam swooped across the yard to the shed.

"Aw, man," Peter said, coming out with his hands up. "You're not supposed to give me away, Lily."

"But now the three of us can look for Max and Marigold together," Lily said.

"You have to go to jail," Zinnie said.

"I won't go to jail," Lily said. "It's too boring in there. Come on, Peter, let's hold hands. Do you want to hear about the flowers I'm pressing so that I can remember this summer forever?" Lily asked him. "So far I've collected impatiens, forget-me-nots, delphiniums, and petunias. I'm going to frame them. I can show you how to do it if you want."

"That'd be great, Lily," Peter said.

Marigold giggled quietly. Lily's crush on Peter seemed to be getting bigger by the hour. Marigold debated relocating to behind the shed. Stealthily changing spots midgame was her signature strategy in flashlight tag, and if she picked a spot that had already been used, she'd really throw Zinnie off. She was creeping out from under the bench when she heard a voice.

"Psst! Marigold! I'm up here."

Oh no, Marigold thought, looking up to see Max halfway up the tree above her. He was a fast tree climber to have gotten all the way up there before Marigold had found her hiding place, and he was even quieter than she was.

"I just want to say that I think you look really pretty right now."

"Uh . . . thanks," Marigold whispered, standing up. "I gotta go!"

"Wait!" Max whispered, jumping down from the tree. He was as quiet and lithe as a cat. "There's something I'd like to ask you."

"Now?" Marigold said. Suddenly she wanted to be

found. She didn't want to be Max's girlfriend, but she also didn't want to have to tell him that and hurt his feelings. She'd done such a good job dodging him all evening. And yet here they were, alone under the stars on a perfect summer night with a soft breeze rustling the leaves above them. Tony and his band might as well have been playing "Can't Help Falling in Love," like they had at least a dozen times during rehearsal today.

"Shh! We don't want them to find us," Marigold whispered loudly.

"Wait! I hear something!" Lily said.

"Where?" Peter asked.

Marigold had a pretend coughing fit.

"Are you okay?" Max asked.

"I'm fine," Marigold said.

"Somewhere over there!" Zinnie said, lighting up the surrounding area.

"Well, this will just take a second," Max said. "I was wondering if, well, maybe you'd like—"

"Gotcha!" Zinnie said, shining the light on Marigold and Max and stopping Max midsentence. Zinnie, Peter, and Lily charged toward the bench.

"Gotcha both!" Lily said. Zinnie shot Marigold a look as if she'd personally invited Max to hide with her.

"We found them both at the same time," Lily said,

not letting go of Peter's hand. "So, who gets the snickerdoodle?"

"We'll split it," Marigold said. "Fair and square."

"No, no," Max said, giving a gentlemanly bow. "Marigold can have the whole thing."

31 · The Summer Triangle

Marigold lifted Lily onto her back as they walked toward the house. She figured that Max wouldn't ask her to be his girlfriend while she was giving her six-year-old sister a piggyback ride. He seemed momentarily distracted anyway; he and Zinnie were walking a few steps behind them talking about a TV show with a time-traveling doctor. Peter was walking next to Marigold, shining a path with the flashlight.

"So what happened with that movie?" he asked.

"Uh . . . ," Marigold said. Things were going well with Peter. The last thing she wanted to do was talk her *Night Sprites* failure. "I was in it, but then I wasn't."

"They took her part out of the movie," Lily said.

"Really?" Peter asked.

"It's a long story," Marigold said.

"That's rough," Peter said.

Marigold felt her stomach clench. "Well, I'm not acting anymore. I'm done with that."

"Why?" Peter asked.

"It's too hard," Marigold said.

"She doesn't want to get cut from any more movies," Lily said. "Can you put me down now?" she asked Marigold.

"Fine," Marigold said, releasing Lily's legs so she could jump off. They were almost back at the picnic blanket, where Aunt Sunny and Tony were drinking coffee and talking quietly.

"I would never give up sailing," Peter said.

"What if you lost, like, the biggest race of all?" Marigold said.

"The nationals?" Peter asked.

"Yeah," Marigold said.

"First of all, if I got to race in the nationals, that'd be amazing. I'd be so happy just to be in it."

"But then what if you lost?" Marigold asked.

"I don't think I'd feel that bad, because it's such an honor just to be on the team," Peter said.

"But what if you lost the race for your team?" Marigold asked, growing frustrated.

"I think I'd still have a good shot at making the team the next year."

"But what if there was no next year?" Marigold asked. "What if the race was canceled?"

"The nationals got canceled? *Nevah* going to happen."

"I just don't want to do it anymore, okay?" Marigold said, walking so that Lily was between them. She took a deep breath and changed the subject. "Let's look up at the stars." There was no moon tonight, and out here in the country the stars were bright and clear. There were so many of them, too. Plus, she knew that Peter liked the stars. Last summer he'd shown her the Big Dipper and Cassiopeia. "Let's see if we can find a constellation."

"I see the Summer Triangle," Lily said. "We learned about it at camp today."

"Where?" Marigold asked.

"Up there," Lily said, pointing at the sky.

"I don't know that constellation," Peter said. "You'll have to show me, Lily."

"Of course!" Lily said, taking Peter's hand. "Okay, so do you see the brightest star in the whole sky? It looks a little bit blue? It's right in the middle."

"Yup," Peter said.

"I think so," Marigold said. "Over there?"

"Yeah," Lily said as they arrived at the picnic blanket.

"Hi, kids, come and join us," Tony said.

"What are you guys looking at?" Max asked as they all took a seat on the picnic blanket. "And where are my parents?"

"They decided to walk down by the harbor," Aunt Sunny said.

"I'll give you a ride home, champ," Tony said.

"I'm showing Peter the Summer Triangle," Lily said.

"Very good," Aunt Sunny said.

"So that big, bluish one is called Vega," Lily said, pointing again. "Everyone see it?"

"I think so," Zinnie said.

"Uh-huh," Max said.

"Okay, well, on the other side of the Milky Way is another bright one. It's kind of yellowish," Lily said. "That's Alter."

"Altair," Aunt Sunny said, gazing up. "But you were very close, Lily. And you have the right star."

"I see it," Peter said. "What's the third one?"

"Denip? Where is it again, Aunt Sunny?" Lily asked.

"Deneb is at the bottom of the Milky Way. It doesn't look quite as bright as the other stars, but—"

"Wait, I want to tell them this part!" Lily said. "It doesn't look as bright as the other stars, but that's just because it's a lot farther away. It's actually a super-giant star. Right, Aunt Sunny?"

"That's right. Deneb is much brighter than the other stars, but it doesn't draw quite as much attention to itself," Aunt Sunny said.

"A shy star," Max said. Out of the corner of her eye, Marigold saw him casting a doe-eyed glance at her. She narrowed her eyes, staring upward, demonstrating an intense interest in astronomy.

"But really it's not a shy star at all," Zinnie said. "It's just hiding its brightness."

"I suppose . . . ," Aunt Sunny said. "With fifteen centuries of light years."

"Or maybe some other star told Deneb to be quiet and not say anything," Marigold said.

"Why do I feel like we're not talking about astronomy?" Aunt Sunny said.

"Do you like this constellation, Peter?" Lily asked.

"It's great. Thanks for showing it to me," Peter said.

"Actually, it's not a constellation," Aunt Sunny said. "The Summer Triangle is a star formation. Each one is the brightest in its own constellation. Vega is part of Lyra, Altair is in Aquila, and Deneb is in Cygnus. The Milky Way runs through the middle."

"And there's a legend that goes with it," Tony said.

"Is that so?" Aunt Sunny said. "Tell us. I don't know it."

"It's a Chinese legend," Tony said.

"Tony traveled all over the world in the Air Force," Aunt Sunny said, resting her head on his shoulder.

"That's right," Tony said. "And before GPS, the Air Force used the Summer Triangle to navigate, only we called it the Navigator's Triangle. Those three are the brightest stars of summer, so during the months of June, July, and August, it's easy to spot the formation and figure out where you are."

"You used stars instead of GPS?" Marigold asked.

"Yup," Tony said. "And I still can."

"Sailors use stars to navigate at night," Peter said.

"That's right," Aunt Sunny said.

"That's so cool," Marigold said.

"It is," Tony said. "I was stationed out in California, where you girls are from. And my wingman, Eddie, call sign Angel, was half Chinese. He's the one who told me about the legend. They have a festival for it in China. It's called Qixi. Q-I-X-I." It sounded like *"Chee shee."*

"What's the legend, Grandpa?" Max asked.

"There are many variations, but here's the one Eddie told me. Vega, the blue star, represents a princess. Legend has it she was the daughter of a goddess. One day the princess was taking a break from her weaving, wandering the heavens, looking for some fun, as you kids do, when she met a lowly cowherd. That's Altair. They fell head over heels in love and secretly married."

"Like you and Aunt Sunny!" Lily said.

"Yes," Tony said. "But Vega's mother was angry when she found out that her daughter married a mortal. So she scratched a silver river in the sky to separate them."

"The Milky Way?" Max asked.

"Yup,"

"The silver river," Zinnie said, taking out her notebook. "I like that. It sounds like poetry."

"But once a year, the magpies—" Tony said.

"What are magpies?" Lily asked.

"They're birds," Tony answered. And they feel sorry for these two. So they get together and form a bridge over the star Deneb. Then, on the seventh night of the seventh moon, if it's a clear night, the two lovers can meet again. That's the night of the festival," Tony said.

"It's very romantic," Aunt Sunny said.

"Yeah, it is," Max said, and he turned to Marigold. "And tonight is a clear night."

"I'm so tired," Marigold said, faking a big yawn before Max could follow this thought any further.

"Marigold," Max said. "I was wondering if maybe—"

"I have to get to bed. And it's getting late for Lily." She stood up, took Lily's hand, and tried to pull her up.

"I don't want to," Lily said. "I don't have to, right, Aunt Sunny?"

"I think we can enjoy the night sky a little longer. But, Marigold, if you would like to turn in, that's just fine," Aunt Sunny said.

Marigold looked at Peter staring up at the stars. She wanted to sit beside him and ask him to show her his favorite constellations. But Max's face was full of courage and she feared, given any more time, he'd find a way to ask her to be his girlfriend. She really didn't want to have to say no. If his smile was so big, what would its opposite be? And then there was Zinnie, who was watching her, her head tilted in curiosity, jotting something in that notebook she always carried with her.

"Zinnie, what are you writing?" Marigold asked.

"Hmm?" Zinnie asked.

"What are you writing down?"

"Oh, the legend," Zinnie said with a smile. "So I don't forget it."

32 · A Little Sadness in Her Happiness

Zinnie woke up extra early the next day. Rain was pattering against the window, sliding down the pane in crooked little rivers and blurring the view of the garden. *Writing weather,* she thought as she stepped out of bed quietly so as not to wake her sleeping sisters. The wooden floor was cool under her bare feet and there was a chill in the air. She pulled on a pair of socks and her Pruet sweatshirt and headed downstairs. Her story was due to Mrs. Lee tomorrow. That didn't give her a lot of time, but she was almost done. All she had to do was figure out the ending. How hard could an ending be?

Zinnie was expecting to find the kitchen empty, but Aunt Sunny was sitting at the table in her bathrobe and slippers, drinking coffee and looking out the window with a thoughtful expression. It was the first time Zinnie had ever thought Aunt Sunny looked old, and it made her heart hurt a little.

"Good morning," Zinnie said softly. Aunt Sunny hadn't heard her come into the kitchen, because she startled.

"Good morning to you," Aunt Sunny said, all signs of age vanishing as she smiled at Zinnie. "Come and join me. Would you like a cup of decaf? It's freshly brewed."

"I'll try it," Zinnie said.

"You don't have to finish it if you don't like it," Aunt Sunny said, fetching a mug with a picture of a piping plover on it. She filled it about a third of the way and added lots of warm milk and two teaspoons of sugar.

"Here you are," Aunt Sunny said, handing her the coffee, which looked more like milk with coffee than coffee with milk. Zinnie smiled as she took a sip of the drink, feeling that drinking coffee was a very *writerly* thing to do. She imagined Virginia Woolf enjoying a daily cup of coffee in her writing room.

"What do you think?" Aunt Sunny asked.

"Yummy," Zinnie said as Aunt Sunny brought over a plate of cookies. "Cookies for breakfast?"

"They'll be our secret," Aunt Sunny said, dunking a cookie in her coffee. "Now tell me, why are you up so early?"

"I have to finish my story by tomorrow and I don't have an ending yet," Zinnie said, dipping a cookie in her coffee as well. The cookie was soft and crumbly and delicious. The bitterness of the coffee made the cookie taste even sweeter.

"Morning is the best time for thinking," Aunt Sunny said.

"What are you thinking about?" Zinnie asked, noticing again that quiet expression she'd seen on Aunt Sunny's face when she'd first walked into the kitchen. "Are you okay? Is everything all right with Tony?"

"Yes, yes. Why are you so worried about Tony, my dear?"

"I just—" Zinnie started, but then she remembered what Ashley had said about causing unnecessary drama. "I don't want him to hurt your feelings."

"I'm touched, but that's not going to happen, Zinnia."

"But you look sad. What are you thinking about?"

"That I've lived here alone for nearly twenty years," Aunt Sunny said. "In just a few days, all of that will change. I suppose I'm a little blue about it. Sometimes even good things, wonderful things like a wedding, can make us a little sad."

Zinnie thought about how she had been so happy to go to Pruet but was also a little sad to be away from her parents. She reached for another cookie.

"A little sadness in your happiness is nothing to

be scared of," Aunt Sunny said, placing a coffee-warm hand on hers. "It brings out the happiness even more."

"Like how the coffee makes the cookie sweeter," Zinnie said.

"Exactly," Aunt Sunny said. "Oh, Zinnia, you amaze me with your astuteness." Zinnie glowed with pride. "And, you know, these cookies wouldn't be nearly as good without a pinch of salt in them."

"There's salt in cookies?" Zinnie asked, taking another bite to see if she could detect the flavor.

"Always," Aunt Sunny said. "Otherwise the taste is too flat. Too plain. Now I need to get dressed and brush my teeth and comb my hair, and you must get started on your work. Your sisters will be awake soon, and then the hustle and bustle of the day will be upon us."

33 · To the Lighthouse

"Forget it," Ashley said when she and Zinnie reached the end of Lighthouse Road. "I've changed my mind. It's too scary."

"But we came all this way," Zinnie said, wiping sweat from her brow. They'd met at the town beach, where Ashley had an extra bike waiting for her. The rain had let up soon after breakfast, but the morning was still cool and misty as they traveled down some leafy country roads. They passed a farm, pastures, and a pond. Ashley even took her through a shortcut in the woods where there was a secret rope swing. They'd finally arrived at the lighthouse, and now Ashley wanted to leave, but there was no way Zinnie was turning back.

"I thought you liked thrillers," Zinnie said. She didn't believe in ghosts even if she did like to write about them, but she had to admit that this lighthouse looked haunted. It was at the very end of a point of land. Some morning fog hung around the bottom of it, creating the illusion that the lighthouse was floating.

"I only like books and movies that are thrillers," Ashley said as she clutched the head of garlic that had been in the basket of her bicycle. Zinnie had only brought a garlic clove, but Ashley said she wasn't taking any risks. "This is a little too real for me."

"But it's the morning," Zinnie said. "I've never heard of ghosts haunting anything in the morning. They only come out at night. Besides, you already told your brothers you were coming out here. What are they going to say if you tell them you wimped out at the last minute?"

"They'll tease me for the rest of my life," Ashley said. "You think having sisters is tough, but it can't be worse than having three older brothers."

"Come on," Zinnie said. She extended her hand and Ashley took it.

They made their way down the rickety boardwalk and over the craggy rocks to the lighthouse door. The lighthouse was much bigger close up, definitely big enough for people to live inside.

Zinnie pushed on the door, and to her surprise it actually opened. As soon as they stepped inside, they heard a hammering sound.

"Oh, lordy!" Ashley screamed. "It's the ghost!"

As Ashley clung to her in paralyzing fear, Zinnie's heart started to pound. It had to be the wind. But then the hammering stopped and the footsteps started.

"Run!" Zinnie yelled. Ashley was frozen. The footsteps were getting louder. "Come on, Ashley! Do I have to carry you?" Zinnie hoped that what she'd heard about getting superhuman strength when you were scared was true, because Ashley wasn't a small girl. Zinnie took a deep breath and bent down to try to pick her up when she heard someone call her name. When she turned toward the doorway, it wasn't a supernatural being standing there.

It was Tony.

"What are you girls doing here?" Tony asked after Ashley had finally calmed down.

"I'm here for a writing assignment," Zinnie said. "What are *you* doing here? Is this why you've been lying to Aunt Sunny?"

"You caught me," Tony said.

"Aha!" Zinnie said. "There's another woman, isn't there."

"Another woman? No," Tony said. "This is the other woman." Tony pointed to the lighthouse. "I wanted to surprise everyone—including you girls—with my gift for Sunny, but now that you're here, I better show you—"

"You're giving your fiancée a haunted lighthouse as a wedding gift?" Ashley interrupted.

"Come on," Tony said. "I'll show you around."

The inside of the lighthouse looked like a regular house, but round and with a giant spiral staircase. Tony gave them a tour of the kitchen and living room and three bedrooms. At the top was a wraparound deck that Tony said wasn't safe to stand on yet.

"Keep in mind that I've barely started," Tony said. "It's going to be a beautiful place when I'm done."

"What about the ghosts?" Ashley asked.

"That's a bunch of hogwash," Tony said. "I have been out here for weeks, and I can tell you that there's no ghosts."

"Are you and Aunt Sunny going to move here?" Zinnie asked.

"I was thinking it would be our little retreat. We could let our friends and family stay here if they liked. Or, who knows? Maybe we could turn it into a bed-and-breakfast."

"Like an inn?" Ashley asked.

"Exactly," Tony said. "Sunny's piping plover sanctuary is almost complete and I'm thinking I'd like to retire soon. It's just an idea. But one thing is certain: you can't beat the view. I might even put up a diving board."

"She's going to love it," Zinnie said. "So this is what you meant when you said 'the old girl'?" Tony looked at her quizzically, and Zinnie blushed, realizing that she'd basically just admitted to evesdropping. "I . . .

um . . . overheard one of your phone conversations."

"I see. You didn't think I was talking about my bride, did you?" Tony laughed. "When Sunny said you had a big imagination, she wasn't kidding. Can you keep this place a secret for me?"

"Yes," Zinnie said. "I won't even tell my sisters."

"Thanks," Tony said. "It'll be my honeymoon surprise."

Before the girls headed back to town, Tony showed them how to catch blue crabs using a chicken bone.

34 · Inspiration

Later that afternoon, the rain started up again. Writing weather had returned for Zinnie as if on cue. She brought a glass of water and a cookie into her writing room. She opened her notebook and read over the observations she'd recorded last night, and then she turned on her laptop. When Peter and his family had stopped by unexpectedly and joined them for dinner, Zinnie was certain that the ending to her story would play out in front of her. But a simple, neat ending had not presented itself.

She'd seen Peter/Pedro sit next to Marigold/Marianna on the picnic blanket, smile at her, and offer to refill her lemonade when she wasn't even halfway done with it. And on their way back to the house after flashlight tag, she'd noticed that Peter and Marigold had been walking so close together that they bumped shoulders. Peter seemed to see the extraordinary in Marigold even if she was determined to hide it. But then, when he asked Marigold about her part in *Night Sprites* and she said that she'd quit acting, Zinnie watched the gap between them widen enough for Lily to sneak into the middle.

And the Max/Lawrence story line hadn't resolved itself either. Max had been chasing Marigold long before they'd started their game of flashlight tag. It hadn't been easy for Zinnie when Max had chosen to stay with Marigold in the boring kitchen to peel boring carrots when Zinnie had challenged him to a tree-climbing competition. Or when he followed Marigold around as she brought the napkins, forks, and plates out to the picnic blanket. Or when he kept glancing in Marigold's direction while Zinnie was trying to talk to him about the last episode of *Tales of the Time Lord*. Then while they were looking at the Summer Triangle, Max had tried to ask Marigold a question and she'd run inside in a huff. This had been a relief to Zinnie. But of course Marigold's absence had done nothing to help her figure out her story.

As she took another sip of her water, Zinnie decided that she was just going to have to use her imagination, try out a few different endings, and see which one felt the most real. In Zinnie's first attempt, Marianna was so inspired by the Summer Triangle that she sponta-neously broke into a modern dance that captivated the hearts of both Pedro and Lawrence. It turned out that Pedro was secretly an amazing dancer, and the two of them led a dance parade through the small town until everyone was dancing on the beach. (Except Lawrence, who was not a good dancer. He was better at singing, so he stayed behind and made up songs with Marianna's friend "Zelda.") Zinnie rubbed her temples as she realized this wasn't quite right. It felt like something she would see in a movie instead of something that would happen in real life or, more important, something she would read in *Muses*. She deleted it.

The second ending Zinnie tried was inspired by the legend about the Summer Triangle. Marianna took a walk along the harbor on the evening of a total lunar eclipse. A dark moon goddess appeared before her and gave her a choice. She could become a star, literally, and be admired forever as an extraordinary galactic being. Or she could lose her talent altogether, live to age one hundred in this small New England town, and have the most normal, ordinary life ever.

Zinnie wasn't sure how the romance element would play out in this version, but she liked how the ending was shaping up. It was an interesting choice, she thought, and Marianna's decision would say a lot about her. But when she read the whole thing over, she realized that it didn't feel like it fit with the rest of the story. And as usual she'd added an element of fantasy, which meant that it wasn't *Muses* material. She deleted it on the spot. She'd avoided pretend stuff so far. She wasn't about to start now.

Zinnie heard her sisters coming down the stairs. It was time for dinner and she still hadn't finished her story. As she brought her hands to her head to massage her brain into coming up with a good answer, she knocked the remaining drops of water in her glass onto the book of Shakespeare's sonnets that Aunt Sunny had left on the desk days before. Maybe it was a sign. She opened the bookmarked Sonnet 18, the poem that Aunt Sunny had chosen to be read at her wedding. Perhaps there was inspiration to be found there. After all, wasn't Shakespeare the best writer, like, ever?

Shall I compare thee to a summer's day?
Thou art more lovely and more temperate:
Rough winds do shake the darling buds of May,
And summer's lease hath all too short a date;
Sometime too hot the eye of heaven shines,
And often is his gold complexion dimm'd;
And every fair from fair sometime declines,
By chance or nature's changing course untrimm'd;
But thy eternal summer shall not fade,
Nor lose possession of that fair thou owest;
Nor shall Death brag thou wander'st in his shade,
When in eternal lines to time thou growest:
    So long as men can breathe or eyes can see,
    So long lives this, and this gives life to thee.

Inspiration not only arrived, it sparked like a live wire. She didn't understand every line (what did "every fair from fair sometime declines" mean?), but nevertheless she could feel the poem in her bones. These words were full of emotion and passion—the image of "rough winds" shaking "the darling buds of May" made Zinnie's brain light up as if it'd been strung with fairy lights. The lines were an actress's dream because they begged to be read aloud with feeling. To be professed in front of an audience. To travel from the heart and be released into the summer air.

Zinnie thought that if she could get Marigold to recite the sonnet, Marigold would remember her extraordinariness. She knew from reading Marigold's diary both how badly she missed acting and how sensitive she was about having been cut from the movie. Zinnie was going to have to walk a fine line, and a Shakespearean sonnet was the perfect tightrope. The sonnet would remind Marigold of her talent, but because it was a poem and not lines in a script, maybe she wouldn't be so set against reading it.

As she heard Aunt Sunny ask her sisters what they'd like to drink, Zinnie realized that she not only needed Marigold to read the sonnet, she needed her to *perform* it. And she needed Peter to watch. She could just picture Marigold saying the words in a way that made Peter listen. Her voice would be clear, strong, and confident. Her face would express the love and brilliance embedded in the words. Peter would not be able to look away. Her talent would be as bright as the Summer Triangle, and he would navigate in her direction.

If Marigold and Peter got back together before the wedding, not only would Zinnie have an ending for her story, but maybe, just maybe, Max would forget about Marigold and he and Zinnie could be friends again. Or maybe even more. She smiled as she imagined slow-dancing with Max.

"Zinnia, it's time for dinner," Aunt Sunny called from the kitchen.

"Coming!" Zinnie answered, getting up from her desk and accidentally knocking the book of poems to the floor. She picked it up, placed it on the table, and skipped out of the room. Clumsy with good ideas, she bumped into the doorframe on her way to the kitchen. She realized that Max was in the band, so they wouldn't be slow-dancing at the wedding. *But we could stare at each other as he played the guitar,* Zinnie thought, as she took a seat next to Marigold and Aunt Sunny placed a plate of stuffed quahogs in front of her. *And that will be almost as wonderful.*

"Just so you know, I'm not worried about Tony any-more," Zinnie told Aunt Sunny.

"I'm so glad," Aunt Sunny said.

"Do we have any more of the cookies left from this morning?" Zinnie asked.

"What cookies?" Aunt Sunny asked with a wink. Zinnie winked back and swung her legs under the table.

Zinnie continued to develop her plan the next day after Aunt Sunny and Lily had left and while she and Marigold searched for wedding decorations in the attic. The girls went through the closet Aunt Sunny said was for "wrapping paper and ribbons and such" and discovered a collection of baskets, big and small and square and round, which Marigold claimed had endless possibilities. There were also spools of ribbons in all shades, widths, and textures.

"We can fill these with flowers and place them along the aisle," Marigold said, holding up some of the baskets. "Let's tie ribbons on the handles."

"Great idea," Zinnie said, though her mind was elsewhere. She was scheming about how to get Marigold to perform the sonnet for Peter. It wasn't like Zinnie could just ask Marigold and expect her to say yes. Aunt Sunny had asked Marigold to read it and she'd said no, and that was for Aunt Sunny's wedding. Now that Zinnie thought about it, had Marigold ever simply said yes when *Zinnie* asked her to do something? She was going to have to be a little sneaky.

"I think the cream-colored velvet ribbon is best," Marigold said after they carried the baskets and ribbons from the attic to the living room, which had been turned into their wedding work center. "And I think we should tie the bows like this. Watch me."

"Okay," Zinnie said, observing as Marigold talked her through how to tie a picture-perfect bow on a basket handle. Zinnie tried one but it didn't look as good. It was droopy and lopsided.

"No, like this," Marigold said, demonstrating the bow-tying moves again and producing another fluffy and symmetrical bow.

I'm supposed to be the one reading the sonnet at the wedding, but I'll get Marigold to coach me! Zinnie thought as she tried tying another bow. As her fingers looped the thick ribbon, she could picture the scene in her mind. Zinnie would read it badly on purpose. Then Marigold would show her how to perform the poem. As she did, she would bring the words to life with her singular and stunning talent. Zinnie would watch the ending of her story play out in front of her and then she'd put it on the page—writing couldn't get more real than that.

"I got it!" Zinnie said, holding out the basket with a Marigold-perfect bow on the handle. Now all she needed to do was to get Peter to witness it. Today.

35 · An Astounding Act of Courage

The rain had stopped by the time Zinnie and Marigold finished tying bows on all the baskets. They had tied the thinner ribbons around the jars they were using as vases on the tables. The living room was a mess, but the wedding decorations were almost done. Marigold had even had time to get started on her project for Pilar. Aunt Sunny had given her permission to use some funky 1970s fabric she'd found in the attic. Marigold cut the pattern and was ready to start sewing as soon as Aunt Sunny showed her how.

When they set out toward town to pick up Lily from camp, the sky was white with cloud cover, but Zinnie could feel the sun pushing through. It was one of those days Mom had said she could get sunburned even though it wasn't sunny. And that gave Zinnie an idea.

"I need to stop in the general store for sunblock," Zinnie said once they hit Harbor Road.

"We don't have time," Marigold said. "Camp gets out at three o'clock and Aunt Sunny said that we can't be late picking Lily up. Besides, it's so cloudy today."

"Mom always says that's when I get sunburned the worst because I'm not prepared. And I'm running low."

"Fine," Marigold said. "I'll see you back at Aunt Sunny's."

"See ya," Zinnie said. Once Marigold was at a safe distance, Zinnie sprinted to the yacht club to find Peter and invite him back to the house for some of Aunt Sunny's delicious peanut butter cookies, which Peter had said himself he couldn't resist.

The streets were slick from the rain, but Zinnie made swift progress as she leaped over puddles. The guy with the clipboard who checked who came in and out of the club appeared to be sleeping at his post, probably because there was hardly anyone here. As she jogged across the lawn, it occurred to her that maybe the sailing team's practice had been canceled because it had been raining earlier. She would check and see. If Peter wasn't at practice, then he was probably helping his dad, the club manager, in the dining room.

Once Zinnie got there, it was clear that sailing practice was still happening. She could see the racing boats with the colorful sails out in the harbor. She walked out to the end of the dock. She was trying to guess how far away they were and whether or not she should just leave a message with Mack, Peter's dad, when she noticed a small boy in the water directly in front of her. He looked about Lily's age. At first she thought he was swimming, but it was strange for a little kid to be swimming here at all, especially without a grown-up by his side. When she saw him flailing, Zinnie knew he was in trouble.

Unlike last summer, when Lily had been carried away by the current and Zinnie and Marigold hadn't known what to do, this year Zinnie was prepared. Her water safety knowledge kicked in immediately. The first thing she needed to do was call for help.

"Help," Zinnie yelled. "Help!"

She hoped that someone heard her, but there was no time to check, as the little boy was now only briefly coming up for air. She had to act fast. *Stay calm,* she told herself, even though her heart was beating rapidly. Their safety instructor had told the class that remaining calm is the most important thing of all. A panicked person isn't nearly as useful as a calm one. *Tell the victim you are there,* she heard the instructor say in her head.

"I'm here to help you!" Zinnie called to the boy. He flapped his arms and gasped for air. This was a good sign. She knew that she should only get into the water to save him if there was no other way to reach him, so she checked the area for a rescuing tool. While the dock was too far from the water to perform a reaching assist with her arm or a pole, there was a life ring nearby. Zinnie took a deep breath, lifted the life ring, which was attached to the dock with a rope, and threw it to the boy.

"Grab this!" Zinnie said. The boy thrashed, but there was no way he could reach it. Zinnie had thrown it too far out. She jerked the ring closer to the boy so that it was within arm's length. "You can do it!" Zinnie called as the boy reached. "Keep trying! Keep trying!" On the third try, the little boy's arm landed on the life ring. Zinnie shouted, "Good job! Now hold on tight!" The little boy was crying but following her instructions. Zinnie reminded herself that crying was a good thing. It meant he was breathing and conscious. "I'm going to pull you slowly toward the ladder," Zinnie said. "All you need to do is hold on." She pulled the ring closer to the dock with steady, sure hands. She almost had him to the ladder when a man called out, "Cameron!" and jumped into the water.

"Oh, thank goodness!" the man said as he resurfaced. He grabbed the ladder with one hand and pulled the boy into his arms with the other. "Cameron! I thought you were in the boat."

"Uncle Phil!" the boy shrieked, his little hands gripping his uncle's neck. The man climbed the ladder with the boy over his shoulder. They were both crying.

Zinnie couldn't help it—she started crying, too.

"I'll call 911," Zinnie said, removing her phone from her pocket with shaking hands.

"It sounds like someone already did," the man said, as a siren sounded nearby. He cradled the crying boy in his arms. "But I think he's going to be just fine."

"I'll call again just to be sure," Zinnie said, trying to catch her runaway breath, but by then the ambulance had arrived on the yacht club lawn.

"He's all right because of you," the man said, placing a hand on her shoulder. "You saved my nephew's life. You're our hero. Today and always." Zinnie nodded, tears of relief spilling down her cheeks. "I can never thank you enough," the man said. "Is there anything you would like? Anything at all?"

"I love ice cream," Zinnie said through her tears.

"I think we can do that," the man said, and as he smiled, Zinnie realized that he was familiar, even without his glasses and with his hair sopping wet. She knew him somehow. "How about a lifetime of ice cream?"

As the team of paramedics came down the dock, and the man pulled her into a wet embrace, Zinnie realized who he was. It was Philip Rathbone. She had saved his nephew.

36 · My Sister, the Hero

"Now, this might hurt a little, so let's count to three and take a deep breath," Marigold said, holding Lily's finger in one hand and a pair of tweezers in the other.

Lily nodded bravely, but Marigold could tell that she was scared. Lily had managed to get a splinter between the time Marigold had picked her up from camp and their getting back to to Aunt Sunny's. It had probably happened when she'd run her hand along the twisted wooden fence on Pleasant Street, even though Lily must not have noticed it at the time. Now, however, her finger was red and tender where the splinter had lodged. And Marigold noticed that Lily's fingernails were filthy. She was going to have to give her a good scrubbing tonight in the tub.

"One, two—" Marigold started.

"Ouch!" Lily cried.

"Lily, I haven't even touched it yet," Marigold said.

"It hurts just thinking about it!" Lily said, and burst into tears.

"Okay, calm down," Marigold said, wondering where Zinnie was. She'd gone to the general store to get sunscreen while Marigold had picked up Lily at camp, but she should've been back by now. The general store was pretty close to Aunt Sunny's, and Marigold and Lily had taken the long way home so that Lily could say hello to the horses that lived on Pleasant Street. She could really use Zinnie's help right now. Zinnie was always able to come up with a funny story or joke on the spot to distract Lily.

"Let's count together," Marigold said as Lily struggled away from her. "Come on, now. We can't leave that splinter in or it could get infected. One, two—"

The screen door slammed and Zinnie walked in with a wild look in her eyes.

"Just in time," Marigold said. "Lily has a splinter. Will you tell her one of your crazy stories while I take it out?"

"I just saved someone's life," Zinnie said, sitting down at the table.

"Oh, really?" Marigold asked dramatically as she aimed the tweezers at Lily's finger. Marigold hoped Zinnie would make this a very entertaining story so that Lily would barely even feel the splinter being removed. "Tell us all about it."

"Yeah, what happened?" Lily asked.

"I was at the yacht club and I saw this little boy in the water—" Zinnie started.

"How old was this boy?" Marigold asked, tilting Lily's hand so that her finger was in the best light.

"Five, I think," Zinnie said. "Maybe six."

"My age," Lily said.

"Yeah, and he was drowning," Zinnie said, getting choked up. Marigold was impressed by her tears. Even the most professional actors had difficulty crying on the spot.

"Drowning?" Lily asked, her eyes wide. This was the time to do it! Marigold took a deep breath and, with precision and speed, gripped Lily's finger and tweezed out that splinter.

"Ow!" Lily howled. "You said we would count."

"Yeah, but I got it," Marigold said, showing Lily the splinter in the tweezers. She kissed Lily's finger. "It's all over. Lily, you were so brave. Good story, Zinnie."

"I'm not making this up," Zinnie said. "I was at the yacht club and I saw a little boy drowning and I . . . I saved him."

Marigold knew that Zinnie liked to pretend that she was a stowaway or a castaway. And she threw herself into those games, imagining a cardboard box to be a hidden compartment aboard the *Queen Mary,* or a soccer ball to be the last remaining coconut on a desert island. But this was different. Zinnie's hands were shaking on the table. Marigold put her arms around her.

"Oh my gosh. Are you okay?" Marigold asked.

"I was really scared," Zinnie said. Marigold felt Zinnie's tears on her shoulder and held her even tighter. Lily squeezed herself between her sisters to give Zinnie a hug, too. "His lips were blue."

Marigold tried to think of what their mom would say. "You must've been terrified, but you did such a good job. Remember what Mom always says? Courage is when you're scared but you take action anyway. That's you. So courageous!"

"It was weird," Zinnie said as Marigold plucked a tissue from the box on the windowsill and handed it to her. "I got really calm and I just knew what to do. I threw him a life ring, like we learned in class—"

Aunt Sunny rushed into the kitchen, her face alive with energy and concern. She dropped her tote bag on the floor and embraced the pile of sisters. "Zinnia, I heard about your astounding act of bravery from Jean. How are you feeling?"

"A little freaked out, and also kind of tired," Zinnie said, dabbing her eyes with the tissue.

"I'm so proud of her," Marigold said.

"We both are," Lily said.

"Add me to that list!" Aunt Sunny said, looking closely at Zinnie's arms and legs to make sure she was okay.

"And hungry," Zinnie added. "I'm very, very hungry. Marigold, can you make me a peanut butter and jelly, but not too much jelly, okay? Just the way Mom makes it."

"Sure." Marigold said. As she grabbed the peanut butter and bread from the pantry, she realized that her sisters needed her. It felt good to be needed. It felt important. It turned out her parents had been right when they'd told her that there was more to life than Hollywood, she thought as she placed the sandwich ingredients on the counter and took a clean plate from the cupboard.

"How did Jean know? No one was there but me and the boy and . . . the man," Zinnie said.

"What man?" Marigold asked, spreading peanut butter on the bread.

"The boy's uncle," Zinnie said.

"Mack saw the whole thing happen," Aunt Sunny said. "He's the one who called the paramedics. He said you were extraordinary. The very picture of grace under pressure." The landline phone rang in the living room. It was such an old-fashioned sound, it always startled Marigold. "I'd better get that."

"Wait. Why were you at the yacht club?" Marigold

asked, pausing for a moment as she held the knife over the sandwich. "I thought you were getting sunscreen."

"I just . . . had to . . . ask Peter something," Zinnie said.

"What?" Marigold asked, cutting the sandwich and handing it to Zinnie. "What did you need to ask him?"

"Um, well . . . ," Zinnie started, but before she could answer, Aunt Sunny returned to the kitchen in a flurry.

"My goodness," Aunt Sunny said. "That's Channel Five. They want to do a television interview with Zinnie for the local news tonight. Should I tell them that you're too tired and not up to it?"

"Me? On TV?" Zinnie asked, the pink returning to her cheeks. "I'm up to it!"

"Okay," Aunt Sunny said. "But only after you rest and have something to eat."

"I'm gonna be on TV!" Zinnie said, with her mouth full of sandwich.

"My sister's a hero!" Lily shouted, jumping around. "I'd give you flowers from my collection, but I can't touch them for a whole month or they'll be ruined."

"That's okay, Lily," Zinnie said. "Thank you for offering."

"Now I have six kinds of flowers—impatiens, for-get-me-nots, delphiniums, petunias, Queen Anne's lace, and larkspur."

"I'll pick out your outfit," Marigold said. "And we're going to have to do something with your hair. After you finish your snack, I want you to take a shower. But don't touch your hair. I'll do it. And I'm sure Mom won't mind if I put just a little makeup on you."

"Thanks!" Zinnie said, devouring what was left of her snack.

"This is so fun!" Lily said. "I always thought *you* were going to be the famous one, Marigold. Because you're so glamorous and you were supposed to be in that movie. But Zinnie is the one who's going to be famous! Zinnie is the star!"

"Uh-huh," Marigold said as she washed the knife she'd used to spread the peanut butter. She knew that Lily didn't mean to hurt her feelings, but as the hot water ran over her hands, she had to hold her breath to keep from crying. Because even though she was happy for Zinnie, even though she was as proud of her as she ever had been, even though it felt good to take care of her sisters just as well as her mom would, Lily's innocent words had pierced her like an arrow.

37 · An Extraordinary Girl

"It was no ordinary day here at the Pruet Yacht Club," Cecilia Lopez, the Channel Five news reporter, said into the microphone as Zinnie stood next to her on the dock. They were shooting at the scene of the rescue for the five-o'clock news. Aunt Sunny, Marigold, Lily, Tony, Max, his parents Paul and Cindy, Peter, and Mack and Jean were all watching from the other side of the camera, along with a bunch of other yacht club people and some of the sailing team. Of course, Edith was there with Mocha Chip, and Ashley was telling everyone around her that she and Zinnie were close personal friends. "She's a very brave person," Ashley was saying. "She's not scared of anything!"

A producer had positioned Zinnie at a slight angle and encouraged her to "stand up nice and tall," and Cecilia Lopez had asked the little crowd to please be quiet during the filming. Everyone was following the rules, though Zinnie could feel them silently cheering her on as she smiled into the camera, confident that she looked as good as she felt.

In the short time they'd had to prepare, Marigold had sprung into big-sister action, picking out a bright-green sundress for Zinnie, pinning the straps in the back so that it fit her perfectly, styling her hair into a chic side pony. Zinnie didn't feel totally like herself— the mascara made her eyes feel sticky and the safety pins were tickling her shoulder blades—but she knew that she couldn't wear one of her old T-shirts or her Pruet sweatshirt for her first TV appearance. Her only regret was that her parents weren't here to see it, but they'd be able to watch it online a little later.

"Tragedy nearly descended upon this small coastal community today when a young boy was discovered struggling in the water near this dock," Ms. Lopez said to the camera. "Though the weather is clear now, today's earlier rain and fog reduced visibility, making it dangerous for boating and other water activities. It was under these conditions that a six-year-old boy wandered away from his uncle's boat here at the idyllic Pruet Yacht Club and off the edge of the dock. It was this very special girl, Zinnia Silver, who saved the day." Ms. Lopez turned to Zinnie. "You were here looking for a friend when you saw the small boy struggling. Isn't that right?"

"That's right," Zinnie said as Ms. Lopez pointed the microphone at her. "I walked to the edge of the dock and saw the boy in the water."

"Was he calling for help?" Ms. Lopez asked.

"No, he was quiet. And in a dangerous situation, that's a sign that someone is in trouble."

"You sound like you know what you're talking about," Ms. Lopez said.

"That's because I do," Zinnie said with a smile. She heard a few people chuckle, but she knew they weren't laughing at her. She was pretty sure that she was being what her dad would call "her most charming self." Zinnie explained, "I took all three levels of water safety at the YMCA this year."

"That's impressive," Ms. Lopez said. "Can you tell us what you did after you discovered the victim?"

"Sure," Zinnie said. A breeze blew her side pony-tail across her face, but it didn't throw Zinnie off. She simply held her ponytail back and continued. "First I called for help. Then I told myself not to panic. I took a deep breath"—Zinnie demonstrated—"and checked my environment. That's when I saw a life ring and tossed it to the boy. He caught it on the third try. A few seconds later his uncle jumped in and carried him up the ladder."

"It sounds like your training served you well," Ms. Lopez said, and turned back to the camera. "The boy's uncle, who wishes to remain anonymous so that his nephew can recuperate in private, told Channel Five that their family is eternally grateful. And the paramedics stated that had this young lady not taken action, the boy's life would indeed have been in terrible danger. So, Zinnia, how does it feel to be a hero?"

"It feels incredible! I'm just so happy that everyone is safe."

Ms. Lopez smiled at her as the crowd on the dock gave a collective "Awww."

"And I don't think that there's a resident of this town who wouldn't call you extraordinary," Ms. Lopez said. "Now, I understand that when the boy's uncle asked if there was anything he could offer you as a reward, you had just one request. Do you mind telling us what that was?"

"Ice cream," Zinnie said. The crowd laughed.

"She saved a life and all she wanted was ice cream, folks. This is Cecilia Lopez, reporting live from the Pruet Yacht Club. Back to you, Chip."

"And we're out," the producer said. "Great job!"

Aunt Sunny and Lily rushed over and congratulated Zinnie. Marigold trailed a little behind them.

"You were so poised," Aunt Sunny said, kissing her cheek.

"And you look so pretty, too," Lily said. "Almost like a grown-up."

"How was I, Marigold? Did I sound okay?" Zinnie asked.

"You sounded really smart," Marigold said. She was smiling, but something seemed off to Zinnie. "You did a good job."

"I did?" Zinnie asked. There was no one whose opinion mattered more to her than Marigold, and she was saying all the right things, but somehow the words weren't landing on Zinnie. They seemed to stop an inch short. Zinnie was just about to ask Marigold if she looked okay when Ms. Lopez tapped her on the shoulder.

"You're such a star!" Ms. Lopez said. "So articulate and charming, just like a pro. Maybe after your career as a lifeguard you can go into journalism."

"Thanks," Zinnie said, and she felt herself blush.

"She's my niece, you know," Aunt Sunny said, beaming with pride.

"And my big sister," Lily said, swinging on Zinnie's arm.

Zinnie looked for Marigold, but she seemed to have slipped away. Before she could see where Marigold had run off to, Zinnie was bombarded with hugs and congratulations from the small crowd on the dock.

"What a champ!" Tony said.

"You really are a hero," Max said, and they did their secret handshake.

"I told you you'd be in the papers, didn't I," Edith said as Mocha Chip licked Zinnie's ankles. "I'll drop by with a pint of your favorite flavor tonight."

"Thanks!" Zinnie said.

"You're wicked awesome," Ashley said, fist-bumping her. "Next ice pop is on the house."

"Cool," Zinnie said.

"I'm impressed!" Peter said, giving her an awkward side hug.

"It's really amazing that you knew how to do that," a girl with a Pruet Sailing Team T-shirt said. Zinnie thought she had to be Peter's girlfriend by the way she was standing so close to him.

"Honey, we just couldn't be prouder of you," Jean said. "Mack and I would love it if you, your sisters, and Aunt Sunny, Tony, and his family wanted to join us back at our house for dinner. We can toss some burgers and veggies on the grill. How does that sound?"

"Great!" Zinnie said. Even after that peanut butter and jelly sandwich, she was still so hungry. "Can we, Aunt Sunny?"

"Ordinarily I'd say of course. But don't you have a story to finish?" Aunt Sunny said, tapping her watch. "It's five thirty."

"OMG!" Zinnie said. She had nearly forgotten about her story. "I need to finish my story tonight!"

"I have to get this hero home," Aunt Sunny said to Jean. "But I know the rest of the crew would love to join you." Aunt Sunny nodded toward the flagpole, where Marigold was talking with Peter, Max, and the girl Zinnie thought was Lindsey.

"Can I go to Peter's house for dinner?" Lily asked.

"As long as Marigold watches you, I don't see why not," Aunt Sunny said.

"Okay," Lily said. "Marigold, watch me!"

As Lily cartwheeled over to the other kids, Zinnie wished she could join her. But she didn't have time. She had to finish her story and send it to Mrs. Lee.

"You don't have to stay with me, Aunt Sunny," Zinnie said.

"Nonsense," Aunt Sunny said, taking her hand. "The hero can't eat alone. Besides, I need to work on my wedding dress."

Aunt Sunny went into the kitchen and fixed them two plates of leftovers. After they ate, Zinnie went into her writing room and Aunt Sunny went into the living room. Because of her extraordinary afternoon, Zinnie hadn't been able to execute her plan of bringing Peter and Marigold together in order to discover the conclusion to her story. She would have to rely on her imagination. Using her observations, her ingenuity, and some bits from the other endings she had come up with, Zinnie pounded out the rest of the story on her keyboard. In this version, Lawrence played Marianna a song that inspired her to dance her heart out. Pedro was then inspired to join her, revealing that he was also a great dancer. The two of them choreographed a piece under the stars, as Lawrence, lonely but talented, played his music. Marianna had discovered that in trying to extinguish what made her extraordinary, she had forgotten who she was. She just had to keep dancing, even if it was only in this small, podunk town. "For she realized that it wasn't the stage that mattered," Zinnie wrote. "It was the dancer."

Oh, that's good! Zinnie thought as she read over the whole thing one more time to check for homophones and poor word choices. Then Zinnie carried her laptop to the edge of the lawn, where there was one little bar of a Wi-Fi connection from the neighbor's house. She had exactly one ounce of energy left, and with it, she did what felt like the bravest thing all day. She typed in Mrs. Lee's email address and hit "send."

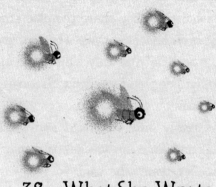

38 · What She Wrote

"Would you mind if I walked you two home?" Max asked Marigold, his brown eyes sparkling with hope under his floppy bangs.

"Um . . . ," Marigold stalled. Hoping some sort of excuse would pop into her head, she looked at Lily, but Lily was busy studying a ladybug that had landed on her arm. "Sure."

Dinner at Peter's was over. The adults were finishing their coffee as they chatted on the porch. The kids had ended their game of croquet in the yard. Lindsey had been in the lead for most of the game, but Marigold's competitive streak had kicked in, and at the last minute she had pulled ahead to victory. It wasn't as though anyone else was really taking the game that seriously. Max was more interested in strumming his guitar than in hitting the ball. He even volunteered to skip a turn. Peter was playing on a team with Lily, who had insisted that they share the blue croquet ball because they both had blue eyes. They were alternating who hit the ball, and Lily's aim was fine for a six-year-old, but Peter had to spend his turns just getting the ball back on course.

So it was really only Marigold and Lindsey who were playing, and Lindsey was pretty good. She was on a field hockey team, she said, so she was used to hitting a ball with a stick. But Marigold was not about to let Peter's new girlfriend win without giving her a good fight. With laserlike focus, she had knocked her yellow ball through those wickets as if she were auditioning for the part of croquet champion of the world. She wasn't sure why it felt so important to win; she only knew that in the last several hours, being ordinary was really starting to lose its appeal.

Marigold didn't begrudge Zinnie the attention. Of course Zinnie deserved every bit of praise she was getting. She had saved someone's life! But something about the whole situation made Marigold feel uncomfortable and awkward and even kind of mad, like she was wearing an ill-fitting pair of jeans. Which, now that she thought of it, she was, because she was still borrowing Zinnie's clothes!

Now Lindsey's mom had called and said it was time for her to come home. Jean was cleaning up the coffee cups. Mack was asking Peter to come help with the dishes. Tony was starting up his old pickup truck. And Lily was yawning as she counted the spots on the ladybug.

"One . . . two . . . ," Lily said through a yawn. "Three, four."

"Grandpa, I'm going to walk the girls back to Sunny's house," Max called to Tony.

"Okay, kiddo. See you back at the ranch!" Tony called as he drove away.

Dusk was settling in. The moon glowed faintly in the darkening sky. Marigold had done her best to stay in the thick of the group all evening, but now she had no choice but to confront Max one on one and tell him how she felt. The moment had arrived.

"I need to tell you something," Marigold said as they started down the driveway. She took a deep breath, gathered her courage, and hoped he wouldn't cry. "I just want to be friends."

"Oh," Max said, his smile disappearing as he studied his feet. "Okay."

"I'm sorry," she said, feeling suddenly like she needed to compliment him and make him feel better. She was going to start by telling how impressive his back handsprings were and then say that she was sure a million other girls would like him. Her own sister, for example!

But before she could say another word, he jumped in front of her and said:

"Big giant slow race you to that tree?" He pointed to a tree at the end of the driveway. That smile of his was like a rubber band. It had bounced right back!

"What's big giant slow racing?" Lily asked.

"Yeah, we don't know what that is," Marigold said.

"You see who can get there the slowest, but you have to take giant steps and you can't stop moving in slow motion. Ready?"

"Okay," Marigold said. They started the big giant slow race and Marigold giggled. It was hard to take giant steps in slow motion and Max was making huge facial expressions also in slow motion. Lily and Marigold were in fits of laughter after only two giant steps. It was the first time Marigold had really laughed, like to the point of a stomachache, since she'd arrived here.

"Oh, you stopped moving in slow motion," Max said. "I win!"

"That was so silly," Lily said, snorting with laughter.

"So, Marigold," Max said as they turned onto Fremont Street. "Grandpa tells me that you've made a lot of the decorations for the wedding."

"I have," Marigold said.

"Marigold made shell designs for tables and picked out the tablecloths and napkins. Oh, and she made these awesome cards with people's names on them out of seed packets from the general store," Lily said.

"Zinnie did, too," Marigold said.

"But Zinnie is more like your helper," Lily said.

"I guess that's true," Marigold said. "And today I designed these baskets with ribbons for the aisle."

"Oh," Max said.

Max didn't seem too interested in baskets, but that didn't stop Marigold from describing her vision of flowers lining the aisle. Lily piped up with her own design ideas along the way, which included a basket with a puppy in it under the archway. Before Marigold could describe the shell designs for the table or the mix-and-match tablecloths and napkins, they had arrived at Aunt Sunny's.

"Sometimes friends dance at weddings," Max said as they lingered by the door.

"I don't know," Marigold said. Zinnie would be so mad at her if she danced with Max, especially if it was a slow dance.

"No, Max is right. That's true," Lily said. "Remember last year at the casino? We danced with friends."

"You can save one dance for me," Max said, leaning against the house.

"But you'll be in the band," Marigold said.

"Grandpa and I are going to trade off playing the guitar for some of the songs," Max said. "A dance with you will give me something nice to think about on those cold New England days. The beautiful, shy girl full of California sunshine."

"Okay," Marigold said. "One dance." She couldn't help but smile. It felt so good to have someone look at her as if she were the movie star she'd thought she was going to be at the beginning of the summer.

"Yes!" Max said, raising a fist in the air in victory. "I've got a dance with a pretty girl! Awesome!"

Then he completely surprised her by bowing like a knight and kissing her hand.

"Wow!" Lily said. Marigold just giggled as she watched him leap over a fallen branch and skip-run across the quiet street.

After she helped Lily with her bath and tucked her into bed, Marigold went to the living room to see how Aunt Sunny was doing with her dress. The lamplight cast a warm glow on her aunt's face as she worked. She was putting the final touches on the lace on the bottom of the skirt and listening to classical music.

"Looks beautiful," Marigold said, admiring her aunt's handiwork.

"Almost done. How was dinner?" Auny Sunny asked.

"It was fun," Marigold said. "Will you help me get started on my bag for Pilar when you're finished with your dress? I cut the fabric using the pattern."

"I can get you started right now if you like," Aunt Sunny said.

"Okay," Marigold said. There was something very peaceful about sewing with Aunt Sunny in the evening. The glowing lamplight, the quiet classical music, the summer breeze from the open window, and the presence of her aunt wove together to create a feeling so relaxing and happy that Marigold felt warm and calm inside.

Aunt Sunny placed her work on a nearby table as Marigold brought her the fabric. She sat at the sewing machine, and Aunt Sunny demonstrated how to thread the needle, apply pressure to the pedal, and slowly push the fabric through. The machine made a satisfying clicking sound as they sewed one edge of the bag.

"I need to finish my dress tonight, but now that you know how to use the machine, you can complete your project anytime."

"Thank you," Marigold said, feeling so at ease that she thought she might fall asleep right where she was. "I'm just going to get a glass of water and then I'm going to bed."

"Pilar is lucky to have a friend like you," Aunt Sunny said as she settled back into her place at the sewing machine.

"Thanks. We're in a fight right now," Marigold said. She glanced at the fabic in her hands. "But I have a feeling we're going to make up."

"I think you will too," Aunt Sunny said.

"Before I came to Pruet, I was having a really hard

time," Marigold said. "Maybe the worst time of my life. But lately, I've been feeling much better."

"I'm happy to hear that, but I'm not surprised. You've been very helpful to me. I've always found that there's nothing like being useful to cheer yourself up. I'll see you in the morning, my dear."

When Marigold went into the kitchen to pour herself a glass of water, she saw Zinnie's laptop on the kitchen table. As she tapped it awake to see what her sister had been working on so hard, a quick glance revealed her own name. Almost.

Her heart went cold as she read the words. It was about her. She realized that Zinnie had read her diary. Now feeling very much awake, she sat down at the table with her glass of water and read the whole story.

39 · Sister Crimes

Zinnie felt weird from the moment she woke up. It was probably because she had fallen asleep before it was dark out and she was still fully dressed. The dress she had worn yesterday was twisted around her waist. She sat up in bed and rubbed her eyes. She had slept hard, without any dreams, and as the faint morning light eked through the curtains, for a moment she wasn't sure what day or time it was. It took her a whole minute of thinking to put together that she had rescued someone yesterday, and been interviewed on TV, and that, oh my goodness, she had turned in her story last night in the nick of time.

Lily was asleep nearby, but Marigold's bed was empty and made. *She's going to kill me when she realizes that I slept in her dress,* Zinnie thought, and wondered where her sister was. As she glanced at the ticking clock on top of the dresser—it was seven forty-five—she remembered that it was the day before Aunt Sunny's wedding. They were going to assemble and frost the cake today, and tonight they were going to have a clambake on the beach. And, best of all, her parents were coming today! Mom had said they were taking an overnight flight. Could they already be here? Zinnie wondered. Was Marigold downstairs with them already?

Zinnie hopped out of bed, hung Marigold's dress in the closet, changed into her own jean shorts and a T-shirt, and headed toward the kitchen. On her way there, she caught a whiff of her mom's perfume. She felt her heart swell. When she walked into the kitchen and saw Mom making coffee in her jeans and green Santa Monica T-shirt, she ran to her.

"Mom," Zinnie said, and gave her mom a huge hug.

"Sweetie!" Mom said, embracing her. Zinnie buried her head in her mom's neck and breathed in the scent of home. She hadn't been away from her parents that long, but that didn't seem to take away from the warmth in her chest at being reunited.

"Hi, cutie! Boy, I've really missed you," Mom said, taking Zinnie's face in her hands and tucking her wild hair behind her ears. "And I'm so, so proud of you. Dad and I want to hear all about the rescue. Do you know how many times we watched that clip from Channel Five on our iPads?"

"How many?" Zinnie asked.

"About a million. Probably closer to a billion. We couldn't get over how we managed to raise such an articulate and heroic and beautiful young woman." Mom took a step backward and looked Zinnie up and down. "Is it possible that you've grown since we last saw you?"

"I think I might have," Zinnie said, meeting her mom's eyes, which crinkled at the corners. "Where's Dad?"

"Right here, hero girl!" Dad said from the doorway. He was carrying two suitcases, which he dropped on the ground as Zinnie ran to him. He picked her up and gave her a little side-to-side swing. Zinnie's toes brushed the floor. "You have grown!" he said, putting her down. "It's miraculous."

"You just haven't picked me up like that in a while, Dad," Zinnie said. She put an arm around his back as they walked into the kitchen. "Where's Aunt Sunny?"

"She's out in the yard. Tony and his friends are setting up the wedding tent," Dad said.

"Is Marigold out there, too?" Zinnie asked. She looked out the window and saw that the big white tent was up now. It looked like Tony and his friends were working on the dance floor while Aunt Sunny hung a garland made of white paper flowers. Soon the whole yard would be transformed, decorated to the hilt with all the girls' discoveries and creations.

"Marigold fell asleep on the sofa last night. Aunt Sunny said she was sound asleep when she discovered her and didn't want to wake her," Mom said.

"Now, before you tell us about your incredible rescue in great detail, I have to know," Dad asked, taking a seat at the kitchen table. "Did you turn in your story to Mrs. Lee?" Mom joined them with two mugs of coffee and handed one to Dad.

"Yes, I finished it last night and sent it minutes before the deadline," Zinnie said. "Oh, and, Mom, I'll have some coffee, too, please."

"Really?" Mom asked.

"Really. It's my new thing. Aunt Sunny makes me coffee like hers," Zinnie said. "Decaf with lots of milk and sugar."

"Oh, okay. Decaf," Mom said with relief. She poured Zinnie a cup from Aunt Sunny's pot and added plenty of milk and a teaspoon of sugar. It wasn't the warm, frothy milk like Aunt Sunny made, but before Zinnie could specify her coffee preferences to Mom, Dad took her hand.

"I want to see this story that you wrote," Dad said. "May I take a look?"

"Um, sure," Zinnie said with some hesitation as she took a sip of her coffee, which wasn't sweet enough. She realized that Dad would recognize the character of Marianna as Marigold, and for the first time since the day she had started her story, she felt the uncomfortable weight of her sister crime. Certainly Marigold had committed one by writing those mean things about Zinnie in her diary. But as Zinnie looked around for her laptop (hadn't she left it here last night?), she wondered if her own offense was greater. Marigold's diary wasn't meant to be read by other people. Zinnie's story was.

"Where is it?" Dad asked, taking his reading glasses out of their case. "You can ask Mom—I've been dying to read your latest work."

"It's on my laptop," Zinnie said. "Which I left right here last night. I think I did, anyway. One second. Maybe it's in my writing room."

"Your writing room?" Mom asked as Zinnie zipped around the corner to take a peek in the room that had become her office. Her laptop wasn't there either.

"Yeah," Zinnie said, returning to the kitchen. "Aunt Sunny made a little office for me." She scanned the kitchen. "That's weird. I don't know where my computer is."

"Check the living room," Mom said. "I think I saw it in there. Maybe Marigold borrowed it?"

"Maybe," Zinnie said, feeling her one sip of coffee rise in her throat. "I'll check." Her breath caught and her hands pricked with sweat as she stepped over the threshold and walked into the living room. There it was. Opened, at the foot of the sofa where Marigold was sleeping.

"Did you find it?" Dad asked.

"Yes," Zinnie said, her voice quavering.

Maybe Marigold hadn't read the story, Zinnie thought hopefully. Maybe she had simply borrowed the computer for some other reason that Zinnie couldn't think of right now. It was totally possible that her secret was still safe, she reassured herself. Zinnie decided that as soon as she got her hands on that computer, she would delete her story and tell her father it had been lost and the email sent to "trash." She would get into Mrs. Lee's Writers' Workshop, quietly and without any fanfare, and she would forget this ever happened.

As she crept toward the sofa to recover her computer, she made a silent pact with the writing gods. If Marigold hadn't read her submission, if their lives could continue without Marigold ever knowing that Zinnie had read her diary, Zinnie would never read another person's diary again. She would devote all her writing from here on out to straight-up fiction. She would never base anything on her sister's life, or anyone else's life for that matter, ever again. In fact, she thought as she neared the sofa and reached for the laptop, all her writing would be dedicated to her sister, written in her honor and with the sole purpose of showing everyone how awesome she was. Zinnie leaned over Marigold and laid her hands on her computer. Without putting any weight on her sister or the sofa, she lifted the laptop, shut it, and pulled it close to her chest. She exhaled pure relief. Marigold hadn't even stirred.

She was just about to pivot back toward the kitchen when small, cold fingers tickled the backs of her knees.

"Ah!" Zinnie said, her legs buckling as she tumbled toward the sofa and onto the sleeping Marigold.

"The tickle monster got you," Lily said, giggling like crazy. "You didn't even hear me coming!"

"Lily, shh!" Zinnie whispered so fiercely she spat. "We don't want to wake—"

But it was too late. Marigold sat up, straight as a board. With her eyes opened so wide and her hair sticking up on end, she looked like a vampire rising from a coffin.

"Um . . . hi?" Zinnie said, testing the waters, hoping against hope.

"YOU!" Marigold said, and she pointed a sharp finger at her.

Zinnie was so scared by the look on her sister's face that she didn't know what to do.

So she ran.

40 · For Sunny's Sake

"Ahhh!" Zinnie shouted as Marigold chased her through the pear orchard and onto the driveway. Marigold's anger seemed to give her extra speed, but it wasn't enough to let her catch her traitorous sister as quickly as she wanted to.

Since Marigold had been Lily's next tickle monster victim, Zinnie'd had a head start out the door. Zinnie also had the benefit of wearing shoes. But despite these advantages, Marigold was gaining on her. Ignoring the small pebbles beneath her bare feet, Marigold flew up the driveway. Her rage, humiliation, and feelings of betrayal mixed together to fuel her cheetah-like strides over the rough terrain.

"He-e-e-e-elp!" Zinnie called, looking back in fear as she whipped past the mailbox and out into the street. She climbed over a stone wall and into a neighbor's yard.

"You can't run forever!" Marigold said, planting a hand on the stone wall and leaping over it like an Olympic gymnast. Breathless with fright, Zinnie backed into the neighbor's hedge.

"Why'd you do it?" Marigold asked, taking an intimidating step closer. Before she took her sister down she wanted answers. "Why'd you read my diary?"

"I don't know," Zinnie said, wiping sweat from her face. "It was . . . an accident."

"Liar," Marigold said in a near whisper. She had learned in acting class that when it seemed like a character should yell, it was sometimes more effective to do the opposite. Sure enough, Zinnie was quaking in her red slip-ons. Marigold said it again, even quieter. "Liar."

"I mean, I didn't mean to at first . . . but then I did, I guess."

Marigold actually heard herself growl as she lunged at Zinnie. Zinnie threw her hands in the air, gasped, and scurried over the stone wall. She headed back down the driveway and toward Aunt Sunny's house. Marigold followed, though her lack of shoes was starting to slow her down.

"Ouch!" Marigold said as the tiny pebbles of the driveway dug into the soles of her feet. She tried to ignore the pain as she stayed on Zinnie's heels. She wasn't sure what she was going to do once she got ahold of her, but it involved making her feel very, very sorry.

"You have to run faster, Zinnie!" Lily said from the back door, where she stood like a spectator at a horse race. "Faster! Faster! She's almost gotcha!"

"I'm going as fast as I can!" Zinnie called. They were halfway down the driveway, headed toward the elm tree and the garage. Marigold swatted at Zinnie's T-shirt and almost caught it, but Zinnie twisted away just in time.

"Mom!" Zinnie called as she raced on. *"Mommmy!"*

"They're not here!" Marigold said when she finally caught up with Zinnie at the elm tree. She grabbed the back of Zinnie's T-shirt, but before she could push her to the ground, she felt herself being lifted up.

"Oh, yes we are," Mom said, standing in front of Zinnie as Dad pulled Marigold away from her sister.

"Mommy and Daddy!" Lily said, jumping on Mom, who with some sort of supermom strength was able to catch her youngest daughter with one hand while holding Zinnie back with the other.

"Dad?" Marigold said as he put her over his shoulder and carried her back toward the house. She was too out of breath to try to fight him. She twisted her body to see Mom, still with Lily clinging to her, talking with Zinnie by the elm tree. She was disoriented, not only because she was hanging upside down, but also from the insane rush of adrenaline that was still pumping through her system, and the unexpected sight of her parents. "Dad, you're here?"

"Yes," Dad said as he took her off his shoulder and placed her on the bench by the back door. "And I have to say I was hoping for a more pleasant reunion. What the heck was that about? And since when do we solve our problems with wrestling matches in this family?"

"She read my diary!" Marigold said, crossing her arms. Dad always seemed to see Zinnie's side of things, but how could he not see Marigold's point of view on this one? This case was clear.

"She did?" Dad bent down to look Marigold in the eye. "That's not okay."

"Yes," Marigold said, fighting tears as the betrayal washed over her again. Dad sat next to her on the bench. Mom was now dragging Zinnie toward them. "But that's not it, Dad. It gets worse."

"How? What else happened?"

"She wrote a story about it," Marigold said, her lower lip trembling. "With this character named Marianna. But Marianna is, like, so clearly me. And anyone who reads the story is going to know it. It's like whoever reads the story is reading my diary. It's the story she sent to her teacher!"

"Oh boy," Dad said as he put an arm around her. "I understand why you're so mad."

"Mad and frustrated and sad and just . . ." Marigold searched for the word, and when she found it, she recognized it from earlier in the summer. The tears came pouring down. "Humiliated."

"It's okay," Dad said. He held her close, and Marigold wiped her runny nose on his T-shirt sleeve. "Shh, shh. It's okay."

"Sorry," she said, wiping again.

"Go right ahead," Dad said. "I never liked this shirt anyway."

Marigold laughed a little, but stopped as soon as she saw that Mom, Lily, and Zinnie were now standing in front of them. Zinnie's cheeks were wet.

"What do *you* have to cry about?" Marigold snapped, rage once again overtaking sadness. Zinnie stepped behind Mom. Lily joined her.

"You're scary when you're mad," Lily said, peering out from behind Mom. "And so fast, too."

"Lily," Mom said, "this is between your sisters. Now, Marigold, I understand that Zinnie violated your privacy, and she knows that's wrong. But keep in mind that you were just on the verge of attacking her. If you can calm down, she has something to say to you. Can you calm down?"

Marigold nodded, though she wasn't sure. Her heart was beating like a drum. Mom guided Zinnie out from behind her so that she and Marigold were standing face-to-face.

"I'm very sorry for reading your diary," Zinnie said. "I understand it was private and I shouldn't have done it."

"And?" Marigold asked.

"And I shouldn't have written a story based on what I read," Zinnie said.

"And?" Marigold asked again.

"And I shouldn't have sent it to my teacher," Zinnie said, hanging her head.

"You sent a story about Marigold to your teacher?" Lily asked, stepping out.

"Lily!" they all said at once.

"Sorry," Lily said. Mom gently pushed Lily back behind her.

"I'm sorry. I'm really, really sorry," Zinnie said. "Sorry to infinity."

Marigold sighed and looked away. She could tell that Zinnie regretted something, but these words didn't feel like a real apology. They felt like she was reading lines.

"Okay?" Zinnie asked. Marigold shrugged.

"She might not be ready to accept your apology," Dad said.

"I'm not," Marigold said. "And I don't know when I will be."

"Fair enough," Mom said. "But do you have something to say to your sister?"

"What do *I* have to apologize for?" Marigold asked.

"Snooping on her laptop? Not to mention starting a physical fight," Dad suggested. "You know better than that."

"Sorry," Marigold said.

"Eye contact?" Mom said.

"Sorry," Marigold said again, looking Zinnie in the eye.

"There you all are!" Aunt Sunny called. The family turned to see her walking toward them with her apron on. "I've been looking for you!"

"Obviously there's a lot more to be said here," Mom said in a low, quick voice. "But you girls have to pull it together for the sake of Aunt Sunny. She's counting on you not only to help her with everything you've promised to do, but to have cheerful dispositions and to walk down that aisle with joyful smiles on your faces."

"Capeesh?" Dad asked.

"Capeesh!" Lily said.

"It's truce time," Mom whispered as Aunt Sunny approached. Marigold and Zinnie exchanged a terse glance and nodded.

"Let's assemble the tiers! We need to do it before it gets too warm or the frosting will be a gooey mess," Aunt Sunny said. "Are my wedding elves ready?"

41 · A Story, Three Tiers High with Cream Cheese Frosting

Before the assembly of the cake tiers began, Marigold took a shower and got dressed. As she toweled off and combed her hair, one thing was certain. She was done being ordinary. She had nothing to show for it but a boring bob and a slanderous story. She pulled an eyelet dress out of the closet and slipped on a pair of sandals. She added a silver cuff bracelet and a pair of studs. Deciding that her outfit required a little more oomph, she took the sash from the dress she'd lent Zinnie yesterday, and which Zinnie had hung up wrinkled and crooked in the closet, and tied it on. A splash of color and a cinched waist. Much better.

Though her anger at Zinnie simmered under her skin, dressing like her old self cooled her down enough to allow her to put on a brave face. She was not about to fall down on the job as wedding coordinator. It had been her idea to come here early and help Aunt Sunny, and she had promised her aunt her dedication and hard work. Not only was she planning to make sure the decorations were perfect, she was also going to keep everyone on a schedule so that Aunt Sunny didn't have to worry at all. And as for Zinnie, well, Marigold would wait until the wedding was over to really let her have it. As soon as they were on their way to the airport, she was going to list all the ways in which she was planning on exacting her revenge. But for now she pushed the thought to the back of her mind.

As she entered the kitchen, she saw that Aunt Sunny, Zinnie, and Lily had already begun to work. The ingredients they had made or gathered since they'd arrived in Pruet were set up on the long kitchen table. There were the twelve-, nine-, and six-inch cakes wrapped in plastic. The jars of blackberry jam. The lemon syrup. The cream cheese frosting, which Lily was taste testing with her pinkie. The blackberries, which Zinnie was slicing in half. The special cake equipment was set out as well: the cardboard rounds, the frosting spreader, the serrated knife, and the big cake-decorating turntable that had been borrowed from Jean and that Aunt Sunny was wiping with a sponge.

Even though it wasn't yet nine a.m., it was already a hot day. Aunt Sunny had the windows open, the back door ajar, and the big fan going fast enough that Marigold's hair was blowing slightly in its breeze. Even with the ventilation and the steady whirring of the giant fan, the tension between Marigold and Zinnie was as thick as the cream cheese frosting that was sitting in the green ceramic bowl.

"You look fetching, my dear," Aunt Sunny said, taking an apron from its hook and handing it to Marigold. "Better put this on. I'm putting you on syrup duty."

"My job is to make sure the frosting tastes just right," Lily said, taking one more pinkie scoop and considering the flavor. "Hmmm. Yes, I still think it's delicious."

"I'm in charge of the blackberry jam and blackberries," Zinnie said, her gaze fixed on the jar of jam.

"And we all have cheerful positions!" Lily said with frosting on her lips.

"Dispositions," Marigold and Zinnie corrected her at the same time. They locked narrowed eyes for a second, and then Marigold turned away. As she tied the apron around her waist, she looked out the window. Her parents were setting up the folding tables that were on loan from the casino. Tomorrow morning the girls would cover them with the tablecloths and napkins they had found in the attic, turning the dingy tables into works of art that were unexpected, fun, and cozy, just like Aunt Sunny herself. Marigold was proud of her design.

"Is it just me, or is it too quiet in here?" Aunt Sunny asked as she cut the twelve-inch cake horizontally with the serrated knife. "Did something happen?"

"Nope," the three girls answered in unison.

"We are helpful and happy," Lily said. Aunt Sunny eyed them with suspicion.

"We're just focused, Aunt Sunny. We want this cake to be perfect," Zinnie said as Aunt Sunny placed the layers on cardboard rounds.

"Let's put on some music," Marigold suggested. She tuned Aunt Sunny's radio to the classical station. "So we can concentrate." *The less we have to talk to each other, the better,* Marigold thought.

"Good idea," Aunt Sunny said as the notes of a piano concerto filled the room. "Marigold, please brush the top of each layer with lemon syrup. Zinnie, you stir the jam until it's totally smooth. Lily, you give that frosting another taste. Make sure it's still fresh."

"It's as fresh as a pinkletink, also known as a spring peeper frog!" Lily said. "They live in the freshwater pond that feeds into the estuary." Aunt Sunny laughed and the tension cracked for a moment.

"I think this cake is like a story," Zinnie said, sighing as she stirred the jam. Marigold rolled her eyes. She'd had quite enough of Zinnie's stories. She dipped the brush into the syrup and began to lightly coat the layers with the sweet golden liquid.

"What do you mean?" Aunt Sunny asked.

"First we found the recipe card, written by your mom. It made you cry to see her handwriting again, remember?" Zinnie said. "And we made the cake layers."

"That was when I first I started camp," Lily said.

"Zinnie, spread some jam on one of the layers, please," Aunt Sunny said. "Right over the syrup."

"We went to the town beach and collected shells," Zinnie said, using a spoon to plop jam on one of the layers and then a special spreading tool to cover the layer evenly.

"And Lily got some glitter in the cake batter," Marigold said, and playfully tugged on one of Lily's curls.

"It was just a pinch," Aunt Sunny said. She placed the layer with jam on the cake-decorating turntable. "Perhaps it will give our cake a little extra structure."

"So some of Lily's story is in the cake," Zinnie said.

"What an enchanting idea," Aunt Sunny said as she carefully inverted another layer on top of the one with jam and removed the cardboard. "Lily, come sit on the table right over here by me and I'll show you how to frost the top." Lily climbed on the table and sat cross-legged in front of the cake. Aunt Sunny scooped two cups of frosting on top of the layer. Lily used her finger to scrape frosting from the cup.

"The next thing we did was make the frosting," Zinnie continued. "That was when Max came over."

"He's why this frosting is so sugary," Marigold said as Aunt Sunny guided Lily's hand with the spreader, coating the top layer with the creamy frosting. "Zinnie was distracted and she added two extra cups . . . because she thinks Max is cute and she has a crush on him."

Zinnie scowled.

"I don't think anyone will complain about extra sugar in the frosting," Aunt Sunny said, raising an eyebrow at Marigold as she and Lily finished frosting the top. Marigold bowed her head in shame. She shouldn't have taken that dig at Zinnie. It had flown out of her mouth before she could stop it. "Okay, Zinnia," Aunt Sunny said. "Scatter a few handfuls of the halved blackberries."

"Jean gave us the blackberry jam," Zinnie said as she added them. Marigold felt a wave of embarrassment as she remembered thinking she was going to get back together with Peter only to find out he had a new girlfriend. "Marigold was just dying to see Peter and—" Zinnie started, but Aunt Sunny cut her off.

"Let's say that the jam symbolizes the friendship that has gone into making this cake," Aunt Sunny said. "And the good fortune of having kind neighbors."

"Great idea," Marigold said, tossing a sidelong glance at Zinnie.

"Move aside for a moment, Lily," Aunt Sunny said. "I need to add the third layer. This will take a steady hand. And I'm going to request a moment of silence for this one."

The girls watched with breaths held as she lifted the third twelve-inch layer of cake off of the cardboard and placed it on top of the cake. They collectively exhaled at the successful execution.

"Phew. Another layer of jam, Zinnia," Aunt Sunny said, dabbing her perspiring forehead with the edge of her apron.

"We made the lemon syrup next," Zinnie said as she added more jam. "The day we washed all those tablecloths. We used some of the lemons to get out the stains. Of course, there are some stains that can't be removed with lemon juice. Stains on the heart made by words."

"Oh, please," Marigold said, knowing Zinnie was talking about the words she'd read in her diary. "Everyone knows actions sting worse than words."

"Girls, may I remind you that the cake story is still in progress," Aunt Sunny said, gesturing toward the remaining cake layers on the table. "The lemon syrup provides exactly the right amount of bitterness. We wouldn't want to add any more."

"Of course not," Zinnie said.

"No way," Marigold said.

"We have cheerful positions," Lily said. This time no one corrected her.

"Okay, here goes," Aunt Sunny said, taking a calming breath as she inverted the final layer of the bottom tier. The girls gasped as it landed two inches off center.

"Not to worry, not to worry. This is a mistake I can fix," Aunt Sunny said. With careful, gentle hands she rotated the layer until it was centered. "Ta-da. Now we'll frost the whole tier, put it in the fridge, and get to work on the other tiers. Tonight we gather the beach roses for the baskets. Tomorrow we'll assemble the cake and add the piping and any other finishing touches."

"We'll write the final chapter," Zinnie said.

"It will be the sweetest chapter of all," Marigold said.

"We promise," Zinnie said.

42 · A Sleeping Dragon

After they finished spreading the filling for the nine-inch and six-inch tiers and placed them in the fridge, Marigold, Zinnie, and Lily went about their other wedding duties until the rehearsal of the ceremony. Zinnie double-checked that there were enough candles, vases, and shells for the table arrangements. Marigold rolled the dinner napkins and tied them with twine, which gave them a rustic charm. Lily gathered the daisies that Mom was going to use to make wreaths for their hair. Mom and Jean hung the fairy lights in the tent while Dad and Mack hung the paper lanterns. Taking several trips back and forth to do it, Tony, Max, and Peter brought eighty chairs over from the casino in Tony's pickup truck. Max and Peter were in charge of setting up the chairs, which would start out in the ceremony area and then be transferred to the tent before dinner.

Marigold supervised the boys as they set up the chairs in front of the stone archway where Aunt Sunny and Tony would exchange their vows.

"The aisle needs to be wider," she told them. "I have baskets to place along the edges. I don't want Aunt Sunny to trip! And, Peter, make sure the rows are neat and even! And, Max, help me tie these ribbons on the chairs on the end. We need some more color!"

"You're not as shy and humble today," Max said as he fumbled with the ribbons.

"Was she *evah*?" Peter asked, using a ruler Marigold had found for him to ensure that the chairs were evenly spaced.

"I don't have time to be shy and humble," Marigold said, distributing the baskets along the aisle to see which arrangement looked best. "I have work to do. And I definitely don't have the time to dress like a slob anymore."

"Huh? That doesn't make sense," Peter said. "What does how you dress have to do with time?"

"Ugly clothes slow me down," Marigold said, dashing back into the house for the craft scissors that cut the edges of the ribbon so nicely.

"What the heck?" she heard Max say behind her. Her statement may not have made sense to the boys, but it made sense to her. It was hard work pretending to be someone she wasn't.

The justice of the peace arrived, and Marigold poured him an iced tea and found him a shady spot where he could relax while she kept everyone else on task. Tony's oldest daughter, Sara, arrived next from New York City. She was followed by Tony's other daughter, Meg, who lived in Atlanta and had twin babies. Marigold set them up on a picnic blanket nearby and made sure they had snacks, lemonade, and toys to keep the little ones occupied. Cindy, Max's mom, joined them and thanked Marigold for being so organized. When the tent was set up with the lights, lanterns, and tables, and the ceremony area was dressed up and organized to Marigold's standards, it was time to practice the ceremony so that everyone knew what to do when.

First Tony and Paul, who was the best man, took their places by the altar. Marigold whispered in Lily's ear when it was her turn to walk down the aisle. "Slow and steady," Marigold reminded her. Lily mimed the tossing of rose petals—it was the moment she had most looked forward to since they'd learned of the wedding. Usually flower girls were the last to walk down the aisle before the bride, but Lily wanted to be first and Aunt Sunny said that was just fine with her. Max walked down the aisle next. He was the ring bearer, though for this rehearsal he was only pretending to carry rings. He would have the real ones tomorrow. Zinnie followed Max, and then Marigold followed. When they reached the archway, the three girls stood by Aunt Sunny, and Max stood by his grandpa.

As the justice of the peace talked Aunt Sunny and Tony through the vows, Marigold slipped away to a chair in the back row to make sure that every seat had good visibility. She surveyed the arrangements of hydrangeas artfully placed by the white rose bushes at the archway, the blue velvet ribbons strung along the aisle, and the baskets lining the path, and she knew that she had kept her promise to Aunt Sunny. While Aunt Sunny had been busy working, Marigold had taken care of all the details, and now that everything had come together, she knew the wedding ceremony was going to look beautiful. Her chest swelled with pride.

Then it was Zinnie's turn to read the Shakespeare sonnet. *Ah! A good time to check for acoustics,* Marigold thought as Zinnie began to read: "Shall I compare thee to a summer's day? Thou art more lovely and more temperate." As Zinnie continued, Marigold felt herself deflate. It wasn't that Zinnie was doing a bad job. She was projecting just fine, though her hands were shaking as they held the paper. And while she didn't have a grasp of iambic pentameter, she read well enough that the meaning basically came across.

The problem was that hearing the words was making Marigold want to perform. She knew how to make words sing, to express them with clarity and feeling. She was certain that she was done being ordinary, but she wasn't sure if she could ever act again. It hurt too much to get rejected, to put herself on the line and be told no. She could feel her talent like a small dragon inside of her. It was sleeping now, curled up in a dark cave in her heart.

43 · A Genie among Wild Beach Roses

Dear Zinnie,

I'm writing with good news. I received your story and you are a finalist for the workshop. I'll be making my decision tonight or tomorrow. I send out this email to make sure that every girl is certain she is ready to make the commitment that the Writers' Workshop requires. Please let me know and I'll proceed with my decision making.

Hope you're having a fantastic time on the Cape!

Sincerely,

Mrs. Lee

Dear Mrs. Lee,

I can definitely promise that I'm ready to make a commitment to the Writers' Workshop! I really hope I get in!

Sincerely,

Zinnie

The good news that she was a finalist for the Writers' Workshop had put Zinnia in a great mood, despite everything that had happened with Marigold.

"I'm the salty sea monster," Zinnie said as she rose above the surface of the ocean water, her hair hanging in front of her face like a wet black mop. "And I like to capture little sisters and eat them for dessert!" She lunged at Lily, who giggled as she pinched her nose, shut her eyes, and dunked back under.

"I'm the Cape Cod kraken," Max said, sticking a pile of green seaweed on his head. "I destroy the sea monsters who eat the little sisters." He dove under the water and grabbed Zinnie's ankle so that she lost her footing and flopped onto her back, laughing. A boy had never touched her ankle before! The thrill of it sent her into a backward underwater somersault.

They were at the big beach with the estuary and dunes, where close friends and family were gathering for a clambake dinner before the wedding. The kids had already had plenty of clams, lobster claws, and corn, and Zinnie, Lily, Marigold, Max, and Peter were playing in the water while the adults watched them from the beach blankets.

Zinnie loved swimming in the evening. It was, she decided, her most favorite thing in the world. At least for right now. The air had finally cooled off. Yet the water had somehow captured the day's sun. Now that she was used to the temperature, it felt warmer in the ocean than out of it, and it was delightful to crouch so that the warm water covered her shoulders. She liked to pop up into the cool air and then huddle down again. They had been hard at work all day with wedding chores, so this evening dip, or "sea bath," as Aunt Sunny would call it, was an especially welcome rest. The only wedding duty left, for tonight anyway, was to gather the bright pink beach roses for the baskets. On the car ride over, Zinnie had volunteered to do it, because she wanted to show her parents that she was still a helpful and good person even though she'd read Marigold's diary.

Though now that she was bobbing up and down in the salty sea, she wished she hadn't volunteered to collect the beach roses. The sun was beginning to set, casting a glow on Max's face and Lily's, and hers, too, she imagined. She wished she could stay in this watery bliss forever, especially since Marigold had headed out, walking toward the shore with Peter. *Good,* Zinnie thought as she watched Marigold and Peter traipse through the shallow surf. *Go.*

Even though she and Marigold had avoided each other all day, except for the cake tier assembling, the Atlantic Ocean still didn't seem big enough for both of them. Especially since Max couldn't take his eyes off Marigold in her one-shouldered turquoise bathing suit, or "maillot," as she called it. ("This is my favorite *my-o*," she'd said when they got to the beach, showing off her French pronunciation.) Zinnie was actually shocked that Max hadn't followed Marigold onto the shore but instead had stayed to play this underwater monster game. She hoped that Marigold and Peter were at this very moment falling back in love with each other so that she and Max could spend the whole wedding having fun together.

"If Zinnie is the salty sea monster, and Max is the Cape Cod kraken, then I'm the magic mermaid who can zap you both with my laser tail," Lily said. Now an expert swimmer, she flipped onto her back and splashed water in their faces with her feet. Max and Zinnie feigned dramatic deaths. Lily laughed so hard she snorted. "Max, are you going to be so crazy when you have your special dance with Marigold tomorrow night?"

"Special dance?" Zinnie asked as she pushed her hair off of her face and planted her feet on the sandy sea bottom. "What do you mean, 'special dance'?"

"Max asked Marigold for a special dance last night," Lily said.

"And what did she say?" Zinnie asked, feeling like the ocean floor was falling out from under her. She knew Max liked Marigold, but Marigold had promised not to like him back.

"She said yes," Lily said. Then she paused the conversation to do an underwater handstand. Zinnie stood absolutely still, staring into the middle distance as the water lapped at her chin. A small wave brought a chilly current. It wrapped around her body, sending goose bumps all the way up to her cheeks. Lily resurfaced and announced, "And then he kissed her!"

"What?" Zinnie asked, unable to hide the hurt in her voice.

"On the hand!" Max said, blushing even though his lips were starting to turn blue. "Jeez!"

"Like this," Lily said, smooching her own hand. Little pecks gave way to full-on slobbering.

"It was not like that," Max said, gently splashing her. "I was as courteous as a knight. A servant of the king, one who rides by night along the perilous shores!" He gave a formal bow. Zinnie could tell he was trying to start up a new game, but she was too busy imagining the kiss to respond.

"I gotta go," Zinnie said, gathering her composure. "I need to pick some wild beach roses."

"Oh, come on, we have plenty of time! Our parents haven't even had their coffee yet," Max said, looking back at the grown-ups. Then he added in a deep, gravelly voice: "And never mind about the knight. The Cape Cod kraken lives! He has seven lives. So even though the magic mermaid killed him, he's not dead!"

"It's actually a really important job. Max, can you watch Lily?"

"Sure," Max said. "I'll watch this mermaid. Then

I'll catch her by the tail!"

"They're not called 'wild beach roses.' They're *Rosa rugosa*," Lily said. She giggled as she swam away from Max. "They're not a native species."

"Whatever they are, I have to get them now," Zinnie said, turning toward the beach. Sometimes Zinnie felt like she was not a native species either. Her teachers called her "unique," her principal called her a "stand-out," and her dad called her a "one of a kind." They all meant it in a good way, but sometimes it seemed like it would be easier to be just a more normal sort of girl. Maybe Marigold was right. Maybe she was too much of a spaz to ever have a boyfriend.

"Honey, you okay?" Dad called as Zinnie wrapped a towel around her waist. He was sitting on a blanket up the beach a bit. Marigold and Peter were walking down the beach, together.

"I'm going to get the beach roses," Zinnie called back as she headed toward the dune. Zinnie knew that if she came within ten feet of Marigold she would want to tell her off, and she had given her word to her parents that she and Marigold wouldn't argue in front of Aunt Sunny.

As she climbed over the dune and out of sight of her family to the patch of beach roses, Zinnie tried to make sense of the situation. Lily said that Max had asked Marigold to dance last night, which meant this happened before Marigold had read Zinnie's story. So

it wasn't just an act of retaliation. It was pure, unpro-
voked treachery!

Zinnie was so lost in her own angry thoughts as
she picked the roses that she didn't even notice the
golden retriever that had decided to join her until he
licked her on the cheek.

"Ah!" Zinnie said, startled by the wet nose in her
ear. It was almost impossible to stay mad as the dog
covered her face in kisses.

"There you are, Bandit!" said a voice. She looked up
to see Mr. Rathbone with a leash in his hand.

"Zinnia Silver," Mr. Rathbone said, his whole face
lighting up. "How fortunate to run into you again!"

"How's Cameron?" Zinnie asked as Bandit rubbed
up against her hand, begging to be stroked. Zinnie
happily obliged.

"He's doing just fine. I can't tell you how grateful
my family and I are. We saw you on the news. You
did a great job. Your parents must be so proud of you."

"Yes," Zinnie said, though they certainly weren't
proud of her for reading Marigold's diary. They had
made that very clear.

"My family and I have been thinking about you
a lot," Mr. Rathbone said. "And I know that you said
that all that you wanted was ice cream, but that just
doesn't seem like enough. I'm fortunate enough to have
a lot of resources—"

"I know who you are," Zinnie said. She almost bit

back her next thought, but Zinnie didn't really care about hurting Marigold's feelings at the moment. She decided to just say what was on her mind. "And I loved the movie *Night Sprites*."

"I'm so glad," Mr. Rathbone said. Zinnie was surprised to see that he did seem genuinely pleased. She thought famous people like Mr. Rathbone wouldn't care about compliments from a kid, but his smile felt real. "And I'd truly love to grant a wish for you. My whole family would."

"Like a fairy godfather. Or a genie!" Zinnie said, smiling as Bandit nosed her neck. Zinnie scratched his back and thought, *Hmmm.*

"Take your time and think about it," Mr. Rathbone said, "and don't be afraid to dream big."

"Thank you," Zinnie said, contemplating this gift of a lifetime. There were so many possibilities. The most obvious one was to ask him to put her sister into another movie, but why should she do that? Why should she give her one wish away, especially when Marigold thought she had no chance of ever having a boyfriend, and on top of that, Marigold was going to have a special dance with the only boy Zinnie had ever been friends with. She was mulling this over when a familiar voice brought her back to reality.

"Zinnie!" Marigold was calling her from the other side of the dune. "Where are you?"

"Coming!" Zinnie called back, and she picked one

last beach rose. She didn't want Marigold to see her with Mr. Rathbone. Not only was it sure to start World War Three, she was not ready to share the news of a soon-to-be-granted wish. She did not want to be pressured or even influenced. The wish belonged to her. Not everything had to be shared with her sisters.

"Let me give you my infor—" Mr. Rathbone began.

"Are you up there?" Marigold called from below. She was getting closer. "Did you get the roses?"

"Thank you so much. I'd really better run," Zinnie said. She ran down the dune as fast as she could, hoping that Bandit wouldn't follow.

44 · Anticipation

Marigold awoke bright and early with her checklist next to her. She sat up and smoothed out the paper, which was rumpled and smudged from having been slept on. She had fallen asleep going over it. She looked out the window and saw a clear sky. The weather was on their side!

Her sisters were sleeping soundly as she looked over her list. There was so much to do. She needed to: (1) Make sure that her ceremony setup was still in shape and give the chairs one more wipe-down. (2) Cover, decorate, and set all the tables. Thank goodness Jean, Peter, and some of the yacht club staff were going to help with that! (3) Assemble the cake tiers that they had frosted yesterday. This needed to happen by noon in order for the cake to reach room temperature. Aunt Sunny had told her that cake tasted best that way. (4) Get her sisters into their dresses and looking presentable. What was she going to do with Zinnie's hair, she wondered as she looked at her sister, with her mass of wild curls spread on the pillow.

Marigold got out of bed and peered out the window at the wedding tent, which, with the dance floor, band platform, tables, fairy lights, and paper lanterns, seemed to be anticipating the party. Even though she was aware that Peter had a girlfriend, she couldn't stop herself from imagining a dance with him, especially since he had been so attentive last night at the clambake.

He'd been able to see something was wrong when they'd all gone swimming after dinner and she and Zinnie weren't speaking to each other at all. It was too hard to pretend to be happy and play games with everyone when she was so mad inside, so she'd decided to walk to shore and sit with the grown-ups instead. To her surprise, Peter followed her.

"I know something's eating you," Peter said, splashing her lightly. "What is it? Come on, spill the beans."

"I'm really embarrassed about something," Marigold said as they walked ankle deep in the calm evening surf.

"What happened?" Peter asked.

"I'm not going to tell you," Marigold said. "That would make me even more embarrassed!"

"My mom once told me that embarrassment isn't

the end of the world," Peter said, stopping to pick up a piece of sea glass for his collection. "And you know what? She was right."

"When were you embarrassed?" Marigold asked, not believing it was possible for anyone to be more embarrassed than she had been recently.

"Last year at the talent show," Peter said. Marigold felt her cheeks warm. That had been her fault. He had said he didn't want to perform and she had pushed him into doing it anyway.

"I'm sorry," she said.

"It's okay," Peter said. "I wasn't trying to make you feel bad. But I was really embarrassed. After that, the whole town knew that I can't sing and that my face is capable of turning as red as a *lobstah*!" Marigold laughed. Peter did, too. "Seriously, I thought I was never going to be able to go out in public again. But you know what my mom said to me?" Marigold shook her head, then turned to him and listened intently. She was ready for some wisdom. "She said, 'No one survives life without getting embarrassed at least once really bad. Better to get it out of the way early so you can learn how to laugh at yourself and move on.'"

Marigold considered this. She had seen how embarrassed Peter was that night, and now he did seem able to laugh about the whole thing. Was this going to be funny one day? Impossible.

Peter tossed the sea glass, which wasn't quite smooth

enough yet, back into the ocean and continued. "Then Mom said, 'It could always be worse.'"

"How could that have been worse for you?" Marigold asked.

"That's easy. Singing it in my underwear," Peter said. Against all odds, Marigold found herself laughing again. In fact, she was in near hysterics.

"What?" Peter asked with a smile. "Is the idea of me in my underwear so funny to you?"

"No, no!" Marigold said. She hadn't even tried to picture that, though now that Peter had put it out there, it was hard not to think about. "I'm not laughing at you. It's just the way you say 'underwear.' '*Undah-weh.*'"

"Hey, that's a good imitation!" Peter said. "No wonder you're an actress!"

For the first time since the *Night Sprites* debacle, she didn't protest the title. At least not aloud.

Now, as she looked at the wedding tent in the morning light, she imagined it tonight after the sun had set, alive with music and aglow with candles. She knew she was going to have her goofy dance with Max, but she couldn't stop herself from wondering: Would Peter maybe ask her to dance, too?

45 · Building a Cake

The whole family gathered in the kitchen for the cake assembly. Later they were going to need to transport the cake from the house to the tent, and Zinnie had the brilliant idea of placing it on Aunt Sunny's old slide projector cart, which they could cover with one of the antique tablecloths. Dad and Zinnie went up to the attic to get the cart, and Marigold and Lily picked out a few lacy tablecloths to layer on top of it. The girls watched as Aunt Sunny and Mom lifted the bottom tier of the cake, which was on the cake decorator's turntable, from the fridge to the cart. Then they carried the other tiers to the table. Aunt Sunny brought out a handful of plastic straws and asked Zinnie to cut them all in half with kitchen shears. These would give each tier of the cake stability. Once they were cut, Aunt Sunny instructed Lily to insert one in the center of the twelve-inch tier.

"Push it all the way to the bottom," Aunt Sunny said. "Marigold, you work on the other pieces. Put them about an inch and a half from the center straw."

Aunt Sunny trimmed the straws so that they were level with the top of the cake; this made each layer sturdy. Aunt Sunny then lifted the nine-inch tier, still on the cardboard, and placed it on top of the twelve-inch tier. The girls repeated the process with the straws for the nine-inch tier.

"Why don't you girls put on the top tier?" Aunt Sunny suggested.

"Oh gosh, Sunny, are you sure?" Mom asked.

"You don't trust us, Mom?" Zinnie asked.

"It's a very important cake," Mom said.

"It's my cake," Aunt Sunny said. "And I trust them. Girls, go ahead."

"Be careful," Dad said.

Marigold, Zinnie, and Lily made eye contact, counted together, and on "three" they placed the six-inch tier on top. Mom exhaled loudly.

"Zinnie, since you were the one who found the bluebird, you do the honors," Aunt Sunny said. Zinnie lifted the bird from the box. The blown-glass object felt cool and delicate in her sweaty hands. She nestled its feet on the frosting and Aunt Sunny pushed them into the cake so that the bird appeared to be resting rather than standing.

"Oh, how I wish Beatrice could be with me here today," Aunt Sunny said as she tucked a beach rose next to the bird. "I really think she would like Tony."

"Me too," Mom said, standing up and putting her arms around Aunt Sunny. Zinnie saw tears gathering in their eyes as they hugged.

"You girls are so lucky to have each other," Aunt Sunny said. "You must never forget it."

"Don't make me cry, too," Dad said, reaching for a tissue.

"You are so sensitive, Daddy," Lily said, and climbed onto his lap. This made everyone laugh.

They all looked at the cake. This wasn't the perfect kind of cake that could be found in a supermarket or a bakery. The middle layer was ever so slightly sloped, the piping was uneven in spots, and the frosting wasn't smooth the way it was on store-bought cakes. Aunt Sunny's cake looked more like the surface of the sea on a breezy day. But Zinnie found it unspeakably beautiful. It had history. It had originality. It had love. It had everything that was not for sale.

"I've got to get my hair done now," Aunt Sunny said, checking her thin silver watch, the face of which she wore on the inside of her wrist. "Marigold, you were so smart to suggest I take a shower early this morning. You were absolutely right about the day getting away from me. Thank you."

"You're welcome. And don't forget about your nails,"

Marigold said, for she had made the appointment at the salon. "Toes, too."

"My first pedicure!" Aunt Sunny said.

"It's in ten minutes," Marigold said. "You'd better get going. I'm going to put the final touches on the table decorations. Lily, you get the first shower. Zinnie, you're after her. And only seven minutes each so we don't run out of hot water."

"I'm on my way. Wish me luck," Aunt Sunny said.

"You've really got things under control, haven't you, Marigold?" Dad said.

Marigold nodded proudly as she marched Lily upstairs.

"She's been like this since we got here," Zinnie said to Mom and Dad. The three of them stood back to admire the cake again.

"I think we should put this out of the way," Mom said. "What with everyone whizzing in and out of the kitchen all afternoon."

"I know. Let's put it in my office," Zinnie said.

"Good idea," Mom said.

Together they wheeled the cake into the room. The only problem was the shaft of sunlight that was coming through the window. In preparation for Tony's move-in, Aunt Sunny had removed the pink curtains.

"It might be better off in the kitchen," Dad said. "It's so bright in here. We don't want it to melt."

"Aunt Sunny has one of those dressing screens in

the attic," Zinnie said. "We can put it behind that."

"Is there anything that attic doesn't have?" Mom asked.

"The internet," Zinnie said, and they all laughed.

46 · An Unexpected Visitor

Marigold had a vision for the seed packets. She'd written the guests' names and table numbers on them, so everyone would know where to sit. Now she was pinning them up by the corners on a bulletin board with thumbtacks. At the top of the driveway, she had set up the desk with a chair and a jar full of sharpened pencils for people to use to write their messages to Aunt Sunny and Tony. She'd just realized that she could add some rulers and other school supplies to really create a scene when she noticed a familiar figure walking down the driveway. It took her a moment to place the man in the dark jeans, white button-down shirt, and round glasses, but once she did, her heart almost stopped. It was Philip Rathbone.

What was he doing at Aunt Sunny's? Was he invited to the wedding? She supposed it was possible, because he had made a large donation to the Piping Plover Society, and anyway, it seemed like everyone in this small town was coming over today. But it wasn't time for the guests to arrive yet. And wouldn't Aunt Sunny have told her if he was coming?

Her pulse sped up as she wondered if he had changed his mind about cutting her out of *Night Sprites*. Although it didn't really make sense, a part of her hoped that somehow he had put her back into the movie, and that a new version would be released— *with her in it*. And all her friends (and enemies) at school would see that she hadn't been lying. She really was a star on the rise! She didn't have time to elaborate on her fantasy any longer, because he was standing in front of her now. Time seemed to slow to a halt as he opened his mouth to speak. Her stomach clenched, her heart pounded, and her eyes refused to blink. Was he going to apologize? Ask her to be in another film? Confess that he had made a horrible mistake?

"Excuse me, is this where Zinnia Silver lives?" he asked.

"What?" Of all the things Marigold imagined he might say, this was not one of them. Even worse, he was looking at her as though she were a stranger. Did he not even recognize her? She put a hand to her short hair, wishing she hadn't cut her signature locks.

"Yes," Marigold said, as her heart seemed to audibly crack. "That's my sister."

"Would you give her this card for me?" He reached into his back pocket and handed her a business card. It had a simple sketch of a movie camera and his name and phone number.

"Why?" Marigold asked.

"I owe her a wish. Like a genie." One corner of his mouth turned up in a smile. "But I can't grant it if she doesn't know how to get in touch. That's my number, and I'll be at the Village Café for the next few hours if she'd like to see me." With that he tipped an imaginary hat and walked away like a cowboy in one of those old westerns.

Marigold stormed into the house, her blood heated to the boiling point.

"Zinnie!" she called, feeling her cheeks color. No answer. She was probably upstairs in the shower.

Everyone always thought Marigold was the mean older sister. But it wasn't true. *Zinnie* was mean. She was worse than mean. She was a criminal. A thief! Acting in movies was *Marigold's* life's goal. It always had been *her* ambition. And now it was all over and it belonged to Zinnie? She had stolen Marigold's dream as if it were nothing but a pair of shoes! How and where and when had Zinnie found Mr. Rathbone and charmed him into being . . . what? . . . a genie? Maybe Marigold was the sister who boys liked, but when it came to adults, Zinnie was some kind of cruel magician.

Marigold's temper was blazing, and this time she wasn't going to tamp it down. She had promised her parents not to fight with her sister for Aunt Sunny's sake, but Aunt Sunny was getting her hair and nails done at a salon two miles away. And their parents were out in the wedding tent setting the tables, so they were out of earshot. Besides, Zinnie had barely even gotten in trouble for having read Marigold's diary and written a story about her most embarrassing moment in life. *If I had done that?* Marigold thought. *I'd have been grounded for life for hurting my poor, innocent younger sister.* It wasn't fair. If their parents weren't going to enforce any justice in this house, she was. Marigold was ready to let her sister know that it was not okay to mess with her like this. She would not resort to wrestling again. As their mother had reminded her, she was above that. But she was not above telling her sister off.

"Zinnie!" she called. "Where are you?" She pulled open the door to the bathroom, startling Lily, who was wearing one of Aunt Sunny's bathrobes and brushing her wet hair.

"Eek!" Lily said, pulling the bathrobe around her protectively. "You scared me. I took a shower just like you said. I washed my hair, rinsed it twice, and even used conditioner." She held up a lock of her hair as evidence. "You can smell it if you want."

"That's okay. I trust you. You're a good sister,"

Marigold said, trying to remain calm. "But I'm look-ing for Zinnie, who's a bad sister. Have you seen her?"

"She's in the office," Lily said, looking miniature in the oversized bathrobe. "Are you sure she's a bad sister?"

"Yes," Marigold said, running down the stairs. "You better stay here." This, of course, just made Lily chase after her—she could hear Lily's little footsteps close behind.

"I like Zinnie!" Lily said.

"I don't," Marigold said, and opened the door to the office, where Zinnie was sitting at her desk with her headphones on, typing something. *More slander,* Mari-gold guessed.

"So, you're trying to get a part from Mr. Rathbone, are you?" Marigold said, loudly enough to be heard over the headphones.

"Huh? What?" Zinnie asked, jumping a little.

"Mr. Rathbone was just here and he was looking for you!" Marigold said.

"Uh-oh," Lily said. "This is baaaaaad."

"I can explain!" Zinnie said, leaping to her feet.

"Why did you do this?" Marigold paced, feeling like the small room could not contain her anger.

"If you can just calm down, I'll tell you the whole story," Zinnie said.

"I don't want any more of your stories!" Marigold

grabbed Zinnie by the shoulders.

"No fighting!" Lily said. "Stop it!"

"I wasn't trying to hurt you," Zinnie said, trying to twist out of Marigold's hands. "I swear."

"Then why did you do the thing that you knew would hurt me the most?" Marigold asked, tightening her grip and lifting Zinnie so that she was on her tippy-toes.

"I didn't," Zinnie said. "Let go of me and I'll explain."

"The rule is no fighting, remember?" Lily said.

"Fine!" Marigold said. Just as she released Zinnie, Lily wriggled in between them and pushed them apart, sending Zinnie into the dressing screen.

"No!" Zinnie cried. But it was too late. Gravity had set her in motion. As Zinnie fell backward, a soft barrier seemed to cushion her landing, and there was the sound of a delicate thing, like a light bulb, breaking. Marigold gasped when a few blackberries rolled out from behind the screen and she saw, by the door, the thin glass beak of the bluebird. They had crushed the cake.

"It was his nephew in the water," Zinnie said from the floor. "I saved Mr. Rathbone's nephew."

47 · The Damage Done

Zinnie lifted up the screen, hoping the destruction wasn't as bad as she feared. Perhaps only one side of the cake was damaged and they could face that side away from the guests? But no. The top tier was on the floor. The middle tier was squished, and one whole side of the bottom tier was flattened. Worst of all, the glass bird was smashed to shards. The three sisters sat without speaking, taking in the wreckage. There was a terrible silence.

"Oh no," Lily finally said. "Oh. No."

"Why didn't you tell me you'd saved Mr. Rathbone's nephew?" Marigold asked, picking up the pieces of the broken bird.

"I didn't want to upset you," Zinnie said. "You were so mad about the movie. But then I saw him last night at the beach—"

"Last night?" Marigold asked.

Zinnie nodded. "He was walking his dog in the dunes. And he told me he would grant me a wish," she said. "Anything I wanted. Like a genie."

"Oh," Marigold said quietly. "I guess that explains it."

"I didn't betray you," Zinnie said. Marigold raised an eyebow. "I mean, it was just the story."

"Excuse me—what are we going to do about the cake?" Lily asked, pulling on her curls. "The cake! The cake! Aunt Sunny's cake!"

"I don't know," Zinnie said. It was too horrible to think about. "I don't know."

They heard the screen door slam.

"Girls?" Mom called.

They locked eyes.

"Uh-oh," Lily whispered, clutching the bathrobe. "We can't let her see."

"Where are you?" Mom asked, her footsteps headed toward the kitchen.

"In here," Zinnie said.

Lily shushed her. "No, we have to try to fix it first."

"There's no fixing this," Zinnie said. This cake could not be made whole again. The bird that had belonged to their grandmother could not be glued back together. Diaries could not be unread. Words could not be unspoken.

"Zinnie's right," Marigold said. "We have to face this."

"We might as well do it together," Zinnie said, stepping between her sisters and taking each one's hand.

Mom opened the door and put her hands over her mouth. Zinnie had never seen her turn this particular shade of white.

The Silver family gathered in the kitchen in the wake of the great cake disaster. Zinnie sat with the bluebird's beak, the one part of the glass sculpture that remained intact, in her hand. They sat at the kitchen table, Mom and Marigold on one side and Zinnie and Dad on the other. Lily, who had changed out of Aunt Sunny's robe, was cuddled on Dad's lap.

Mom and Dad hadn't used angry voices or a single time-out. There had been no need to discipline the sisters. They felt so awful, looked so distraught, and had cried two oceans (the Atlantic and the Pacific) of tears between them, that it was clear they were punishing themselves enough.

"You two need to talk," Mom said, looking at Zinnie and Marigold.

"Who's going first?" Dad asked.

"I will," Zinnie said. "You hurt my feelings, Marigold. The things you wrote about me were mean and thoughtless. Do you really think I'm such a spaz that I'll never have a boyfriend?"

"No, of course not," Marigold said. "A diary is a place to write things that you don't think anyone will read. Sometimes people write things they don't mean or would never say aloud. I didn't mean it. It was just something I thought for a second. Does that make sense?" She sighed and added ruefully, "I honestly don't know anything about boyfriends."

"Why did you say you'd dance with Max?" Zinnie asked. "Why did he kiss your hand?"

"It was just as friends," Marigold said. "He kissed my hand in this silly way, like a knight. You know how Max is. He was being ridiculous." Zinnie did know Max. He was ridiculous. That's what she liked about him. Marigold leaned on the table and looked Zinnie in the eye. "People like you, Zinnie. Everyone likes you. I know that will mean boyfriends will, too." These words felt so true. "Do you think I'm as stuck up as Marianna?" Marigold asked.

"No," Zinnie said. "Especially not after what you've been through this summer." Marigold nodded. "I'm finalist for the Writers' Workshop," Zinnie continued. "I got an email from Mrs. Lee today."

"I knew you could do it," Mom said.

"But I'm going to write to Mrs. Lee and tell her my submission isn't valid. I'm going to withdraw it," Zinnie said.

"That's a very nice thing to do," Dad said. "I'm

impressed by your integrity. But are you sure? I know that means the world to you."

"I'm sure," Zinnie said. "It's the right thing to do."

"You still wrote that story, Zinnie," Mom said. "I really want you to think about this."

"You don't have to do that," Marigold said.

"I don't?" Zinnie asked.

"I don't want to take your dream away from you. That happened to me, and it was the worst."

"Thank you," Zinnie said. "That means a lot."

"And I'm sorry for snooping on your laptop. I shouldn't have done that," Marigold said.

"I forgive you," Zinnie said. "Let's both promise not to snoop anymore. Deal?"

"Deal," Marigold said. She walked over to Zinnie and they embraced.

"Okay!" Lily said. "Now that you guys made up, let's fix the cake!"

"I don't know if that's possible, sweetie," Dad said. "That cake is in bad shape."

"I know making up was hard," Mom said. "But the hardest part is still ahead of you. You're going to have to tell Aunt Sunny."

"She's going to be back any minute," Marigold said.

"Ruining the cake was awful. But ruining Grammy's bird . . . ," Zinnie said, shaking her head. "That's going to break her heart."

"I wish we didn't have to tell her," Lily said. "Can we at least try to fix the cake?"

Marigold and Zinnie went to the office and wheeled out what was left of the cake.

48 · Breaking the News

"Marigold, are you saving the cake? Can it still be our present to Aunt Sunny? Even without the bird?" Lily asked.

Marigold and Zinnie were using the extra frosting to try to salvage the bottom tier.

"We're just making it worse," Marigold said, stepping back from the cake.

"I think you're right," Mom said, placing a hand on Marigold's shoulder.

"We have to think of another present," Marigold said.

"You don't have a lot of time," Dad said.

"We still have four hours before the wedding starts," Zinnie said. "Four whole hours!" She was determined to make it up to Aunt Sunny—somehow.

"But you guys haven't even taken your showers yet,"

Lily said. "I've washed, rinsed, and conditioned my hair."

"I can take a thirty-second shower," Zinnie said. "I've done it before. Once I even took a twenty-second shower."

"I can take a thirty-second shower, too," Marigold said. The whole family gave her a look. "Fine. Sixty seconds. One hundred and twenty seconds tops."

"That would still leave us three hours and fifty-seven minutes or something to figure out a new present," Zinnie said.

"I don't know, girls," Mom said. "I wouldn't be too worried about another present right now. I think you should apologize from the heart and then promise to be your best selves for the rest of the day."

"Mom's right," Marigold said. "We don't need any more shenanigans. There's still some tables that need to be decorated and some odds and ends to be taken care of."

"I know, but—" Zinnie started, but was silenced by the sound of the door opening. Aunt Sunny was home. Zinnie clutched her stomach, which ached with anxiety. Marigold bit her lip and looked at the floor. Lily buried her head in Dad's shoulder.

"It's time," Dad said, peeling Lily off of him. "You girls know what you need to do."

"What are we going to say?" Zinnie whispered. "How are we going to explain?"

"The simple truth is the best explanation," Mom said.

"I'm back," Aunt Sunny called from the living room. Mom nodded at the girls and they stood up, together, in front of the cake. "I barely recognize myself, but I have to admit my toes have never looked—" She stopped midsentence as she walked into the kitchen and saw the line of somber-looking sisters. "Heavens. Why the long faces?"

"We're sorry," Zinnie said.

"We're so sorry," Marigold said.

"We've never been so sorry in our lives," Lily said.

"What's happened?" Aunt Sunny asked.

The girls parted like curtains, revealing the damaged cake.

"We were fighting, and we lost our balance, and then we just—"

"We ruined it," Lily said, bursting into tears.

"We're so, so sorry," Marigold said.

"Oh. Oh my," Aunt Sunny said, placing a hand on her heart. The pink nail polish, as subtle as it was, made Aunt Sunny's hands look foreign. Even though her hands looked elegant, Zinnie preferred them without the polish and with some soil beneath the nails from working in the garden. Zinnie's eyes traveled from her aunt's hands to her face. Aunt Sunny's voice was soft and laced with hurt as she said, "It's only cake. It was my mother who always said, 'Don't cry over something that can't cry over you.'"

"But it's your wedding cake," Zinnie said.

"And our present to you," Marigold added.

"The real gift was not the cake, but rather making the cake with me," Aunt Sunny said quietly. "I will always have that."

"And Grammy's bird," Zinnie said, holding up the piece with the beak. "We broke that, too."

"Oh dear." Aunt Sunny covered her mouth.

"We're so sorry," Marigold said. "It was my fault."

"No, it was mine," Zinnie said. "I should have told you about Mr. Rathbone."

"It was my fault," Lily said. "I'm the one who pushed you two apart."

"It doesn't matter whose fault it was," Zinnie said, turning back to Aunt Sunny. "The point is that we're sorry."

Zinnie saw the sadness in her aunt's eyes just before she closed them and said in a quavering voice, "Excuse me. I need a moment." Zinnie's heart constricted as she watched Aunt Sunny walk toward her bedroom. Marigold squeezed Zinnie's hand.

"Is Aunt Sunny crying?" Lily asked.

"I think so, honey," Mom said.

"On her wedding day," Marigold said in a shaky voice.

"Because of us," Zinnie said, hanging her head.

"I'm going to check on her," Mom said.

"I'm going to set the tables outside," Dad said. "I trust you girls will help me as soon as you're ready. For now, Marigold, why don't you give me your checklist?"

Marigold handed over her checklist and Zinnie placed an arm around each sister, drawing them more tightly together.

49 · The Plan

"Zinnie, get your notebook and follow us," Marigold said, taking Lily by the hand and heading toward the stairs. "We need to come up with a plan."

"Okay," Zinnie said, darting into the office for her plan-making supplies before following her sisters up to the attic bedroom.

Once the three of them were inside and seated on her bed, Marigold advised them to take deep breaths—a focusing technique she had learned in her acting class. "In, two, three . . . and out, two, three . . . ," she said, guiding them through the exercise ten times.

"Okay," she said, once she felt that she and her sisters were calm enough to think straight. "We have three and a half hours before the ceremony starts. How are we going to make this up to Aunt Sunny? Zinnie, let's make a list."

"We need a new cake," Lily said.

"Cake," Marigold said, pointing to Zinnie's notebook. Zinnie dutifully wrote the word.

"But think of how long it took us to make that cake. Where are we going to find a wedding cake in three hours?" Zinnie said. "Besides, I have to practice the sonnet again. I messed it up at the rehearsal."

"I'll read the sonnet," Marigold said, realizing as she spoke the words that not only would she do it, she wanted to more than anything in the world. She had so many feelings inside her—sadness, regret, despair, and great love for Aunt Sunny. Her soul seemed to be shaking from all the emotion inside of her. She wanted to do something with those feelings besides making checklists and decorating tables. She wanted to do what she did best. She longed to spin those feelings into words and breathe them out into the world. She longed to *act*.

"Phew," Zinnie said. "You'll be so much better at that than me."

"Isn't that what Aunt Sunny wanted as a present from you anyway?" Lily asked.

"Yes," Marigold said, remembering when Aunt Sunny had asked her to read the sonnet and she had said no. She felt a stitch in her side. How could she have refused? How could she have put her desire to be "ordinary" in front of Aunt Sunny's wedding wish?

Sure, she was embarrassed about being cut from the movie. But as Peter had said, there were many things in life worse than being embarrassed—like hurting Aunt Sunny's feelings.

"And she asked Zinnie to write something," Lily said, turning to Zinnie.

"Oh, yeah," Zinnie said. Marigold could see that Zinnie's mind was already working. "Of course I can write something."

"But, Zinnie, you have to promise me it won't have anything embarrassing in it," Marigold said.

"I promise," Zinnie said.

"What about the cake?" Lily said. "We need a cake!"

"I wish time travel were real," Zinnie said. "I wish we could go back and stop that cake from falling. I wish, I wish, I wish."

Something about the word "wish" seemed to be sticking in Marigold's mind, accumulating energy as Zinnie repeated it. And then she remembered something in her pocket. She reached in and pulled out Mr. Rathbone's card. Zinnie smiled, her eyes lighting up.

"He said he'd grant any wish, right?" Marigold said.

"Like a genie," Zinnie said. "But is it possible? In three and a half hours? We spent days on that cake."

"We won't actually eat the cake until at least eight o'clock tonight," Marigold said.

"You're right," Zinnie said.

"He said he was going to be at the Village Café for the next few hours," Marigold said. "If you run, you still might be able to catch him. In the meantime, I'm going to finish helping Dad with the tables."

"What about me?" Lily asked. "What am I supposed to do?"

"You're going to help Mom with the bouquets," Zinnie said.

"The bird!" Zinnie said as she tied on her sneakers. "We need a bluebird."

"I don't think we can glue Grammy's one together again," Marigold said.

"Maybe I can find a way to bring her sisters into my speech somehow?" Zinnie wondered aloud.

"Brilliant," Marigold said.

"I have an idea," Lily said. "I'm going to tell a real bluebird to come to the wedding. Bluebirds are a pretty common species, though there aren't as many as there used to be. We learned about them in camp. I bet I can find one."

"That's great," Marigold said, and patted Lily on the head. She wanted Lily to be a part of this, but there just wasn't any time to go looking for birds.

"Okay, so we all have our jobs. I'm going to rehearse the sonnet, finish the tables, and take a thirty-second shower. Zinnie, you're going to ask Mr. Rathbone to get us a cake and you're going to write something for the ceremony and take a thirty-second shower. And Lily, you're going to help Mom with the bouquets and—"

"Find a bluebird!" Lily said.

50 · The Story

Because Marigold was so organized, they finished their tasks early. Zinnie brought her computer to the spot in the yard with Wi-Fi to write to Mrs. Lee. Even though Zinnie liked the story she had submitted and Marigold had told her that she didn't have to withdraw it, the situation just didn't feel right to Zinnie. If she were accepted on the basis of that story, she would always feel like a traitor. She typed a thoughtful email explaining why her story wasn't a valid submission. She also explained how hard it was to withdraw her application to the Writers' Workshop because it was her dream to participate, but she couldn't do so at the cost of betraying her sister. She pressed "send."

She was then overcome by an urge to write that was so powerful that she couldn't stop herself. The words flowed like water from the estuary into the sea.

She thought back to Mrs. Lee's first prompt, the one she hadn't used yet, about writing about an argument she'd had from the other person's point of view.

Zinnie wanted to write about her argument with Marigold, only she didn't want to write about it in a "real" way. Instead, she wanted to write about it in a way that let her be a little more creative. A little more . . . her.

Zinnie wrote a story that was inspired by the legend of the Summer Triangle, but she put her own spin on it. Instead of being about people in love, it was about a goddess named Zuli and her sister, Mandu. In order to shine more brightly than her incandescent sister, Zuli stole Mandu's secrets and spilled them across the sky. The whole world could see them, for they had frozen in a dazzling constellation. Mandu was so furious and embarrassed that she fled to the earth to live the rest of her days disguised as a humble mortal.

Writing from Mandu's point of view, Zinnie found herself describing with clarity and passion the shame and anger Marigold must have experienced when she read Zinnie's story. She barely lifted her fingers from the keyboard as she wrote about how Zuli shouted apologies to her sister, telling her that she would sew a cloak in which she could hide and regain her privacy. But Mandu knew that it was useless, for what has been seen cannot be unseen. Besides, she was enjoying her time among the humans, learning there was more to life than being a shining star. She'd found a job in a café, serving pancakes and coffee. It was a humble job indeed, and Mandu sort of liked it—especially all the free maple syrup and bacon.

Meanwhile, Zuli worked furiously and without stopping on the cloak, so that her needle burned through the night, creating a fire in the sky that was so brilliant, the mortals forgot all about Mandu's secrets. Touched by her sister's hard work (and growing tired of maple syrup and small tips), Mandu accepted Zuli's apology and returned to the sky. Despite its dark beauty and exquisite detail, Mandu didn't wear the cloak. She knew that she was a true goddess and a star that longed to be seen. Instead, it hung on Mandu's wall, and she tucked her secrets beneath it. Sometimes, however, Mandu missed her time as a mere mortal. Once a year, she and Zuli descended to the earth, where they feasted on pancakes and always left a big tip. The mortals who were lucky enough to catch a glimpse of their fall never failed to make a wish, because everyone knows that double shooting stars are twice as lucky as one.

It was, Zinnie thought, her very best writing. She couldn't imagine it in *Muses*, but it had felt so good to write it that she didn't really care. She decided to send it to Mrs. Lee in an email titled "Writers' Workshop Submission, Take 3 (I *really, really* want to get in!)."

Then, with that feeling of satisfaction that comes

with something having been done right, she closed her laptop and placed it aside. A calm breeze rustled the leaves of the great beech tree above her. Lying back in the sweet-smelling grass, Zinnie watched the Cape Cod sunlight dance in patterns all around her as it filtered through the branches. She might have drifted off to sleep if she hadn't been so excited for the events ahead.

51 · I Will

As the guests chatted and found their seats, Max played sweet melodies on his guitar. Zinnie peered out from behind the hedge where she and her sisters were waiting to walk down the aisle before Aunt Sunny made her grand entrance. Aunt Sunny was still inside the house, not wanting anyone to see her before the ceremony. In the hours leading up to the wedding, Marigold had practiced the sonnet, made sure there was plenty of soap and hand towels in the bathrooms, and assisted Dad, Jean, Mack, Peter, and the helpers from the yacht club in putting all the finishing touches on the dining tables. Lily had disappeared for a while, but had reappeared before anyone became too worried and just in time to help Mom tie the bouquets with velvet ribbons.

Zinnie had made it to the Village Café just as Mr.

Rathbone was leaving. While he had been surprised by her cake request, he'd said that one of his specialties, as a Hollywood director, was making the seemingly impossible possible. Once he'd had to locate a trained alligator and bring it to the set within forty-five minutes, so five hours for a wedding cake to be delivered to her aunt's house was not as crazy to him as it might have been to someone else. They weren't in L.A., where he had all his connections and the world moved much more quickly, so he was going to have to pull some strings. But by gosh, if this was Zinnie's wish, he would make it happen. She had saved his nephew, and there was nothing he wouldn't do for her.

"And I also need sparklers," Zinnie said, thinking on the spot. "A hundred of them."

"You got it," Mr. Rathbone said.

After meeting with Mr. Rathbone, she ran home and took her thirty-second shower. Then she went into her office and wrote a wedding toast.

Now the moment was finally here. Aunt Sunny was about to get married to Tony! On the guitar, Max transitioned into "Wonderful Tonight," which was the song that he'd said he would play before the processional. Marigold gave Zinnie and Lily a once-over, straightened the bow in Lily's hair, and adjusted Zinnie's sash. Once the guests were seated and quiet and facing the stone arch, Aunt Sunny sneaked out of the back door, down the stone pathway, and to the hedge to join her bridal party, her nieces. She looked beautiful in her simple white tea-length dress and crocheted shawl.

"Girls," Aunt Sunny whispered, "come close." The sisters gathered around their aunt as she took their hands in hers. "I want you to know that I forgive you." She gave them a smile so warm and familiar that Zinnie felt completely at home in this spot in the garden, at this moment in time.

"Even for Grammy's bird?" Zinnie asked.

"For the bird, for the cake, for the fighting the past few days. It's all water over the dam. I was emotional this afternoon, but I would never want you to think you took away from my happiness on this day. You are here with me and it brings me so much joy that I can hardly contain myself." She kissed them each on the head. "Cake is nothing compared to the sweetness of nieces."

Max began to strum "I Will" by the Beatles, which meant it was time for Lily to begin the procession.

"That's your cue, Lily," Zinnie said.

Lily was about to head down the aisle, but instead of preparing to scatter rose petals, she reached into her basket and grabbed a handful of the strangest-looking mixture.

"Lily, what the heck is that?" Zinnie whispered as Marigold pulled their sister back behind the hedge.

"It's a mixture of canned mealworms and raisins,"

Lily said with a smile. "It's what bluebirds love to eat more than anything. Just like you love French toast and bacon. We learned about it at camp. My counselor helped me get the stuff today."

"You can't throw worms down the aisle!" Zinnie said, peeking out at the guests. Max raised his eyebrows in a *What's going on?* look. Zinnie mouthed, *Keep playing!*

"Don't worry," Lily said. "They're dead."

"Oh my goodness!" Zinnie said.

"Where are the rose petals I put in your basket?" Marigold asked.

"I sprinkled them around already. Birds don't eat rose petals," Lily said. "So that would never work."

"Why didn't you tell me?" Marigold asked, her voice high with frustration.

"Oh no!" Zinnie said when she saw tears running down Aunt Sunny's face, but before she could freak out, she realized that they were tears of laughter.

"Lily, my young scientist, I think it's a brilliant idea," Aunt Sunny said, wiping the tears from her face. "You just may be the niece to take after me the most. Try not to sprinkle worms on the guests, okay?"

"Got it," Lily said, as Marigold turned her around and sent her down the aisle. Zinnie, Marigold, and Aunt Sunny giggled as they watched her tossing bits of mealworm and raisins in time to the music. One at a time, Zinnie and Marigold followed and took their places at the archway. As they turned to face the hedge, Max segued into "Here Comes the Sun." The guests stood up as Aunt Sunny walked down the aisle. The song was still playing when a bluebird landed not two feet away from where Aunt Sunny stood, and it didn't fly away until after the vows were exchanged.

52 · The Twist

All my hard work really paid off, Marigold thought as she took in the reception scene. The wedding tent was alive with conversation and music. Candles flickered. Paper lanterns glowed. Fairy lights twinkled like a parade of lightning bugs. The tables, with their arrangements of seashells and flowers, were the perfect combination of fancy and homemade. The whole tent felt unique, in a way that was personal to Aunt Sunny. Marigold was proud of having put it all together. And in such a short time! It gave her an idea. Maybe, when she went back to school in the fall, she could join the social committee, which organized all the school dances and fund-raising activities. It would be a way to fit in while doing something she thought was fun and was good at, unlike swimming. She was still nervous about seeing the Cuties, but as Aunt Sunny said, there was nothing like being useful to cheer yourself up. Marigold would be very useful putting together social events. And she would just have to see how things went with Pilar. As her mom had said, they'd been friends for a long time, and that wasn't easily forgotten. Marigold hoped Pilar liked the bag she'd started to make for her and was planning on finishing in the next few days. Just thinking about giving it to her made her feel hopeful about the situation.

She was still glowing and happy from having read the sonnet during the ceremony. She had practiced that afternoon as she had gone about the wedding preparations. In the second before she stepped in front of the wedding guests with the sonnet in hand, she panicked. She wondered if she had no talent, if she was just a girl who'd had a bit of luck for a while and whose luck was up. She realized it was a fear that had been living within her since that dreadful moment in the movie theater when she felt that her existence had been erased along with her character.

Pretending to be "ordinary" was just a way of hiding from that fear. But it had turned out that there was no need to be afraid. The fear passed as soon as she took a deep breath and began to read. She performed the sonnet with emotion, meaning, and confidence. She felt the collective attention of the wedding guests hold her as if in an embrace. A sense of ease returned to her and filled her up. She was herself again. Of course she was, because this was how acting made her feel, and no movie director could take that away from her.

Naturally, a part of her wished that Mr. Rathbone had arrived with the cake just in time to see and hear her read. He would have been blown away, and Marigold was certain that he wouldn't have been able to stop himself from offering her another part on the spot. But the cake had not arrived until a half hour ago, long after she'd read the sonnet. And the cake had been delivered by a team of Rathbone's assistants, not Mr. Rathbone himself. It had arrived exactly in time for dessert. It was three tiers of perfection. Too much perfection, the sisters agreed. They needed to add something to it to make it their own. They placed some of the beach roses around it, but it still somehow didn't look complete.

"I know what to do," Lily said. She ran into the house and brought out her pressed flower collection.

"But you were going to keep these forever to remember this summer," Marigold reminded her. She didn't want Lily to regret giving the flowers away.

"I will remember this forever instead," Lily said. "Especially if you take a good picture with your iPad when we're all done. But these are not edible flowers, so we have to tell the guests not to eat them. They're for decoration only!"

"I'll make an announcement," Zinnie said, and she grabbed the mic before anyone had a chance to ingest any flowers.

"The cake is gorgeous," Aunt Sunny said. "Lily's pressed flowers are the most perfect addition. But you know what I'm looking forward to even more than tasting it? Hearing every detail about how you three made it happen. But I want to wait until after the honeymoon, so you don't have to skip a single moment."

"Do you know where you're going yet?" Zinnie asked.

"It's still a mystery to me," Aunt Sunny said. Marigold noticed that Zinnie was smiling ear to ear.

In the end, Marigold had decided that it didn't really matter if Mr. Rathbone saw her or not, because when she turned to her aunt after the reading, tears of love were streaming down Aunt Sunny's face. She nodded at Marigold with deep appreciation and even, Marigold thought, a touch of awe. And Peter, Marigold noticed, couldn't take his eyes off her for the rest of the ceremony. She had smiled at him from the archway and was not just a little bit pleased that he turned his signature shade of red.

She searched for Peter now among the dancing wedding guests. Paul and Cindy were laughing as they held each other tight and spun around the dance floor. Sara and Meg chatted by the punch bowl, each holding a baby. The justice of the peace was swaying to the music while enjoying his cake. But she couldn't spot Peter. At that moment, Max took Tony's place on the band platform. They started to play "The Twist" and soon everyone was twisting away: Mack and Jean, Lily and Zinnie, Mom and Dad, and Tony and Aunt Sunny. *I should remind Zinnie that it's almost time for her toast,* Marigold thought. Just then she felt a tap on her shoulder. It was Peter.

"Would you like to dance?" he asked.

"I'd love to," Marigold said, feeling her cheeks fill with color as he took her hand to lead her to the dance floor. What a gentleman!

"Are you coming back next summer?" Peter asked.

"Of course," Marigold said as they did the twist in unison. "Maybe this year we can keep in better touch."

"That'd be awesome," Peter said.

"We could chat once a month online," Marigold said.

"We could even make a time right now," Peter said. "How about sometime during the Perseid meteor shower? It starts in the beginning of August."

"Cool," Marigold said. "We can describe what the shooting stars look like from opposite sides of the country."

"Wicked cool," Peter said, taking her hand and spinning her. She felt so light on her feet, so happy and free, a part of her wondered whether, if Peter let go, she would continue to twirl and twirl all the way up to the moon.

Later, Marigold and Max fast-danced. After a few minutes, Marigold motioned for Zinnie to join them. Then she stealthily danced away, leaving the two of them to do some crazy moves together. Zinnie was definitely a spaz, but so was Max. They made a perfect couple, Marigold thought. By the look on Max's face, which was one of pure joy, he'd soon realize that the best sister for him was the one he hadn't even thought to ask to dance. If he hadn't figured it out by next summer, Marigold thought, she would help him. After all, she had a good history as a matchmaker.

53 · Stand by Me

"Now," Zinnie whispered to Max as soon as he and the band finished playing "Wake Up Little Susie," a number that had everyone on their feet. The moment was perfect because Aunt Sunny was dancing near the band and Tony was standing all the way at the other side of the tent talking to Paul. In order for the dramatic effect of her toast to be achieved, Zinnie needed there to be some distance between them. "I'm ready to give my toast."

"And now the fabulous Zinnia Silver, Sunny's niece, would like to give a special toast," Max said into the microphone before he passed it on to Zinnie.

"Hi, everyone," Zinnie said, feeling nervous as the crowd of guests faced her. She had her notebook in her hand but decided on the spot that she didn't need it. She was pretty sure she knew by heart what she wanted to say. "Um, so, you all know how great Sunny is. Some of you know her as a teacher. Some of you know her as a neighbor. Some of you know her as your new grandma," she said, and looked at Max, who played a little riff on his electric guitar, to the crowd's delight. "But to my sisters and me, she's Great-Aunt Sunny, and she's the best. Whether she's teaching us how to make a cake, or letting us search for treasure in her attic, or telling us a story of how things were a long time ago, she does it with so much love."

Zinnie heard many of the guests say, "Awww." Mom and Dad were holding hands. Mom's head was on Dad's shoulder, and Dad gave Zinnie an encouraging *keep going* nod.

"I could talk all night about the many things Aunt Sunny has taught us," Zinnie went on, "but tonight I'm going to tell you about something that she and Tony taught us together, the Summer Triangle.

"'The Summer Triangle' is the name of the star formation made up of the three brightest stars in the summer sky, which, as you may have guessed, form a triangle. Aunt Sunny told us about the science of the stars, Altair, Vega, and Deneb, and Tony told us that when he was in the Air Force, they used the star formation to navigate their planes."

Max played a guitar riff that actually sounded like zooming airplanes. Zinnie smiled at him and he smiled back. They hadn't planned this part in advance, but it was working. Zinnie felt something in her tummy. Butterflies. Definitely butterflies. She wasn't ready to do anything about those butterflies, but it was kind of great just knowing that she could get them. She still wasn't sure if she liked him as a boyfriend or a boy-who-is-a-friend, but she decided she was having so much fun it didn't matter. Maybe she would try to find more boys-as-friends when she went back to Los Angeles.

And Aunt Sunny and the guests loved Zinnie and Max's collaboration. They clapped and whooped.

Zinnie continued, "Tony also told us about a Chinese legend associated with the Summer Triangle. The legend goes that the two lovers, Altair and Vega, are separated, except for one night of the year. On that one night, all the magpies—"

"Those are birds," Lily shouted from the dance floor. Everyone laughed.

"Thanks, Lily. The magpies come together to form a bridge over the silver river—"

"That's the Milky Way!" Lily said, to more laughter.

"Yes, the magpies, which are birds, form a bridge over the silver river, which is the Milky Way, so that the lovers can be together again for this one night," Zinnie said. Max played a little background music on his guitar as Zinnie continued. "Tonight, I'd like us all to be like the magpies, and make a bridge for Sunny and Tony to come together, not just for one night, but for the rest of their lives. If you look under your chair, you'll find a sparkler. If everyone will light their sparklers, we can make a bridge of stars."

As Max continued to play music, the guests found their sparklers and began to light them. Marigold brought a sparkler to Tony, and Lily brought one to Sunny. Then they all created a fiery passageway for Aunt Sunny and Tony to walk through. Everyone's face glowed as Sunny and Tony approached each other from opposite sides of the dance floor. When they met in the middle, they kissed.

"Now for a dance!" Zinnie said. "If you know the words to this song, please sing along."

That's when Zinnie gave Max the signal and he began to play "Stand by Me," the song that Sunny and her sisters had listened to over and over again that one summer Aunt Sunny had described as the best summer of their lives. It seemed like everyone knew the song. Sunny beamed as she danced with Tony. They broke apart briefly so that Sunny could kiss and hug her nieces, and then they reunited. Max launched into the song one more time, and people coupled off as their sparklers fizzled out and the music continued.

The sisters stayed in their own little group. They huddled together and swayed for a few measures, but soon silliness took over. They twirled, spun, and dipped one another, until they collapsed in a giggling pile on the dance floor.

During one of the last slow songs, Zinnie brought her laptop to the edge of the yard, just in case Mrs. Lee had written back—and she had. Zinnie's heart leaped when she read the note. Mrs. Lee really liked the first submission, and the second submission, but the third submission was the best, she wrote. It was so good, in fact, that she offered Zinnie a place in the Writers' Workshop. She also said that one of the reasons the final piece was better was because it felt authentic for Zinnie. "I've been hoping that this year's writers would be a more diverse group in lots of ways, including style. Your talent for fantasy and science fiction will expand our horizons. I think your work might inspire the other girls I teach to take more risks with form and genre. Looking forward to seeing you in the fall!"

Later, after the party, after the guests had gone home and Sunny and Tony had left to spend the night at the lighthouse, and Mom and Dad had fallen asleep on the pullout sofa in the living room, the girls brought the old sleeping bags down from the attic and spent the night under the stars, just like Aunt Sunny and her sisters had. They stayed up laughing and talking and looking at the sky until one by one they crossed a bridge of stars to their dreams.

Acknowledgments

Many thanks to my brilliant editor, Alexandra Cooper, my stellar agent, Sara Crowe, the superb Alyssa Miele, and the whole team at HarperCollins. Lots of gratitude to my writing group, Vanessa Napolitano and Kayla Cagan, for their insight, support, and friendship. I could not have finished this book without the help of Cecy Lopez and Maria Moran, who took such good care of my infant son while I wrote. Many thanks as well to my parents, Elyse and my Mommy & Me classmates, Holly Shakoor, Penny Hill, the St. Timothy School community, and my family—my heart—Jonathan and Henry.

For a sneak peek at the latest book in
the Silver Sisters series,
turn the page.

The *Forget-Me-Not Summer* brims with hilarity and sisterly hijinks.
— Rita Williams-Garcia, Newbery Honor and Coretta Scott King Award–winning author

the
**Silver Moon
of Summer**

A Silver Sisters Story

LEILA HOWLAND

1 · Dive In

"One . . . two . . ." Zinnie's toes were curled up on the edge of the lighthouse diving board. Her palms tingled with anticipation, and her heart was in her throat as Marigold, Lily, Aunt Sunny, and Tony all counted together. Zinnie gulped a breath of air and plugged her nose as they all said, "Three!"

"Woo-hoo!" Zinnie shouted, and jumped. The air skimmed her body. Then she plunged into the cold, salty water. As it engulfed her, she felt the possibility of all that was ahead in the next two and a half weeks.

The Silver sisters were back in Pruet, Massachusetts, for their third summer, and Zinnie was certain it was going to be the best yet. The town was celebrating its tricentennial—its three hundredth birthday—and there was going to be a ton of activities, like an epic sand castle building contest; a parade from Charlotte Point all the way to the town beach; a sailing race with Omgansett, the next town over; a clambake at the yacht club and a dance at the casino. This first dip into Buzzards Bay was just the beginning.

Zinnie flipped onto her back and gazed up at the clear blue sky. After their long plane ride from Los Angeles—during which Zinnie had read the entire third novel in the Dream Weavers series, Marigold had watched two and a half movies, and Lily had mostly slept—the cold water was refreshing. It was six p.m. here, but only seemed like three o'clock because they were still on West Coast time. She felt like she had the whole day in front of her to think and dream about what she would be writing for her blog.

As an eighth grader in the fall, Zinnie would have the chance to be the editor in chief of *Muses*, the school's literary magazine. During the first meeting of the school year, the members of Mrs. Lee's Writers' Workshop would nominate candidates, and at the next meeting they voted.

Zinnie loved being in the Writers' Workshop, and she really wanted to be the editor in chief. She'd noticed that it was mostly just the members of the Writers' Workshop who read *Muses*. Zinnie was hoping to create something that everyone wanted to read, and couldn't put down until they'd devoured the whole thing, like one of Aunt Sunny's surprise brownies.

Muses should live up to its name and inspire people. As editor in chief, Zinnie felt she could make that happen.

But first she was going to have to get nominated! And then, of course, she'd have to win. The blog that Mrs. Lee assigned each member of the Writers' Workshop to keep over the summer was Zinnie's opportunity to prove not only her talent for writing, but also for connecting with readers. She needed to think of what Mrs. Lee called a "hook," a clever way to get the audience's attention, and then she'd have to find a way to keep her readers hooked. "A hook with legs," Mrs. Lee had said during the last meeting before school let out.

Zinnie had brainstormed on the beach in Malibu, bouncing some ideas off her dad, before they left L.A. She'd also journaled about it, and of course, she'd been obsessing about it on the plane ride to Boston, even while she was reading her book.

So far nothing was coming to mind, but she was hopeful that was going to change soon. Pruet was where she found some of her best ideas. As she swam her way back to the lighthouse in the smooth, even strokes she'd been practicing all winter, the salt pleasantly stinging her skin, she was sure her mind was opening up.

"Is it freezing?" Marigold asked as she watched Zinnie climb the ladder up the side of the lighthouse to the porch.

"It was invigorating," Zinnie said through chattering teeth.

"Was it scary?" Lily asked as Zinnie climbed onto the wooden porch, which was warm from a long day in the sun.

"More like thrilling," Zinnie said, patting her little sister on the head.

"You dripped on me!" Lily said. "It *is* cold."

Aunt Sunny stood nearby, holding open a striped beach towel. Zinnie left wet footprints as she ran into her aunt's toweled embrace.

"I'm so delighted you're back, my dear," she said, squeezing Zinnie tight.

"Me too," Zinnie said. Something about Aunt Sunny's hugs was deeply reassuring and comforting. It was as though she could hold the whole world still for a moment with her arms. "There's nothing like summer in Pruet."

"Summer is our reward for getting through the tough winters," Tony said.

"Especially this winter," Aunt Sunny said as she rubbed Zinnie's back. "The storms were vicious."

Aunt Sunny had told them all about the blizzards that she and Tony had endured. There had been three in a row, knocking out the power for days. Tony and Aunt Sunny had had to sleep in the living room in front of the roaring fireplace to keep warm. Luckily,

Aunt Sunny's house had withstood the high winds, but not everyone had been so fortunate. Some of the houses closer to the shore had to be rebuilt, and the roof of the yacht club had been seriously damaged.

But now the sun stretched their shadows, and birds sang back and forth above her sisters' voices. They were discussing who would jump off the diving board next.

"You go," Marigold said to Lily. "I need to be a little warmer."

"But you're bigger than I am," Lily said. "And it's so high!"

"Zinnie already said it wasn't too scary," Marigold said.

"There's no reason to bicker, loves. You don't have to jump today," Aunt Sunny said. The lines around her eyes seemed more deeply etched than usual.

"Is it true that the Pruet town council chooses one boy and one girl to lead the parade at the tricentennial?" Zinnie asked, trying to distract her sisters. Zinnie didn't like to see Aunt Sunny looking worried, so she changed the subject to something she'd read about in the *Buzzards Bay Bugle*.

"That's right," Tony said. "The town council will nominate a young man and young woman who embody the spirit of James and Eliza Pruet, the town's founding family."

"Wait, what?" Marigold asked.

Zinnie's tactic had worked—her sisters had stopped fighting.

"They were said to be hardworking, spirited, and of course, very civic-minded. And the town council thought it would be fun to pick two people who embodied these same qualities to lead the parade on horseback," Aunt Sunny said.

"Horses? Wow. What does 'civic-minded' mean?" Lily asked.

"It means that you care about the community," Marigold answered. "Do they have to dress up in an old-fashioned way or get to wear anything . . . special?"

"There won't be any costumes, if that's what you mean. But Jean has offered to make a floral wreath for our Eliza and a matching corsage for James," Aunt Sunny said. "She's been taking a lot of courses on flower arranging this year. She says it's the new yoga."

"Cool," said Marigold with a dreamy look in her eyes. Zinnie felt pretty certain Marigold was imagining that she and Peter Pasque would be picked to be Eliza and James.

"I didn't know about the horseback part," Zinnie said with a smile. She didn't care about wearing a floral wreath on her head, but she did think it would be fun to ride on a horse next to Max down the main street. Max was Tony's grandson and Zinnie's

first boy-who-was-a-friend, though Zinnie had sometimes wondered if he might be her boyfriend. Now, she
looked down at her arms and noticed she had goose
bumps. Was it the breeze that had given them to her
or the idea of seeing Max again soon?

"So, Tony, when is Max coming?" Zinnie asked.

"They'll be here in a couple weeks," Tony said. "I
think they arrive a few days before the tricentennial."

"That'll be fun," Zinnie said, though she felt disappointed. She and Max messaged back and forth
sometimes, so she knew that he was going to be living
in Italy for a while. The last time she'd heard from
Max, he wasn't sure how long their summer visit to
Pruet was going to be. It all depended on his dad's
time off from the military. As the sting of disappointment sharpened, she realized how much she'd been
hoping he'd be here the whole time she was, not just
for a few days.

"You really want to see Max, huh?" Marigold asked
in a teasing voice.

"So, are you going to jump or not?" Zinnie asked,
embarrassed that Marigold had seen through her so
easily.

"There'll be plenty of time for swimming," Aunt
Sunny said. "But now I think we should go get you
girls settled in."

"This year I'd like the bed near the window," Lily
said.

"Hey, that's always been my bed!" Marigold said.

"Just because you're the oldest doesn't mean you always get what you want," Lily said.

Zinnie realized that she wanted that bed as well—the view might inspire her. She was about to put in her two cents, but decided against it.

The sisters had plenty of arguments at home, but for some reason their worst fights happened here in Pruet. Maybe this was because their parents weren't around to stop them. Or perhaps it was because they were all sharing a room. Or possibly it was because summer, with its freewheeling days and long twilights, simply had more room for everything—happiness, dreams, ideas, and even conflict. Their first summer here, Lily had almost drowned because Zinnie and Marigold had been fighting. And then last summer, they'd ruined Aunt Sunny's wedding cake because of another big argument. The idea of another big fight this year made her feel seasick. And the crease in Aunt Sunny's brow was getting deeper by the second.

"Hey, guys, can we make a deal?" Zinnie asked.

"Depends what it is," Marigold said.

"Come here," Zinnie said, and motioned for her sisters to join her in a huddle on the far end of the porch.

"Let's not fight this summer in Pruet. Let's promise to get through the two weeks in peace," Zinnie said. "For Aunt Sunny."

"Fine with me," Lily said. "But can you two really handle it?"

"Of course we can," Marigold said, visibly annoyed that her younger sister was questioning her.

"Shake on it?" Zinny asked, extending a hand. Marigold took her sister's hand in her own. Lily used both hands to cover her sisters', and the three of them shook.

"So then," Lily asked, "who gets the bed?"

2 · Three Wishes

"I can't sleep," Marigold said into the darkness of their attic bedroom. With its three narrow beds, one shared bureau, and the dollhouse that had been Aunt Sunny's when she was a girl, the room was exactly the same as she remembered it. "Anyone awake?"

Marigold held her breath and listened, but no one replied. She tucked her hair behind her ears, sat up, and gazed out the window—which was right next to her bed. Marigold had won the number guessing game they'd devised to see which sister would get the best bed. And as she pulled back the curtains to get a better view, she was satisfied she'd prevailed.

The sky was a dazzling array of stars. It seemed to be practically begging her to make a wish. She located the North Star, which was easy because it was the brightest, and thought for a moment. Then she said to herself, *I wish to find a perfect friend in my new school.* She had been thinking about transferring schools ever since the clique of mean girls in her class had started excluding her in seventh grade, and after another year of it in eighth, she'd finally decided to switch schools.

The event that really put her over the edge was when her former best friend Pilar officially ditched her for the Cuties clique last September by not inviting Marigold to her fourteenth birthday party, which was a sleepaway weekend in Big Bear Lake, a nearby mountain town. When she asked Pilar about it later, she'd told Marigold that she thought she wouldn't have fun because she wasn't in the clique. Marigold not only felt like she'd been punched in the gut, she'd also lost some respect for her old friend.

For her own fourteenth birthday, which had been in the spring, her mom had taken her and her sisters out for a fancy tea at a hotel in Beverly Hills. It had always been her mom's rule that Marigold either invite the whole class or only her best friend. Since she didn't have a best friend anymore, and she didn't want the whole class to come, she decided to just celebrate with her family. They all got dressed up, and Zinnie spoke in a British accent the whole time. It was fun, but it didn't feel much like a birthday.

That was when Marigold announced to her mom that she really wanted to make a switch for high school. To her surprise, her mom agreed with her on the spot.

Marigold was thrilled when she got into the prestigious Performing Arts Magnet school, also known as PAM, where she was going to be able to focus on all her favorite things: acting, design, costumes, and even directing. She was looking forward to all the other artists she was going to meet at PAM. She knew that artists weren't like the Cuties. Everything was going to be better there. The school was across town, close to the beach, but her parents were willing to drive her.

As hopeful as Marigold was about her friend wish coming true, and as happy as Marigold was about her acceptance to PAM, she was also sad she was *really* losing Pilar now. Different schools were like different universes. They'd probably never see each other again.

Suddenly, here in her bed at Aunt Sunny's, she was anxious. She'd gone to school at Miss Hadley's since kindergarten! She would be starting school with absolutely no one she knew, traveling to a campus that was completely unfamiliar and three times the size of her old school. And she'd be going to school with boys for the first time since preschool! Boys! Marigold's heart pounded. She took several deep breaths. Boys weren't so bad, she told herself. Actually, she really liked boys, or at least one boy: Peter Pasque.

Oh, Peter Pasque! Her heart fluttered faster at the thought of him! It was amazing how quickly anxiety could transform into delightful nervousness. She smiled, picturing him on his sailboat. When would she get to see him? Tomorrow, she hoped! Yes—she would go to find him at the yacht club after sailing practice, which she knew ended around two thirty in the afternoon. She'd taken some sailing lessons in Redondo Beach over the school year. It would be so much fun to surprise him with her sailing skills this summer. And it would happen soon. Tomorrow was not so far away at all. At least, not if she could get to sleep. And then of course there was the dance during the tricentennial. Would she and Peter be chosen to be Eliza and James Pruet? It would be so dreamy to ride on a horse next to him, especially with a wreath of flowers in her hair! Would she even be eligible to be Eliza if she was merely a summer visitor?

She and Peter had kept in touch during the year, emailing and chatting online once or twice a month, especially when certain constellations were in the sky—they had a thing about the stars. Their families sent each other cards over the holidays, and Marigold had placed the one from the Pasques, which had a picture of Peter in a fisherman's sweater, in a special box of private things. For some reason she had trouble picturing him in anything but that fisherman's sweater now.

Could she make two wishes tonight? She didn't see why not. After all, there were plenty of stars in the sky! She needed to find another good star to wish to see Peter as soon as possible! Oh, and she also wanted to wish that he didn't have a girlfriend already. Make that three stars. She pressed her face against the screen and searched for the two next brightest stars. Thinking she'd have a better selection if she could lean out a little farther, she unfastened the clips that held the screen in place and gently put the screen on the floor.

Feeling as romantic as Juliet on her balcony, she leaned out the window to look around. In the story, Juliet was fourteen too, Marigold remembered. The air was still and warm and smelled green and fresh, just like country air should. An idea occurred to her—a wonderful, summery idea. Maybe she and Peter could be like Romeo and Juliet this summer. And he could secretly visit her outside this window late at night! She took a deep breath, imagining the sight of Peter calling up to her from below. Just as she leaned out a little farther, something small and dark and fast as a bullet whooshed by her ear.

"Ahh!" she shrieked as she watched the dark form darted around the room. "Aaaaaahhh!"

EXPLORE THE SUMMER MAGIC OF CAPE COD WITH THE SILVER SISTERS!